PRAISE FOR REBECCA LIM

'Subtly bea...   ...'s
Mercy series brims with mystery and romance that
pull readers through the veil between worlds real
and mythical.' Andrea Cremer, *New York Times*
bestselling author of the Nightshade series

'Gripping…by the end, you can't help but wonder
who this angel of Mercy will become next.'
Sunday Herald Sun

'What is compelling about this novel is not only
its tightly constructed plot but the lyrical quality
of the writing…Not to be missed.' *Reading Time*

'*Mercy* is a page-turning mystery. Readers will be
begging for the sequel.' Laurie Faria Stolarz

'This thriller has a creepiness that keeps
the pages turning.' *Kirkus Review*

'Mercy['s] sarcasm, courage and determination
will hook readers.' *School Library Journal*

ALSO BY REBECCA LIM
Mercy
Exile
Muse
Fury
The Sweet Life

Rebecca Lim is a writer and illustrator based in Melbourne, Australia. She worked as a commercial lawyer for several years before leaving to write full-time. Rebecca is the author of fifteen books for children and young-adult readers, and her novels have been translated into German, French, Turkish, Portuguese and Polish.

THE ASTROLOGER'S DAUGHTER

REBECCA LIM

TEXT PUBLISHING MELBOURNE AUSTRALIA

textpublishing.com.au
The Text Publishing Company
Swann House
22 William Street
Melbourne Victoria 3000
Australia

First published in 2014 by The Text Publishing Company

Cover and page design by Imogen Stubbs
Cover photograph © Lia & Fahad / Stocksy United
Illustrations on pages 25, 26 and 66 by Rebecca Lim
Typeset by J&M Typesetting

Printed in Australia by Griffin Press, an Accredited ISO AS/NZS 14001:2004 Environmental Management System printer

National Library of Australia Cataloguing-in-Publication entry:
Author: Lim, Rebecca (Rebecca Pec Ca)
Title: The astrologer's daughter / by Rebecca Lim.
ISBN: 9781922182005 (paperback)
ISBN: 9781925095005 (ebook)
Dewey Number: A823.4

This book is printed on paper certified against the Forest Stewardship Council® Standards. Griffin Press holds FSC chain-of-custody certification SGS-COC-005088. FSC promotes environmentally responsible, socially beneficial and economically viable management of the world's forests.

This project has been assisted by the Commonwealth Government through the Australia Council, its arts funding and advisory body.

To Michael, Oscar, Leni and Yve.
Always.
Love.

To leave this world behind, is death.

John Donne

PART 1

Your life takes an unexpected turn this week. Stay alert.

1

My mother always called it *the eventuality*.

Not the *maybe*, or the *probably*.

'It's going to happen,' she would tell me calmly. 'I even know when. It's a twist in my stars. It's written there, and we have to accept it.'

My mother, Joanne Nielsen Crowe. She has a name, she's not a *was*.

I'm struggling to recall what she was wearing. I'm struggling to recall her exact state of mind. She always drills into me how important every moment is, each one trembling with potential. 'One minute,' she will say, 'one degree rising, can change everything, darling. Remember.'

I have to get the story straight or they'll think I'm

deranged and won't listen, won't care. I have to be credible. I have to be coherent, orderly, the way *she* is.

She's beautiful. And kind. Small, and sort of frail-looking, but the hardest worker. She never sits still, she always has to be doing something, or making something, with her blue-veined, fine-boned hands. You would forget, after a while, that she was missing five joints on her right one. You just stop noticing, so industrious she is, with what she has left.

'It's like you've got a condition,' I tell her in mock disgust, whenever she sews or draws or types, and Mum will laugh.

But she's a bad cook, a really bad cook. I took over doing that for the both of us when I was ten and she was trying to hold down the country-town bakery job and the thing at the doctor's clinic that didn't work out because some sleazebag called Graham kept inventing illnesses just to harass her for a date. It was the only thing I could do to help, cooking, and I've just kept doing it, through every move, every new upheaval. We had to leave town, I remember, because of that man, Graham from Rainbow, with his isolated farmhouse, extensive gun collection and pack of pit bulls. There was nowhere to go, everyone knew everyone; they all had an opinion. And everywhere my mother turned, he'd be there; taking up her time, wanting her all to himself. It was suffocating.

4

People always attach themselves to Mum. They get addicted. It only ever goes one way; always in her direction. Eventually, women *and* men find themselves craving her, like a drug. And she, *we*, have to leave and start over.

But for her, there was only ever one love in this life, one drug, and he's gone. I never really knew my father, although I have this memory: of waking in the dark and walking into the glow of him watching the television, alone in a room somewhere, the sound turned down low so as not to wake the two of us. He'd touched my hair and we'd sat side-by-side in the flickering light. And that's it. I remember my father as an instance of light, just a presence beside me. But I'm told I have his long, dark eyes and eyelashes, the same dimple in my right cheek. Though the rest of me is *some new animal altogether*, Mum said once, laughing.

Some new animal. That's me.

'There won't be another like him, you know,' she'd added, her expression going still and inward, the way it always did when she thought about Dad. 'It's kind of nice, to have so much certainty. It means I don't have to try anymore. I can just *be*. It's a relief.'

But that's what she is known for—*trying*. Trying to squeeze everybody in; trying to make people feel special, and seen; trying to find the truth in amongst the chaos that makes up the singular state of existence. Mum helps anyone and everyone. She's always giving away our money and our belongings: to strangers in the park; to people she gets talking to in queues at the bank or down the shops; to weird, dead-eyed Jehovah's Witnesses with greasy hair who come looking for converts and end up converted themselves to The Way of Joanne. She always says that every single life is a struggle against pre-determination, and she has the proof; case after case, chart after chart, annotated with strange hieroglyphs in her own delicate half-hand. 'If you let it,' she always tells people sternly, 'it will happen. Only the strong-willed can change what's in the stars. It's always, and only ever, up to you.'

She's persuasive, Mum. People see the big blue doll's eyes and the long, white-blonde hair worn with a poker-straight centre part, and don't realise at first what they're dealing with. She's iron and velvet in human form. She's a magus.

Everywhere we go, word gets around that she's *good*, that she never gets it wrong. When she says it will happen, it *will*; like white water, it will suck you down if you let it. Maybe things don't pan out the way the person hearing it expects them to, but her readings always fit, *always*. When people look back at what's just hit them like a semi bearing down on them standing helpless in the road, the answer would always have been there in their forecast, all along. They just hadn't been seeing it.

'You just have to know what to ask,' Mum will mutter as she works her arcana at night, always at night, with a bowl of tinned soup, or a bitter black coffee on a tray beside her—no milk, no sugar, because she'll buy me sweeties to eat at the drop of a hat but she won't touch them herself. 'You just have to know where to look.'

Strangers come from all over. I open the door, or answer the phone at some God-awful hour, and it is always some new client who is quietly, though more often openly, desperate. And the questions they want answers to are always urgent, always *life and death*, need-to-know, let me at her, I gotta see her, now, now, *now*.

And most of them don't pay. Or can't. Not in money, anyway.

Mum's 'reading room'—where hearts are set at rest, or mended, or broken all over again—is really just our meals area, only separated from our open kitchen by a vinyl-covered breakfast bar. All the reading room contains is an overflowing bookcase, a couple of mismatched chairs and a battered antique card table covered in a plastic tablecloth with a lacy, doily pattern embedded in it. The kind of 'fabric' you can buy by the metre from a haberdashery store that's easy to wipe down.

'It's the only way to keep the only table we have in the house clean enough for us to eat off,' she said once. 'Fear and stains go hand in hand. You'd do well to remember that in this line of work.'

Our place is full of things like that tablecloth. Things that speak of making-do and desperation and aspiration. When people can't pay Mum's fee, there's almost an unspoken rule that they bring knick-knacks in lieu: pot plants, porcelain dolls, wonkily hand-painted ceramic platters, crystal figurines, feathered dreamcatchers, cheesy vases only big enough for tiny rosebuds, and commemorative coin sets by the score…You get the idea.

These things rest on every available surface in our apartment; line the narrow hallway to the front door like an honour guard comprised solely of kitsch. It has always been that way for as long as I can remember. Necessity causes us to shed things from move to move, but bric-a-brac is drawn to us somehow, as if my mother and I are especially magnetised. There are too many things to make out in the darkening bedroom I am now sitting in; they peek out one behind another, hanging off the cabinetry, probably breeding furiously in the dark, exclaiming to each other, to the silence:

> *You're a star.*
> *Thanks a bunch!*
> *Happiness is.*

They are the gifts of grateful people with no taste, or no idea. It's almost like the Franklin Mint, or a home shopping show, has set up a showroom in the place where we live.

'And I wouldn't have it any other way,' Mum said once, firmly, in her *end-of-discussion* voice. 'Don't look at them as *things*. They are realised *emotions*: like relief, anger, sadness, gratitude. You are surrounded by thanks—a powerful thing to have about you.'

Yeah. And look at how it has protected her.

I'm like that tablecloth, I've decided. A repeating pattern, embedded in plastic, frozen in place. Fully functional and easy-care, but so unlovely.

It's hell to keep clean, this home. Which is only *home* because my mother and I were together in it, and not even for long enough to catch breath. Just five lousy months, a record of brevity, even for us. Without Mum here tonight, our tiny apartment seems cavernous and strange, every grinning, dancing bear and ceramic clown wearing an air of darkling menace.

I know I've waited long enough, but my hand hesitates over the handset, fearful that I've misread her absence as something more than it is. She might be making a special house call, which she has done before. Maybe she's still stuck on a country train, somewhere, someplace without mobile coverage. It's possible: she goes to those lengths to see something through, even though she can't afford to care as much as she does. Mum hates fuss and attention; has made a life out of casting the spotlight back onto others.

What I'm about to do would horrify her.

But she's never left me alone without explanation. Knowing what's out there has made her hyper-cautious, made her a great note-taker and note-leaver. On the bathroom mirror, on my bedside table, on the kitchen bench:

> *Love you.*
> *Take care.*
> *Call me?*

It's been twenty-eight whole hours since her last message went straight to my voicemail. There had been a minute of static, threaded through by the sound of a moving car, maybe the rumble of a man's voice on the radio? Afternoon noises. Just a mistake message left by her hip hitting her bag, or something inside it shifting and speed-dialling me by accident.

I've searched everywhere at home, looked under every stupid trinket and scuffed article of furniture, rifled through her sacred cabinet of futures foretold, and found nothing to say where Mum is, or what she could be doing.

I have a photographic memory for words—I could sit down and write out the whole of page 52 of *Chemistry Matters!* right now—but Wednesday, the day I last saw my mother, is an immediate blank. Which means she never said where she was going or I would remember. I would.

It's time to call. Every minute is vital; everything can change in just one minute. She taught me that.

I pick up the handset, the faint purr of the dial tone radiating out of my palm. Night shadows and reflected neon from street signage play across my frozen figure, my olive skin that is more like his was, than hers.

It's a powerful thing, fear, the *not* of not-knowing. After they get to know my mother and what she can do, no client ever calls her *Jo* again, not even *Joanne*. They're too afraid to call her anything, really, by the end, when they're walking away with their progressions and transits and retrogrades clutched in their cold, trembling fingers. All the knowledge brought down by one small woman in a flannel shirt and faded pedal pushers.

Over time she's come to be known as *The Astrologer*.

And me? *The Astrologer's Daughter*.

When I answer the door, see, that's what they say.

And though I, more than anyone, should know that the stars are impersonal—they wheel and grind and turn without reference to our wants or needs or desires—my mother, Joanne Nielsen Crowe, didn't deserve what's already come to pass, just because she let it.

She *let* it.

That's what has shaken me most. She did not fight it. She stopped running, and let *it—the eventuality*, the black hole she foresaw in her own future that she would never tell me about—take her. When I pressed her about it once, all she said was: *Death isn't just a person dressed all in black, darl. It's a place we're each of us heading to.*

I've never understood that. But the words have always stuck with me: that she thinks death is a country with its own topography, horizon, stars and moons and planets, just like our own.

In a flurry of bile and nerves, I dial.

'My name is Avicenna Crowe,' I tell the woman who answers, her voice crisp and emotionless. 'I'd like to report a missing person please.'

2

Since I'm in *no immediate danger*, two officers come out first thing in the morning. A tall, heavy-set man with sandy hair and a compact woman who looks only a year or two out of the academy, still fresh-faced and curious. Both are bristling with holsters, gadgets, ripstop nylon.

They recoil when I answer the door, and my hand rises to my ear. But, of course, it's too late. The young woman's eyes narrow thoughtfully on the melted, stumpy thing that is all that remains of my left ear, then on the waxy-looking pattern burnt into my left cheek that pulls my eye down a little at the outer corner. I see her thinking, as clearly as if a thought bubble has formed over her neat, blonde head: *Abuse?*

Then: *Motive?*

Before two lots of official ID are even folded away, I find myself babbling, 'Ipswich house fire, late 90s; it's on the public record.'

What's also on record is that my father died trying to save both of us, but I don't tell them that part. They can look that up themselves.

'Uh, come in,' I add, belatedly releasing my messy topknot and finger-combing all the wavy dark hair down off the top of my head and over my ruined ear.

I look like hell today. Like Hollywood-grade demon spawn in my fiery tartan pyjamas with matching craniofacial scarring that grew and stretched as I grew and stretched. A teen serial killer in faux-sheepskin slippers.

We all sit down, the male officer across from me in the orange tweed armchair, the female officer beside me on the matching couch because it's the appropriate thing to do: I'm eighteen years and thirteen days old today, the least fully formed 'adult' you'd be likely to encounter. The front desk coppers who took my call at Melbourne East station—passing me around like a hot potato—got that right away. When Constable Lara Brand now tries to take my hand, it makes a panicky, crablike gesture of escape, and she doesn't try again. I'm striving so hard not to stare at the real live gun she's carrying in a thigh holster on her right leg that I'm practically sitting with my back to her.

'Sergeant Sam Docherty,' the man says, rushing to fill the silence that follows. And I'm glad he does, because I'm unable to frame in words the awful realisation that I've somehow lost myself *two* parents. I only seem to have misplaced the most important person in my life not once, but twice. A feat for anyone, surely.

Docherty summarises the specifics of my call-in, refraining from mentioning that it was both hysterically brief and largely non-sequential. I nod and nod and nod as he speaks, like a nodding doll.

They make me describe Mum in detail. How tall she is, dress size, skin tone, hair and eye colour, and I'm racking my brains again over the vital question.

What had she been wearing yesterday morning? Had I even lifted my head to grunt as she lingered by my bedroom door? I'm not what you would call a morning person. I have not yet discovered the time of day at which I am optimally functional. But you can't find a person you can't describe, so I say, 'Dark blue?' with so much uncertainty I sound like an uncaring flake.

Docherty frowns. 'Can you go one better than that?'

'Some kind of pants-suit thing,' I add hastily. 'White blouse, with a foofy collar or scarf?' I fluff around at the base of my neck as if I have wattles, like a chicken. 'Flat shoes because she was walking to work,' I resume threadily, lowering my hand, 'at the bank. She always walked.

Though she may have been packing heels for a meeting. Hair down.'

I only know that part because I have a vague memory of squinting through my open bedroom door and seeing the early morning sun flaring in the ends of her hair, turning them a pale red. That was after the bit where I'd pretended I was still asleep when she'd said quietly, 'Love you, my girl,' and got no answer.

While I've been talking, I've caught the officers flicking surreptitious glances at each other. I don't blame them—I'm tall and broad-shouldered, dark and busty and solid. The exact opposite of the woman I'm describing. *You wouldn't even know you're related!* the TattsLotto lady in the shopping arcade across the road from our place had exclaimed, the first time we'd met her. *No, you wouldn't*, Mum had replied cheerily, rubbing the back of her wounded hand against my face with affection. The unconscious gesture had caused the TattsLotto lady's eyes to flick away.

The sergeant underlines something in his small police-issue notebook. 'Your mum have any identifying marks?' he asks. 'Like tattoos? Evidence of childhood illnesses, accidents? Scars, is what I mean. Someone may see them on her, jog something.'

I pause, diverted by Constable Brand's light-hazel gaze skimming across all the surfaces in our apartment. Her eyes fly up the smoke and grease-stained walls, taking in the knick-knacks, the dust, the general air of poverty and neglect. I'm sitting so close that I catch her nose wrinkle minutely at the smell of old food and vicious rising damp masked by an ambient layer of lavender oil. She takes in the books on astral projection and *fate versus free will*, the tomes on reincarnation, Chinese astrology and foretelling the future Occidental versus Oriental style, and I see more thought bubbles quickly forming that say: *New Age fruitcake?*

And: *Bad mother?*

'She wasn't,' I interrupt sharply, unable to stop myself. 'She was the best mother you could ever, ever have. She's been through so much. You have to find her. *Please*.'

There it is again, the past tense, slipping out. Sudden panic squeezes my throat closed.

Constable Brand averts her eyes and asks if she can see the rest of the apartment but is gone before I can reply. I hear lights going on in Mum's bedroom, mine, then the combined toilet/shower/laundry room at the far end that almost always feels like you're stepping into the tropics regardless of what the weather's doing outside. Only one window opens in our flat—it overlooks the street— and I've broken more nails than you can count trying to jimmy it open.

The sergeant clears his throat gruffly and repeats the question about identifying marks. 'Not that we hope it will come to that, mind, but anything you can give us is always useful.'

The room goes airless as I tell him about the small broken heart, inked onto her right shoulderblade. 'No colours,' I whisper. 'Just black. A heart with, like, a white lightning bolt through it.'

Loved him, she did. Was cut through, just like that heart, when he died. None of *that's* on the public record. They were both heroic that night. I shouldn't have survived. But I can't make the extra words come out, to explain: the depth of her love, the depth of his.

Docherty holds out his notepad, asking me to sketch the tattoo. I was there when she had it done, my eyes wide, near fainting when the beads of blood welled up on her white, white skin. I'm no good with blood.

'Not that I'm likely to forget,' was the only thing Mum said as the needle had bit in.

'That's marvellous,' Docherty mutters, studying what I've drawn, adding, 'She was a part-time, ah, *fortune-teller*, you say?'

He sounds disturbed, as if I've just declared my mother a nudist and notorious con woman, rolled into one.

'She was—is, *is*!—an *astrologer*,' I cry, teary-angry, as he makes a *Whoa there, lassie* hand gesture at me. 'An *astrologer*. Not a "psychic", or some cheap tarot-reading faker you call on a 1900 number. There's a *difference*.'

I'm almost spitting, though I can tell from his face he can't see it, the difference.

'And she accepted monetary payment for these, these... services?' he ventures delicately. 'Routinely doled out bad news, did she? People not liking what they were hearing? Enemies?'

'She worked as a bank teller for money,' I say, voice rising, 'because we needed to eat. Everything else she did from the heart. Ask everyone, they'll tell you. PEOPLE LOVED HER.'

I fling one arm out at all the stupid, ugly trinkets positioned lovingly around the sitting room. 'This! This! This!' I shout, jabbing at two leaping crystal dolphins forming a heart shape with their bodies; the porcelain ballet dancer with rose-filled flower basket; the sad-eyed, clay bloodhound with the ginormous head, 'is how she got *paid*.'

Docherty glances down dubiously at a family of pink elephants marooned in the centre of the cheap white cube we use as a coffee table, and I know I'm making no sense at this point, everything's disjointed, just like the call I made that brought him to me. And I cry then, loud and gushing; I can't help it, it's like I've finally been given permission.

At the raw, animal sound, Constable Brand shoots back out of whatever dismal corner she's been nosing around in and looks sharply into her partner's face, before drawing him into our cramped galley kitchen.

I hear everything, of course, there's nowhere to hide in here. I used to sit in my bedroom with the door shut, willing all the strangers with their desperate eyes to *go the hell away*. But I still heard it all: infidelities and breakdowns; miscarriages and hasty marriages; accidents, crossroads. Death. All delivered in Mum's calm, authoritative voice, peppered by frantic outbursts across the table.

It's always the women who overreact and imagine the worst. A man gets bad news? He's already trying to slide out from under it. But, by and large, a woman only hears what she wants to hear, and then she's never the same again. She twists it, it twists her. The end.

'Please let that not be *me*,' I wail through hot, salty tears, my fingers interlaced over my mouth.

They are kind, and let me cry. And through the sound of it—which goes on and on and seems somehow quite separate from my body—I hear Docherty rumble: *I didn't say anything I don't say to all the others. But she's only a kid. She's got every right to be taking it hard.*

Brand replies, low, but harsh: *She's an* 'adult'. *And it might not be a coincidence, the timing. I mean, look at this place! Anyone would do a runner, honestly. There's something in this. They should see this while it's fresh.*

While Docherty excuses himself from the room to make calls, Brand takes my hand firmly and will not let me pull away. Writing with her free hand in the notepad she's balanced on one knee, the constable shoots question after question at me.

Jewellery?

Don't know. Never wore much. Didn't have much.

Aliases?

What? God, no idea.

Car?

No, no, not for years.

Medical conditions?

She had, like, a cold last year, but that's it. She was good, fit. Happy.

(I howl out that last word, *Happy*, so that it's got extra vowels in it, extra syllables.)

D.O.B.? P.O.B.?

Don't know, don't know, she would never tell me, though we celebrated in November, different days, always.

Why? Why on earth would you do that?

Didn't want me to do her chart and find out, I suppose.

The constable's eyes fly to mine. 'Find out what?'

I swipe at my nose with the back of my hand. 'What was coming for her. Yesterday.'

Brand stares at me, astonished. 'Sorry?'

I say, in a mad rush, 'I didn't know it was supposed to be yesterday, she never said there was anything different about yesterday, but I suppose yesterday must have been *the day*. The day *the eventuality* was supposed to happen.

It was *the goddamned day* and she never said anything. She just woke up and went out and met it—in a suit and foofy blouse. Head on. *God.*'

'What are you talking about?' Constable Brand insists, shaking me by the arm. 'What was *coming for her*? What *day*?'

I'm deep into an explanation of the Joanne Nielsen Crowe school of predictive astrology when Docherty comes back through the front door with a hard-faced, kind-eyed man in a dark suit and stripy tie. 'Detective Senior Sergeant Stan Wurbik,' he says. 'Missing Persons Intelligence.'

3

Constable Brand, who hasn't let go of my hand this whole time, says urgently, 'Tell Detective Wurbik—about the work your mother did.'

So I start in again, still sniffing into my cuff, about the astrological clock and progressions and transits, the significance of solar and lunar returns, eclipses, nodes and the significance of the Pleiades when directed towards the ascendant—and he's lost, she's lost. Docherty's got his mouth hanging slightly open.

After I falter to a stop, the detective says into the silence, 'Could you maybe sketch out what you're talking about? It will give us a…better idea of what your mum does.'

I'm about to go in search of a pen and notepad when

my mobile phone goes off in the kitchen. The sound of it makes me go cold, reminding me that time has not, in fact, come to a standstill. I am due at school to do a witness cross-examination role-play with my creepy Legal Studies teacher and two other sacrificial victims. On top of this? I'm already the late-entry new kid with a tragic backstory no one can make me go into. I stick out enough without sticking out more.

I have to shake Constable Brand's hand off in order to get up from the couch. Conscious of three sets of eyes on me, I turn my back on them and pick up.

'*Frankencrowe?*' Vicki hisses down the line. 'Mrs Clarke's ropable. You've been late five days in a row. She's gunna get the office to call your mum again. She's talking detention*s*, plural.'

'Can't talk, Vick,' I say softly, hunching over to make my broad, tartan-clad back less visible. 'But you tell Clarkey and anyone else who asks that Mum's gone missing…' I make a weird mewling noise in my throat, swallowing to hold the tears down. 'And I'm not sure when I'll be back.'

'That's rich, even coming from you!' Vicki says incredulously. 'They'll never buy that.'

'Will if they log on to the Victoria Police media website in the next…?' I glance towards Wurbik.

'Twenty-four hours,' he replies, voice loud enough to carry. 'Probably faster. Time's everything with cases like this.'

I hunch over the phone again. 'You get that?' I say into the sound of Vicki's rapid, open-mouthed breathing. 'That's the *Police*. Got a room full of them right here. With guns. Remind Clarkey that I'm *fast*, the fastest she'll ever have the privilege to work with—she'll still be talking about me when she's in a nursing home—and that I'll catch up.'

I hang up before Vicki's breathing can turn into questions, because with Vicki Mouglalis it always turns into questions. Sinking back down into the couch with a black felt tip and a bit of paper, I pull the coffee table closer, upsetting the elephants walking across it, and begin drawing the very first thing I think I learnt to draw:

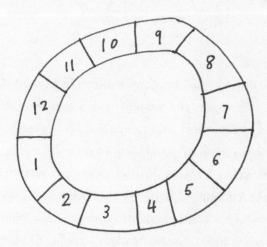

Then around that I add two more wheels, making a mess
of all the lines, leaving them both blank.

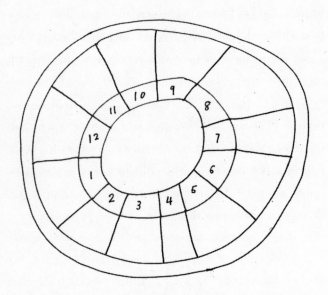

I stare down at the thing my mother blithely called her
canvas. She could draw this blindfolded, every ring almost
perfect, without even using a single one of her compasses.
On this diagram she could hang an entire life.

Brand, Docherty and Wurbik cluster around the series
of shaky, concentric circles I've sketched out. The detective pushes the felled elephants to one side as he crouches
beside me, tapping the centre of my drawing. 'This some
kind of clock?' he asks.

'Kind of,' I say, voice back under control. 'The centre wheel—the one with the numbers around it—represents the natal chart, or *radix*. That's where a person's story begins. Twelve houses, two-hour intervals, like a clock face with midnight at the cusp of the fourth house, noon at the cusp of the tenth. It's calculated based on the birth information the client gives you: you fill the interior with a map of the heavens as it was at the exact time, date, place of birth. It's all about themes and influences, Mum says, not specifics. They have to be teased out, or the chart will tell you very little about how a person's life will really unfold. Just writing up the radix tells you nothing really concrete: probably unlucky, overly chatty, a bit of a stress head, might have a career in finance. Why bother, right?'

I quickly trace the next wheel out from the centre. 'It's in the progressed chart that the themes and influences come into their own,' I continue. 'Will you have the male children your mother-in-law desires? Does your porkable secretary think you're hot stuff, or a bit of a bastard? Will your husband leave you for a man? Will you lose your teeth, your lustrous hair, your fortune, win one? Mum's been asked all those things.'

Docherty shakes his head, flicking a finger at my sketch. 'You can tell that from *this*?'

I look up into his faded blue eyes and realise he's only seeing the blanks on the page, not the possibilities, because no one's ever trained him to see them. The detective crouched beside me taps my diagram again. 'And the very outer ring? The thin one without lines? What's that for?'

'Fine-tuning,' I reply. 'It's like a kind of lens, or magnifying glass. It brings what's in the central wheels into sharper focus. It can help to foretell actual events. To the extent you could have a specific question answered, to the date. They're called *horary readings*.'

Beside me, Constable Brand inhales. Wurbik leaves the room and I hear the sound of the filing cabinet in Mum's bedroom opening.

'Some people don't move without them,' I add quietly. 'They're the neediest. If they could come live here with Mum and me, they would. Just to have her on tap.'

'That so?' says Docherty, leaning in, and I'm instantly defensive.

'Mum told me that as far as she knew, she'd never been wrong. Maybe they wouldn't tell her themselves, but word got back if she was right and it seemed like she always *was*. People talk. Good fortune, misfortune, we all love hearing about it. People always tried to follow her. No matter how many times we moved, or where we went, clients from years back would look for her. She was spooky-accurate. Is, *is*.' I could punch myself in the mouth.

Docherty mutters, 'I still don't see it.'

'You wouldn't,' Detective Wurbik replies, coming

28

back into the room, 'because that thing is missing quite a bit of…detail.'

He throws a stapled document onto the coffee table and I register with a jolt that he's got rubber gloves on, the disposable kind. The top sheet is dated roughly a month before today and headed: *Carson Watters, age 59. Horary reading: move interstate?* There are the same three wheels on it, and a dense forest of numbers and astrological symbols, or glyphs, laid over the top, that to the uninitiated might look like code.

'I remember him,' I murmur, scanning the top page before flicking through the typed-up notes Mum stapled behind, without really seeing any of the words. 'Big guy, booming laugh, smelled like cigarettes. Said to call him *Cars*: "Cars by name, Cars by trade." He wanted to sell his business, move to Cairns. Asked Mum whether she thought the stars were beneficial for the day he had in mind.'

'And were they?' Docherty interjects, sceptical.

'Yeah,' I say, running my eyes again over the glyphs Mum annotated freehand onto the top page. 'Surprisingly good. He was lucky. A couple of afflictions, nothing major. She said: "Do it." And I think he took her advice.'

'Come with me,' Wurbik says abruptly to Docherty.

I hear them opening the filing cabinet again, their voices pitched so low I can't catch the words. When they return, Wurbik picks up right where Docherty left off. 'Bank account details? Place of work?'

I stand up and head towards the overflowing filing tray on the kitchen bench, handing him an old bank statement of Mum's and a pay slip with the bank branch she works at, printed across the top. 'Her work called me, yesterday, asking where she was. But we're doing a musical, at school, and I was painting the backdrop. Didn't check my messages all day, not until after five. I mean, who calls someone asking whether they've seen their *mum*? I wasn't expecting it. I'm still angry at myself.'

I should have said something, back when she was at my bedroom door. Regret is sharp in me. I pivot, suddenly reminded of the accident-message Mum left. 'Listen to this.'

Turning on the speakerphone, I let them all listen to the date and time stamp, the static-filled call from Mum's phone to mine.

Detective Wurbik hands me his card. 'Can you forward that message? To the number here?'

While he watches, I do it, then Wurbik goes back into Mum's room and comes out with an armful of charts, asking if he can take them. I shrug. 'I guess,' I say, feeling like I've said the wrong thing because they're not really mine to give.

'They all look...finished,' the detective says, holding

them out to me in a fan, like an oversized deck of cards he's just pulled out of his sleeve, *ta da*. 'Am I right?'

I flip through them and have to agree. 'Mum's works-in-progress aren't typed up like this. When she was done with someone, she used my laptop for word processing, but she always kept a handwritten journal for "open" cases.'

Wurbik's eyes sharpen on me instantly. 'There's no journal in her room. You see one?' he asks the others, and they shake their heads. 'Where are the old ones? If you still have any.'

'In the hallway closet by the front door, stacked up,' I reply. 'I'll show you. Half our problem is Mum never throwing stuff away. Especially not info that might come in handy down the track; if the client came back. And lots did.'

There are dozens of journals in the narrow broom closet in the hall, all different shapes and sizes, going back years. After scanning the pile, Wurbik follows me back into the living area and I finally remember to tell them about Mum's hand.

'Father's name?' Docherty interjects gruffly, still shaking his head at the fact I could leave something so important out of Mum's description. *Only just about half her hand missing, wouldn't you say?*

'Greyson,' I say quietly. 'Kooky, right? Greyson Zhou. But he wanted me to have Mum's name, I don't know why, so that's what she had put on my birth certificate. *Avicenna Zhou* would have sounded all right. *Crowe* and *Zhou* rhyme, which is weird, even though they're spelled completely differently.'

It's turned into a stifling hot autumn day. Forensics people start trickling in, with their gloves and brushes and flash-lit devices, asking me things I can't remember answering a second after the words have left my mouth.

Before all of them finally leave, spiriting away my laptop and armloads of journals and paper, Detective Wurbik asks for a photo and her toothbrush. And that's when it hits me like a solid punch. It's official: she's really missing.

Numbly, I retrieve the toothbrush, also handing them the photo of Mum and me from the fridge. It's the most recent thing I have of her. Someone at school took it, just after they told me I'd made it through the bastard-hard Collegiate High entrance exam with flying colours, full marks—didn't happen too often, I should be real proud. In it, Mum's beautiful, the way she's always beautiful, wings of hair like white-gold, and we're both grinning manically. I've got my arm around her neck like I'm putting her in a headlock.

Wurbik assures me I'll be cropped out of it, and I say inanely: 'I don't mind, really, it's up to you,' but of course I need to be out of the picture or it will be like it's me that's missing too.

He gives me all the numbers I need if I can think of anything, promising to have the laptop back to me ASAP. And all I can say is: 'Thanks, you've been really... thorough'.

No one was talking homicide—*Not yet, early days*—but I could see them entertaining the idea because I'm observant. They took so long tearing our place apart that I knew, as if they'd straight out said it to my face, that they held grave fears for Mum's safety.

4

I don't like to be alone and I'm afraid of the dark.

There it is. I've never told anyone that before. It's at odds with the way I look, the way I have learned to conduct myself in public—with hauteur, and a certain amount of swagger, as if I am a pirate.

I work out that I've been awake for roughly two days. It might go some way towards explaining the hammering in my ears, and the heat I seem to be generating, as if I'm made out of pistons and cogs and steam.

In the end—even though I had nothing more pressing to do at home than stare at the ancient soot stains on my bedroom walls—I didn't go to school, didn't even make it down the hall to the toilet, or eat. After the police left,

I shut my door and climbed back into bed, because I knew that night would eventually fall and no one would be here to mark it with me. Or bear it with me. On their way out, I almost begged one of them to stay, but it would have sounded pathetic.

I haven't left home for more than a day, based on the irrational fear that I will go out and somehow miss Mum popping back for something, then leaving again. If I'm not here, I won't catch her, and it's important I catch her and tell her not to go outside again, that it's dangerous to leave home, to leave *me*.

I feel disgusting, and it's only feelings of self-disgust and bladder-as-ticking-time-bomb that finally propel me out from under my blankets. I crack open my door and am greeted with the kind of darkness that could hide... anything.

Skin prickling, I run through our apartment towards the front entrance, palming on every light along the way. The air smells stuffy and ancient and dead in here, like how a tomb might smell, and panic makes me throw the front door wide open to catch a draft, any sort of draft. Or just to catch my mother, walking back through it, throwing her battered tan leather handbag down and saying, 'Phew, Avi, that was the longest train ride in recorded *history*.'

We live on the top floor of a three-storey Victorian-era brick building in the heart of Chinatown, listed as the registered place of business for the *Mei Hua Bean Sprout Company*. A tarnished brass plaque right by the residents' entrance at street level says so. The bean sprout people are very quiet. I often imagine, as I pass by the locked wooden door on the second floor, that they are practising a kind of Zen farming, nurturing their seedlings in absolute silence.

When we came here—with our scratched meals table, mismatched chairs and boxes of journals, books and bare essentials—I'd shrieked, 'No, what, *seriously?*'

And Mum had replied fiercely, 'We're lucky to have this. *Lucky.* You don't understand how perfect it is for you.'

But it hadn't seemed that way. And on days when the Chinese restaurant next door is cooking up a stinky new batch of XO sauce? It still doesn't. An old Chinese medicine practitioner takes up the whole ground floor of our building; there's a street entrance to his shop, but also a separate doorway leading into his business from our stairwell. Sometimes, when I look in on my way out of our building, I see him taking shrivelled-up things out of Perspex canisters for the benefit of whoever's just walked in. But we live in our own little bubbles, the bean sprout people, the old guy, and us. And bubbles can't touch or they will burst, so I haven't introduced myself, even though he looks animated and kindly, with his wrinkly face and ring of crazy-scientist white hair surrounding a freckly bald spot. There's really no point. We always leave.

I don't know how Mum found the place, but it's fifteen minutes door-to-door to my school by tram, so she's right, it *is* perfect, even though she'll never get me to admit it and I might now never get the chance.

I should have said something, yesterday. Like *hello* or *good morning*.

Or *goodbye*.

A squeal of pain escapes my throat, like the sound of a wild pig in fear for its life. I have to lean against the doorframe for support, conscious my breathing sounds ragged, as if I'm trying to outrun something.

But it's inside me, and I can't.

God, she could be anywhere—I can't make myself think past that—while I'm *marooned* here, in a city I barely know.

The weak kitchen fluorescent barely penetrates the darkness beyond our door. I take a tentative step forward and peer out and down into the stairwell. It could be an actual *well* out there. Maybe if I set foot past the threshold, beyond the thin puddle of light, I will fall straight through the earth.

Below, the bean sprout people are silent. The air outside my apartment is heavy with the scent of dust and the mouldering cardboard boxes that are stacked on every landing in the building. But I breathe it all in gratefully because it does not smell like *inside*, everything stinking of nerves and fruitlessness and *waiting*.

Which is what Mum's clients have been doing. She only ever has two or three on the go at a time, but no more. I know that, because she told me once that it was exhausting—the constant expectation. 'If I don't keep it down to manageable numbers, love,' she said, 'I make mistakes. And precision is everything.'

She had a waitlist *that* long to see her. Lately, she'd been turning people away; I know because I heard her on the telephone being apologetic, but firm. And we've had so many hang-ups I knew people were pissed. Some would just call to see if she was answering. I'd say my name, get a second of breathing, then dial tone.

The waitlist, the live cases, will all be in Mum's missing journal. I described it to the police: dark red, bound in fake leather with gold scrollwork on the front cover and the spine. Mum couldn't believe she'd gotten it for a dollar from the five-dollar shop across the road that doesn't live up to its name; everything's so expensive. 'Donny must have missed this one when he was repricing everything,' I remember her laughing as she held it up for me to see, flicking through the unlined, white pages with the thin edge of gilt around each one.

I think I'd mumbled something sarcastic back, like: 'Well, doesn't that look *special*.'

But I would do just about anything right now to get hold of that book. Next to talking to Mum? It would tell me what was going on inside her head before she...

I cut that thought right off at the knees and go back through our apartment, turning on all the table lamps for extra company. I paw through the kitchen cupboards first, then Mum's reading room. Ransack her bedroom and the hall cupboards next, before digging through the bathroom cabinets, which are full of shed hair and half-finished bottles of Bio-Oil, for the scarring. She never would have hidden anything in here, where the air smells constantly of mould. But still I look.

Then I look at everything again, everything she might have touched, even under the couch, running my hands through the dust balls and staples and crumbs; peering inside all the seat cushions for things that might be secreted there. As if Mum was some kind of spy who had to hide all the information she was putting together on people, or risk having it fall into enemy hands.

Nothing.

The only pieces of paper with Mum's brittle-looking handwriting on them are in her filing cabinet, which is filled to capacity with superseded notes, finished charts, all past history. The police took all her old journals away and skimmed off the most recent forecasts for further study.

And because the police have taken my laptop for

analysis, I can't access the half-arsed English presentation on John Donne I'm supposed to have finished, like, yesterday, with Simon Thorn who is, literally, a thorn.

I think it's safe to say we felt an immediate visceral, mutual dislike; just one of those chemical things you can't explain. *I* think Simon's a know-it-all with a God complex because he will not leave me alone in class—the moment I open my mouth he will chase and badger, bait and harass, trying to make me look stupid, it's almost reflexive—and *he* thinks I'm visual pollution because he stuck me with *Frankencrowe* the moment I walked into our form room for the first time. And now everyone at school calls me that, even the people who claim to be friendly. So I've got nothing better to do right now but freak out about where my mother might be.

The only place I haven't searched is my bedroom, because I was in it, pretending to be asleep, the morning she walked into thin air. Suddenly, I hear screaming and realise—after one disorientating, out-of-body moment— that it's coming from *me*. I'm just standing there, on the narrow bit of hallway connecting our two bedrooms, my fingers curled into claws, and I'm screaming like I'm that wild pig, but with a spear lodged deep in its guts. I have to force myself to stop. I actually put my hands around my throat in order to choke the sound off, and the tears overtake me again, from nowhere. I feel them falling straight out of my eyes onto the speckly brown carpet worn so thin I can make out the yellow underlay in places.

You have to understand, I'm not a crier. It's something I've trained myself not to do, but what has taken me years to perfect has all been undone in one day.

I'm falling apart. I'm a mess. I need to pee. A door banging somewhere far below causes me to sprint for the bathroom and lock myself in. The Chinese medicine man closes up late on Fridays. Mum and I have gone out for late suppers before and seen him moving calmly amongst his shelves and medicine chests, putting things away, the lights in his shop half-dimmed to deter persistent traffic. Mum said he was good, too; that his appointment books were always full weeks ahead. He could cure anything, any hurt, she said. Physical, spiritual, you name it. He had magic hands.

Like, yeah, that's possible, I'd snorted, pointing at the webby skin on the side of my face. *Magic hands can't fix* that.

But she'd just started belting out the chorus from that Whitney Houston song about miracles, and I'd been forced to hit her with a cushion, right in the mouth. Only when we'd stopped laughing had she said: *That's your trouble. You're a sceptic. You're a straight line, my darling, in a very circular world. Things will not go easy on you in this life if you do not unbend.*

And I'd said tightly: *It's not that I'm a sceptic, per se, Mother. I just don't want to know any more than I have to.*

And then she'd said, *Fair enough, but you'll have to agree it's a necessary evil*, in a funny little voice, before disappearing somewhere for a while. Never for long, which is exactly what I told the police. Just long enough for her to *commune with my dead*, as she liked to put it. I never knew where she went, and I never asked, and now I think I should have.

Ignoring the hard ache in my bladder, I throw myself onto the closed plastic toilet seat and wrap my arms around myself, knees tucked in hard under my chin. The blue-green tiles beneath my toenails swim indistinctly in the ebb and flow of my salt tears, straight lines reforming into curves and back again. *Please, please, let the nice old man not have heard me losing my head up here.*

Perched there, I rock back and forth while the tears continue falling straight out of my eyes. It's something habitual and comforting, the rocking. Mum told me I've always done it, since the fire. The rocking helped me get to sleep in the beginning, and I still do it after I climb into bed each night, or else the sleep won't come. Just another thing that isn't common knowledge about me. It's what I do when I'm at home, and I can let it all hang out, and there's no one to judge, because she never did. She accepted me and loved me and called me: *the most precious thing in the whole world*. Another sob escapes me then, harsh and monstrous.

I'm still crying noisily, steadily, when a deep voice, male, calls through the bathroom door, 'Hello? Joanne?'

It's like magic, the man's voice. Instantly the tears, the rocking, the noise winding out of me, it all stops.

I am a single pent-up breath.

The guy tries the bathroom doorknob but I shot the bolt out of reflex, and the steam-warped door rocks in its frame, but doesn't budge. I almost fall face-first off the top of the toilet, scrambling for the taps above the sink. I turn them both on, full force, to disguise the sound of my desperate breathing. But he is undeterred by the loud sound of running water. *Rattle, rattle* goes the door.

'It's Hugh,' the voice calls out—male, posh, *drunk*, because it comes out:

Ish Hee-yooooooo.

'You said I was supposed to come back and see you.'

Statement, not question; all the words slurring together. It takes me a beat extra than it should to work out what he's saying. Was she expecting him today?

Trapped like an animal, I half-turn from the basin towards the ancient washing machine in the corner, as if I might somehow take shelter inside it, and hear someone else outside laugh, 'Maybe she's in the shower?'

The way my skin is prickling now actually *hurts*.

43

A third voice butts in. 'Bet you'd like to see that, Charlie, you dog.'

Charlie, the dog, laughs and says, 'We can wait. We can wait all night, right Hughey? Because you're worth it. Don't you wanna know how *much*?'

My eyes fly to their own bulging reflection in the medicine cabinet mirror, scar flaming in the water-stained glass.

Men. Three. In my house.

Hugh, Charlie and a third one, whose confident sneer had made my skin crawl. What if they try to force their way in?

I hug myself, rocking, as the water runs and runs noisily down the plughole. For the second time today, I am outnumbered by strangers in my own home. It's as if time and sound are magnified, made elastic, by my fear.

The doorknob rattles again and I almost tip over into the mirror, in horror. *Leave me alone.* My throat works at the words, but they do not come.

'Now you bastards have got me here,' the one called Hugh snarls imperiously, 'what's supposed to happen *next*? Jo-aaa-anne?' he adds sharply, singsong. 'Is everything o-kaaaay?'

Everything is not okay, *it is not okay*, but I pitch my voice higher than usual, like I'm doing a comedy version of my mother's voice, and quaver, 'Now's not a good time, young man. Come back another day.'

Then I turn the water off, listening hard, fingers tangled in the spokes of the taps, which feel like the only things keeping me up.

'She can't be decent,' sniggers the nameless one. 'Maybe the hot, naked, psychic lady needs a hand?' He doesn't bother lowering his voice.

The male equivalent of giggles erupts outside—*hor hor hor*—and I feel my face flush right up to the hairline.

The door jumps as a fist is rammed into it. 'I *told* you this was a waste of time, Rosso. She hasn't even done it. I let her take my money, Jesus. *Get my birth chart done to find out how my life's going to "turn out"!* It's going to be a *sterling* life, and I don't need a bullshit psychic to tell me that. Only morons believe in this stuff.'

Hugh, Charlie, Rosso.

Mum took this guy's *money*?

He sounds like a born-to-rule arsehole. Mum usually gives shitheads like this a miss. She has a meter. She can just tell. How did she let this one through?

I can't explain what happens next. The words just tumble out of me.

'I'm a busy person, *Hee-yoooooo*,' I roar, dizzy with fury and distress. 'Leave your natal details on a piece of paper on the table on your way out and call in this time Monday. *Alone.* Leave the Greek chorus of wise guys at home. *If you're game.*'

I'm so angry I'm not even rocking now, though the room seems to tilt in and out of focus at the edges.

'Oh, I'm *game*,' Hugh replies immediately through the door, 'because, like I said, only *morons* believe in this stuff and nothing you can do has the power to change a single thing about *me* or my *life*. Later.'

He punches the door again, and I recoil into the pink enamel sink rim like the punch actually reached through the wood and landed on me. More shuffling and laughter, followed by the sound of something being shoved aside, or someone being shoved into someone else.

The heavy *tock, tock* of the bathroom clock tells me only minutes have passed, but it feels like hours that I stand there, waiting: for the creaking and snickering and shuffling outside to stop; for the sound of my own heartbeat to die out of my ears.

Why did I offer to do the guy's *chart*? Mum's never been able to get me to do one from start to finish, not even for a bit of pocket money, not even when I know how, like, backwards; because I refuse to be influenced, or to influence others, using some 'science' I don't even truly believe in. And here I am promising to do the guy's radix out of, what, *anger*?

But then I work out that some small, vicious part of me wants there to be bad news in Hugh's stars, and for me to be the person who delivers it. I want it so much to be true, it is a feeling as fierce as pain. I will find something. I will twist him, and he will never be the same.

Feeling stupid, I pull open the medicine cabinet and grab the black-handled hair scissors off the first shelf. Cranking the door open an inch or two, I survey the narrow slice of hallway with the blades raised, letting out the breath I hadn't realised I was holding.

I push the door open more fully, and the *creak* it makes on the outward swing is like a chill breeze across my skin. It's quiet now, and so very bright. The dim of the pendant light in the bathroom hasn't prepared me to re-accept the light blazing down the length of the corridor, out of my room, Mum's, everywhere. So much light. It's like I released the sun in here. But all I can think is that I need to lock the front door; that I have to make it there first.

I'm moving down the hall before my feet know they've started. It is somehow like the light's inside me, hot and unsettling, crowding out all conscious thought save the need to protect myself. How could I have been so dumb to leave the place wide open like that? I find myself standing in the connecting doorway to the living room, just across from Mum's room, and I can't immediately process what I'm seeing as I look towards the kitchen. It's all coming to me in pieces, stark and backlit.

A fallen reading lamp. On the floor.

A fan of papers, kicked out, like leaves, leading from

the sofa towards the reading room, the kitchen bench beyond it.

Cushions every which way. Did I leave the place looking like this? Or did that pack of malicious pricks kick them around for good measure on their way out?

A man, bent so low over the meals table that the tip of his nose is almost touching it. A voice in my head says quite clearly and calmly: *Leave him for now, he won't hurt you, you know that.*

My gaze slides right on past him—and he's standing there plain as life, I mean I can see him, I can't explain what I'm doing—and comes to rest on the long white envelope in the centre of the table with big, bold words and figures slashed across it.

What kind of wanker, I hear myself thinking, *writes with a permanent marker?*

And the conversation I'm having with myself goes exactly like this, as if circumstances have caused me, somehow, to split down the middle: *Date of birth, time of birth, birthplace. It'd better all be there, just like I asked, the stupid shit.*

But there's a man!

Even his handwriting looks like an arsehole was responsible.

But there's a man! The old man from downstairs.

He looks up suddenly and sees me, his face going as shocked and rigid as mine must be. He steps back, squinting, one hand rising up before him as if I am an apparition,

48

and the light is a halo in his ring of fluffy, colourless hair.

I can't really make out his face for the light when he says, 'I warned her! I warned her this would happen!'

The words rain down on me like little pebbles, having no innate sense to them, only an irritant quality. Time and distance, all sensation, are magnified once more by my fear. Perhaps my heart stops; I don't know.

I remember sliding to the ground, having enough sense not to fall on the scissors I am still loosely holding. But that's all I remember.

∽

There's a telephone in my thoughts, ringing loudly. I follow the sound of it, like it's a rope, until it brings me to the sharp realisation that I'm sprawled along my side across the floor, the greasy feel of the brown shag pile against my face.

But then I'm no longer on the floor, I'm in the air; lifted effortlessly by someone with hands that are slight, but hard with muscle. I'm laid across the couch and everything *pings* inwards, and I remember.

She's gone. I'm alone.

No, I'm not. There's a man. *The old medicine man, from downstairs.*

'Avi-*cen*-na?' he says, shaking me slightly. He sounds like he's stepped out of a Chow Yun Fat movie.

He knows my name. That surprises me—because I've never introduced myself, never even talked to him—but I play dead for a bit longer, fighting the impulse to curl up in a ball and rock until the old man walks out in disgust, or dismay, unable to fathom what I could possibly be doing. Once, when I was nine and sleeping over at a friend's house, someone caught me doing it and that was pretty much the end of sleeping over. People think you're mad, you see, and they think that madness is catching.

The telephone stops then starts up again, loud and jarring, and the old man snaps, 'I know you are awake. Aren't you going to answer it?'

I ignore that, too, eyes jammed resolutely shut to indicate: *I do not want your help; I do not need you here; I will 'come to' when you have gone.* The man makes a *hunh* kind of noise and walks away, and I feel myself start to relax as he crosses the room.

Then he actually *answers my phone*. My eyelids spring open as he says calmly, 'Avicenna's phone, Boon speaking.'

'What are you doing?' I say, appalled, scrambling upright, as Boon adds, 'Okay, okay, uh huh, she's home, no problem.'

He gently replaces the receiver, looking at me across the length of the apartment, his head slightly tilted.

'You've got no right!' I snarl.

He shrugs. 'It could have been your mother.'

That stops me like a bullet.

'I saw some men leaving your apartment,' the old man says, expression softening. 'Naturally, I was worried. You should really be locking your door. I told your mother, when she insisted on moving back here, that the city is a lot crazier than when she lived here with your father.'

I feel the muscles of my face sliding into shock. He knew both of them?

'You have his eyes,' the man adds, as if he can read my mind. 'Oh, and your school friend, Simon Thorn—that was him on the phone. He wants his book back. He says he's coming over now to collect it.'

Then the old man's gone, and it's all I can do to make it to the toilet in time.

5

Basic Premise #1: *Simon Thorn knows where I live.*

If Vicki Mouglalis was the one who told him my address, I will kill her myself using some fiendishly diabolical and highly complex methodology involving pulleys, notwithstanding that she is my closest friend (and that's not saying much).

Basic Premise #2: *Simon Thorn cannot come up here and see how I live.*

I can imagine his lips twisting hatefully as he says to his second-in-commands Buddy Sadiq and Glenn Tippett on his way over: *Getting a glimpse of the Frankencrowe in her native habitat? Priceless.*

The things you see, you can never unsee. He's not

allowed that much power over me. I've got to catch him on the street, before he even sets foot on the stairs.

Bolting out of the bathroom and into my bedroom, I look for my backpack and that stupid *Compendium of Classic English Poetry* that I was forced to borrow off him to write my half of the talk because I was too cheap to source myself a copy. I remember the collective gasp that had gone up when Mrs Dalgeish allocated talk partners midway through first term. I'd only been there a few weeks, but already I knew who was safe, who wasn't.

'But it's worth ten per cent of our final mark!' Simon had protested, skin pale with fury, refusing to look me in the eye.

'Maybe you got lucky,' Adam Carney had snorted from behind, 'because she's going to carry your sorry arse over the line, Thorny. She's got the Tichborne covered; ask anyone. *I'll* take her if you don't want her.'

Lots of people had joined in the haggling, while I burned and burned at my desk, until Dalgeish had rolled her eyes under her unnaturally black Jazz-Age bob and matching eyebrows and put a stop to it. Cornered, Simon's gaze had snapped to mine with an *All right, bring it* kind of look which had made me so mad I had asked him for his stupid book in front of everyone, and he'd had to hand it over.

I tip everything in my daypack onto the carpet and I'm

looking at a coin purse, a plastic zip-lock bag full of panty liners and a squashed banana that's ninety-nine per cent black. None of which remotely compute when taken in combination. Where *is* everything?

While I'm staring down at the banana, whose off-white insides have started leaking out through the broken skin like pus, I'm frantically jiggling on the spot. Tearing off flannelette every-which-way and pulling on jeans, a yellow turtleneck and a shapeless fleecy navy hoodie with kangaroo pockets I'm hoping will convey just the right amount of disdain for Simon Thorn, eternal champion of the free-market system and school captain of the biggest boatload of dysfunctional so-called high-school geniuses in Melbourne.

Every girl nerd and polysexual at Collegiate High—a name that says it all, because every day at Collegiate *High* is exactly that!—has a metaphorical hard-on for Simon Thorn, who like some mystical Indian shaman goes by many names: The Thornster; Greased Lightning; Simo; Lucky-as-fuck.

He's the man most likely to steal your girlfriend and charge you for the privilege, via some complex betting/ Ponzi scheme he's come up with. I can imagine the swing-ing, cashed-up household he hails from: half an acre on The Avenue in Parkville, with a louche barrister father who doesn't believe in having to pay a cent for education, and a fruitarian artist mother who used to be a neurosurgeon.

Can Simon Thorn *argue*. He has a mouth like a sub-artillery machine gun and looks like one of those ugly-beautiful French boys: the kind with interesting bony faces and long, off-kilter noses who model kilts and combat boots on the runway. All grey-green eyes, nuclear-winter pale skin, straight dark brows and slicked-down, side-parted short hair that's long on top. Whatever the weather—maybe because he's trying to prove he's really one of us, one of the proles—he wears worn-looking jeans with beaten-up leather workboots and a rotating handful of faded, button-front Henleys that show off his boxer's shoulders and broad-spectrum pectorals to perfection.

We're all scholarship kids, see, every single one of us. Get past the fiendish entrance exam and show proof you live within two kilometres of the place—established for the offspring of the inner-city working class by some 19th century sadist—and you're in. There's no uniform, few rules. You don't have to possess basic levels of personal hygiene or even a loose idea of how the social contract is supposed to work. Based on the way people eat at The Caf, the entire student body has never been taught how to hold a fork properly and can't afford three square meals a day.

But Simon's not sloppy like the rest of us. He's not content just to coast. He lives by his own set of internal guidelines, and occasionally you get glimpses of the iron that rules him. But only glimpses. He cuts through the rest of us like an icebreaker on its way to leaving the known world behind.

He looks too hard and too clean. He wants to know everything from every angle and he wants to know it *now*. And he never stops trying to crush me in public. It's like a blood sport with him.

He'll be here, any moment and *he can't see how I live.*

Where is his damned book?

The last time I felt normal levels of anxiety it was Wednesday afternoon and I was in the Leppitt Gymnasium, painting a crowd scene. Lots of pink, tan and brown faces. *Fuckin' fifty shades!* Ozzie Palomares had grunted, down on his massive knees—each one thick as a Christmas ham—beside me, amongst the paint pots.

I had made one of the spectators red-faced, and frizzy-haired, just for him, and Ozzie had given the woman he was painting enormous tits, as a gesture of affection for me and my D-sized rack. We'd grinned at each other like lunatics then, and proceeded to paint moustaches on all the women.

Slow down, rewind. Gym. Start there.

I was already in the gym before the working bee started. I'd helped move the balance beam out of the way to get the backdrop down.

Everything has to be in my sports bag. The one

prominently marked with the word *Champion* on both sides, which must operate as some kind of visual joke once I've got the thing slung over my shoulder.

I pull the duffle out from under my bed and squat beside it, before undoing the long zipper that runs the length of the bag. I toss out my wallet, shin guards and the plastic box-on-a-rope that holds my bright yellow mouth guard, digging down through tracksuit, socks and dirty runners until I hit the smooth cover of a textbook.

There are others beneath it, and I tip everything out onto the floor. The weight and motion of upending the bag puts me on my arse on the carpet and two things leap out at me: Simon Thorn's bloody poetry *Compendium* and a dark red, A4-sized journal, bound in fake leather with gold scrollwork.

I feel like I'm on fire as I grab hold of both, and my wallet, and my house keys. Slamming the door behind me, I run, shaking, down the stairs to head Simon off at the pass.

∾

It's chilly now, in a way I've only just started to recognise as the way night falls in Melbourne in autumn—bitter and immediate, from sun to shade in a heartbeat—and my feet are soon frozen lumps inside my Explorer socks.

But it isn't long before Simon materialises out of a crowd of start-of-weekend, out-for-thrills street traffic in his usual worker-chic garb—six foot plus of wiry, rock-solid muscle, a fresh bruise under one eye—and I don't bat an eyelash or even say, *Hi*.

I just ram the compendium into his sternum so hard he gives an audible *ouf*, then step off the front stoop of my building, job done, crib protected, crisis averted, and turn on my heel to cross the street. The arcade over the road is only open until midnight, but beyond it, one block over, is a 24-hour grease-pit where I can sit and feel like I'm part of the living, but still be left alone with Mum's journal, a lamb gyro and something to drink with sugar in it.

I'm so hungry, so grainy-eyed and tired, I'm light-headed. Or maybe it's the feel of the journal, burning like acid into my palms. I have to resist opening it right now and devouring it while I walk.

'Hey, wait, *wait*,' Simon growls, grabbing my arm just as I'm about to step onto the road. His hand is red-raw, so damaged from doing time on the bags at whatever designer gym he frequents that the knuckles are practically smeared together into a single puffy line. Simon's hands are the ugliest part about him, and I don't want them near me.

'How dare you come here!' My voice sounds thick and strange with rage. 'How dare you *touch* me. And how,' I add, elbowing him in the ribs to make him let go but getting only a small, ragged intake of breath in return, 'do you even know where I *live*, you creep?'

Simon's fingers bear down harder around my arm as he snaps, 'I can't believe you *bent* the front cover of my book right back!'

I'm not a short person, but he makes me feel short, and so angry I see stars. Running on instinct, I reach below my left armpit with my right hand and pull out sharply on his battered little finger. It's a trick Mum taught me. Simon gives a wounded bellow and lets go.

'Now it's two for two,' I snarl, and a taxi blares in passing as we tussle for a moment on the edge of the bluestone kerb.

'*I'm not going to carry you!*' he shouts, and an Asian girl coming our way, in fluffy Mukluks, skinny jeans and a black hooded puffer, opens her eyes wide and swerves around us.

'And I'm not asking to be carried,' I splutter, 'and especially not by *you*. I'm *out*, you've *won*. There's nothing now standing between you and the R. M. Tichborne Prize! Field's clear, best of luck with your life.'

It's true: I don't care anymore; he can have it, that thing we both wanted so badly. Suddenly, I feel lighter: *One less thing to consume me.* Simon is so shocked that he drops my arm and I'm across the road before he can work out a reply.

'That's it?' he calls, frowning over the rooftops of the cars passing between us. 'One bad thing happens and you give it all up? You don't come back? Where's your *fight*? You're supposed to be a fighter.'

I turn and look back at him, hugging Mum's journal to me. Beneath it all—the big hair, the swagger, the sarcasm-as-full-body-armour—I'm no better than any of them, the people inside her book. I am the sum of my vanities and my faults, my cravings and my weaknesses, just like they are.

All I want is my mother. I need her to come *back*.

One moment Simon is standing there, glaring at me, and then the sea, the sea that is in my eyes, washes him away, and there are only colours. I don't hear him cross the road, but then he's right in front of me, stepping up under the bright white of the arcade signage, and I can't understand why he isn't *glad*. The Tichborne Prize is worth $10,000 to the top student in their final year. It's a no-strings, no-questions-asked windfall. You can use it to fund your tertiary studies or your raging coke habit. For the lowlifes of Collegiate High, it's a big, *big* deal; no one's ever seen that kind of money in their lives. But I am prepared to walk away.

That's what I tell Simon, mumbling the words in the vicinity of his chin. He stares down at my scar tissue with fascination and I feel it burn. Up close, it's like crocodile or ostrich hide, quite alien.

'It's bad, really bad what happened with your mum,' he says in a low voice. 'But we have until Wednesday, and it's important. Dalgeish got me your details and gave us an extension because of the circumstances. It's a *joint* thing, remember? *Marks given for ability to work with others.* Which indicates more than one person must participate. We're the last two. That's what I came to tell you: there's still time.'

I tap the back of the journal. 'Maybe for you,' I tell him jerkily, 'but time's everything in cases like this. This was Mum's. We've been looking everywhere for it. It was in my gym bag!'

He can hear the confusion and bitterness in my voice, and frowns.

'I must have scooped it up with everything else on the kitchen bench before I left the house that morning,' I say, shaking my head. 'It could tell me everything, or nothing, but this is where I turn and swim out, partner.'

I don't care that I'm not making any sense, flinching as he moves forward until he's so close I can smell the sandalwood and citrus and sweat on his skin. I don't really want to know anything more about him. We two are ships. I hold his gaze as I back away.

Eventually, Mum liked to say, hands on hips, surveying the mess of our possessions as we geared up for yet another move, *you have to give things up, even if it hurts.*

I know I will have to give up Mum's book, but not yet. Not when I'm the only one in the whole world who spoke the same language she did, and can maybe read this thing to work out what happened to her. It's almost as if I was created to do it, and I will not fail.

I look up into the clear, cloudless black of the night sky, the muted stars, and say fiercely, 'I do not *submit*.' Then I turn and enter the glaring white tunnel of the arcade teeming with late-night shoppers heading home, uncaring of whether Simon is with me or not.

6

Simon looms at my shoulder as I queue at the sweaty display window of fried foods and ask for the special of the day: a Turkish pide stuffed with shanklish, pickled pineapple and pulled-pork. My mouth is watering so badly I can barely get my order out. It sounds like all kinds of wrong: salty, sour, sweet, meaty, and loaded with carbs and melted cheese. But it's the only meal I'm going to manage today, and it covers every one of the food groups, so, hey.

For a moment grief overwhelms me. I close my eyes and lean my chest and belly against the hot glass on the pretence that I'm feeling cold. There's the sound of a vacuum seal separating, and a rush of warm air against my face, as the mournful-looking man behind the counter takes the pide out of an oven nearby. The background clatter of falling cutlery could almost be Mum, fumbling haphazardly around our kitchen for something to boil water in because she burnt through the bottom of another kettle. She could literally burn water, my mum. Didn't I say she was magic?

I smile, but it's a smile that pulls down at the corners, like I'm going to cry. In my head, I can hear her tutting: *You've got to take better care of yourself, love.* I make a small noise, like a hiccup, before I get my throat under control.

'Drink?' the man barks and I open my eyes, pointing to a fluoro-coloured jumbo bottle of sports drink in the fridge behind him, which covers all the food groups, too.

The front door's just about rusted open at this place, and tonight the draft is fierce, so I settle for an inside table against the far wall, near the swing door to the toilets. Taking a seat where I can see the flat-screen TV screwed into the wall, I uncap my bottle, distracted by grainy CCTV footage on the news, of a tall man in a cap and tracksuit robbing a servo. Behind me, Simon's voice is diffident, jokey. 'I think I might be related to that guy.'

I turn, skewering him with a look of disbelief. 'Mr Clean? No way.'

I don't remember telling Simon he was welcome to join me, but he does anyway, sitting across the table over his own mound of oozing meat and pastry. He slides the compendium out of the space between us—its bent cover sticking up at a weird angle like an accusing finger—and I centre Mum's journal in the space it has vacated. The journal doesn't quite lie flat because there are things interleaved through the middle.

Scrapbooking with the stars, Mum would mutter as she pasted in the backstory to some stranger's life. It was crazy the stuff they thought was important to show her. I remember one woman bringing in a cake-baking trophy, another one a Grade 5 piano certificate. Like it had any bearing on the outcome of her life.

I stare at the cheap leatherette cover, wolfing down the pide so quickly that I'm missing my mouth and hitting my chin, wanting to get the eating out of the way so that I won't leave stains on the pages. Simon raises his eyebrows, fascinated, as I chug half the bottle of electric-blue drink in one hit before wiping my hands clean. But then I hesitate over the journal like it's a live grenade.

'You won't know if you don't open it,' Simon observes mildly through a mouthful of chewed food.

Stung, I flip the journal open so forcefully there's a hollow *clap* as the cover hits the Formica tabletop. There are marbled endpapers pasted on the insides of the book in a vomity pattern of pale blues and reds, like an oil slick on water. On the facing page, over the general impression

65

of vomit, I see that Mum has taped a small diagram. It's an astrological chart without any identifying attributions: no name, date, natal longitude, latitude.

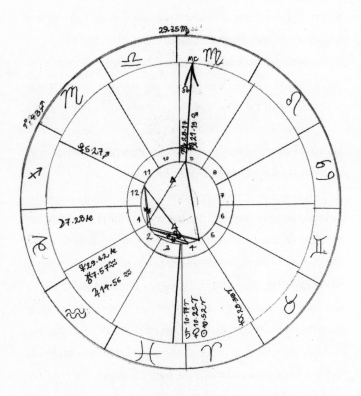

Just a bleached-looking photocopy, so pale it could be a bad photocopy of a bad photocopy. But the drawing is in Mum's hand, and the chart must have been important to her because it's the very first thing in the journal. I can't stop myself from reaching out and touching it as though it might speak to me and tell me where she has gone.

But, of course, it doesn't.

'It could be for anyone, from any time,' I say aloud, my eyes running across the signs and annotations.

Simon swallows loudly, leaning forward with interest, and I swear I almost hear his fearsome, gigantic brain kicking up a gear, ready to suck down and master something new. *'What—?'* he begins.

I make a duck beak with my hand to shut him up, the same way Mum and I used to silence each other, and he actually laughs. Flushing, I run my finger over the photocopied glyphs, one after the other, and I'm talking before I realise I'm talking. 'Sun in Aries and the fourth house indicates ambition, obstinacy, restlessness, brilliance, sensitivity, quickness to anger, a desire for greater security, a strong maternal influence.'

Simon has stopped eating now. The usual faint expression of scorn he wears around me is curiously absent. What did he declare once, during Physics? Oh, yeah: *He who dies with the most skills, wins.* I feel a savage satisfaction that he will never, ever get *this* the way I do.

'Moon in Capricorn,' I continue, 'and Capricorn ascendant indicates a reserved person with few friends.' The words tumble out of me as if I am channelling *her* voice.

'Pisces and Saturn in the fourth house says the person may be marked for life by a tumultuous upbringing, and this area here?' I jab at the sign:

'It's roughly moon square Saturn indicating a disturbed relationship with the maternal; family problems, abandonment, *lack*.' I run my finger over the chart, seeing this pattern repeated in Saturn square the ascendant. 'Life will be difficult for this person, and solitude will be forced upon them, rather than looked for, or wanted.'

It's like I'm reading it all aloud from a book. Except that *I* am the book and the words are somehow written in my blood. All these years I have denied *the knowledge*, as Mum rather grandly called her skill, but it soaked in anyway, because I'm a freak.

Things come back to me, all the time. I'll be asleep, and then I won't be; and there will be these words in my head: from an advert or a song, or a book about time travel that I haven't held for years. I might look them up, hours later, and see them repeated on the internet, or on the page, word-for-word, and feel a wave of absolute coldness.

Like the time I passed a woman asking her friend if a movie she'd seen was any good, and the friend had replied,

'Shit yeah! It's really deep, and it's got all these underlying themes and shit.'

That happened years ago, before I'd even grown boobs, on a train platform in Nowra. All I'd done was walk past these two women and now those words are stuck in my head, for always. Whenever I see a deep film—one with themes and shit—I'll think about those two women and wonder what they're doing, whether they're still engaging in filmic discourse, on a distant train platform, in the sun.

Snippets eavesdropped from strangers: all that's in me, along with the jingles and the songs, the poems and the passages. I can't run away from the words. I carry them with me, like a carapace: my curse, and my armour, growing heavier and heavier.

With a groan, I plunge my hands into my heavy fall of loose, wavy hair and shove it back again over my shoulders, making sure my left ear is covered. Simon pushes his plate away, even though he's only eaten half his meal. He wipes his mouth carefully, steepling his fingers together on the table in front of him. 'You know,' he says, 'that could be *me* you're talking about. No shit.' My eyes fly to his over the top of the photocopied chart. His mouth quirks up at the corners when he sees he has my attention. 'Brilliant, ambitious, friendless, marked by tragedy.'

'Don't be ridiculous,' I say sharply. 'This can't be *yours*. She didn't know you. She never even met you. You have plenty of friends. You're the school freaking *captain*.'

To forestall him saying anything more, I turn over to the first of the internal pages of the journal. It's headed by an underlined name: <u>*Elias Herman Kircher*</u>. Under it, Mum has written: *Horary reading. Date he is ordained to die? And how.*

'Why would you even want to *know*?' Simon breathes, coming around to my side of the table and forcing me to shove over.

What follows are pages and pages of notes. How many pets the man had, the stupid things he'd called them. The names of his estranged adult children, the houses and places he'd lived in, the money he'd made and assets he owned. Names of companies, names of old girlfriends, ex-wives, people he thought had swindled him, people he thought he'd swindled. Mum had a way of loosening people up so that they talked and talked and talked. People told her everything: their deepest, darkest secrets, things they'd been carrying around for years. None of it might have anything to do with their actual horoscope, but whatever they told her gave her an idea of the kind of person she was dealing with, and how to frame the message she was about to give them: short and sharp, like a slap, because that's the way they liked to take their bad news, straight up; or vague and sweet, because anything harsher than that would completely undo them.

Based on Kircher's birthdate, he was seventy-one years old and had never been hospitalised, never taken a day off work. He lived to work. He'd ruined just about a million marriages to prove the point. Every woman he'd ever come into contact with hated his guts. The guy had enemies from every walk of life, stretching back decades.

Mum had drawn a little cartoon in one margin; a small stick-figure dog with a balloon coming out of its mouth that said: *He seems proud of this?!*

I can't resist needling Simon. 'Play your cards right,' I say snidely, 'and one day this could be *you*.'

Simon shoots me a dark look and keeps reading.

At the end of Mum's running notes on Kircher, we come across a rough sketch of the astrological wheels she'd worked out for him. There is no indication that she'd ever scheduled in the guy for the final face-to-face to give him the news, whatever that had been. Maybe she was working from the drawing I was looking at straight into my laptop. When she...

I feel a pang. The police can correlate all that. They have my computer.

'Can you read this thing?' Simon asks, glancing from Kircher's roughed-out astro chart to me. 'Those questions he asked, could you answer them, do you think?'

I nod, but quickly turn the page, to stop myself doing it. It's none of my business if someone's got a death wish, or whatever. People are mental. The next two pages are filled with taped-in photocopies of old newspaper clippings. My scalp prickles.

Simon helps me hold one of the pages flat as I smooth out a large article folded into an upper corner. There's a date handwritten along the margin in blue biro: *9 July, 1984*. It isn't Mum's writing.

'Somebody must have given her this,' I murmur. 'As background.'

We start reading the article and I feel myself shrinking in my seat, my face and body going hot and needly with distress. *Fifteen-year-old girl found naked, brutalised. Clubbed to death on neighbour's property.*

Fleur Lucille Bawden would have been around my Mum's age now, if some sick bastard hadn't used her like a wet wipe and thrown her away. He'd used a golf club, apparently, in all sorts of inventive ways.

I fold the newspaper clipping up hurriedly as soon as I'm done, not checking to see whether Simon's finished because I'm feeling panicky and breathless. I flip backwards and forwards, briefly scanning every article, and he lets me do it, without complaining. All date from a six-month period from mid-1984 to early 1985; there's nothing later than that.

I slump in my seat. There is a feeling in the pit of my stomach, an almost pain, for this girl. I can see why

Mum would have wanted to take this one on. Sometimes the news made her cry. I would look up from the meal I was balancing across my knees and there would be tears streaming down her face. She'd see me looking and hurriedly pretend there was something in her eye, a big something. Or she'd *whoosh* to her feet and say she needed to go to the bathroom, and go cry in there.

She lived like all her nerves were on the surface of her skin. If someone was rude to her at the bank, or in the street, it would hurt her for days. She'd circle back to the incident like a dog worrying at a wound, always resolving to be a better person, saying she must have deserved it somehow, that it was karma coming back on her.

Someone had called her a *chink-lover* once, on the streets of Dimboola while she was pregnant with me and walking with Dad. This stranger had leaned over and hissed it right into her startled face. She'd never gotten over it. Such a small, random unkindness, but she could still access the pain fresh, like it happened five minutes ago. Since we moved here, she'd mentioned it more than once, like it was on her mind a lot.

On the page after the taped-down news stories is a list of names and birthdates, times, all with birthplaces attached. There are four names, all male, ranging from a forty-eight-year-old to someone who would be eighty-seven later in the year. I see Simon's eyebrows rise when he gets to that one, doing the math as quick as me.

On the facing page, Mum's written: *All horary readings. Any likelys? Contact Don Sturt for more background. Two instalments, first down.*

There's a mobile number for Don Sturt, written underneath, but nothing more. No charts, no workings. It was hard to see whether Mum had gotten very far with this one, but easy enough to figure out why someone would still want to know, even after all this time.

Time's like a concertina, Mum said once. *It has a habit of folding in on itself. You come back to it, and back to it, the same point where everything went off course. It's a song with only one verse, one chorus.*

She'd been talking about what happened with Dad. But she could just as easily have been talking about Fleur Bawden, with her long, skinny limbs, long golden hair and wide brown eyes.

'She was unrecognisable,' I find myself whispering, unable to forget the words. 'Like she'd been in a bad car accident with no seatbelt on. Blunt force trauma to the body, to the face; but *especially* the face.'

'They must have been desperate, hey? To consult a, um, ah…' Simon's voice trails off awkwardly.

'Witch doctor?' I say waspishly, regretting it when I see the look on his face. 'Yeah,' I murmur. 'Desperate. They always are.'

I look back down at the list of names, times, dates, places. To anyone but the Crowes, they would just appear to be a harmless arrangement of letters and numbers, flat and unrevealing. But if there was anything in them, Mum would have been able to find it.

I turn to the next page and take in the name: *Hugh Athelrede de Crespigny.*

Birthdate: *19 October, 1992.*

Birthplace: *London, United Kingdom.*

'Well, that figures,' I say automatically, understanding dawning at once. 'Dickhead.'

Out of the corner of my eye I see Simon's eyebrows shoot up. 'You *know* this one?'

'He came calling this evening,' I mutter, 'while I was on the toilet.'

'*What?*'

Mum's written: *Wants a simple radix done—emphasis on wealth, health, love. Paid in total.*

Nothing more beyond that. I flick through a few more pages and they're all blank. All up, Mum only got a third of the way into the journal.

'Wait!' Simon insists as I fan through the rest of the book impatiently until I reach the queasy-looking endpapers at the back and shut it. 'I think I saw something.'

He takes the journal out of my hands and thumbs carefully back through the end pages. Taped all by itself, on a page near the end of the book, is a small business card that reads:

THE ARK OF
A – Z
WUNDERKAMMER & EMPORIUM
SCIENTIFIC & NATURAL ODDITIES BOUGHT AND SOLD

I lever the card a little off the page and peer down the gap I've created, spotting an address in Little La Trobe Street on the back. It's about three blocks away from my place.

'I've never heard of it before,' Simon mutters, 'and I thought I knew—'

'Everything?' I interject quietly. 'Keep thinking that, mate.'

Simon sits back, looking slightly wounded, and I almost say to him: *What is it about you that makes me say these things?* Instead I close the journal, looking up at the TV without really seeing it. Outside, in the intersection between Russell and Bourke, someone gives someone else a serve on their car horn. I hear abuse, a flare of squealing tires, but I don't turn.

She said I would love it here, because she did. She lived here before, with my father.

The old man, Boon, had let that one slip. Mum had never told me herself that she had any history with this city. When I'd been looking at it all with fresh eyes, like a wide-eyed bumpkin in the big smoke, I'd thought she had been too.

I lay the flat of my hand against the journal's cover. 'I have to give this to the police,' I hear myself saying faintly. 'First thing. One of these people may have, may know…'

It's the enormity that gets me the most: of her absence. It crowds out everything. I swallow, and the sea beneath the surface of me trembles.

Simon tugs on my sleeve and I look down at his damaged hand, reminded afresh how weird it is that he is here, of all people. We're sharing pineapple-pork pides together like we're *friends*. If we aren't defending our positions vigorously, poisonously, we barely talk in class. Just look dagger eyes at each other in a constant struggle for verbal and written supremacy.

He's exhausting to be around, pushy. I'm reminded of this as he says, 'You need to come back to school, finish the talk.' His voice is low and urgent. 'Just *finish*, you're that close. It won't take more than an hour, two at most. We'll get it done—even if it means we have to stake out a corner of the library and I have to put up with your ugly mu…'

Simon actually tries to suck the words back in, pulling away from me in horror, and I find I've got that smile again, the one that draws down a little at the corners that I have trouble holding steady. Abruptly I stand up and jam the journal under one arm, my wallet under the other. Then turn on my heel with a hiccupping sound. This time, he doesn't try to follow me when I walk away.

7

I slept like I was falling into a pit. But something woke
me. My alarm clock reads 5.41am and there'll be no going
back to sleep now. I'm *on*, that's the way it always is.
On till I'm off and have run out of hours in the day.

The darkness is absolute in my windowless room and
immediately the light has to go on, too, or I'll feel like I'm
drowning.

I can't just leave it to them to find her.

The thought makes me sit up. I fumble for my phone,
speed-dialling Mum. I go straight to voicemail for, like,
the fiftieth time. It's a long shot—the longest—but I tap
open the app, just to see whether she has played. In the
absence of an actual life, I play *Words with Friends* a lot.

Mum's one of them, one of the *friends*, that's how hard up I am for mates. She'll be sitting out at the meals table—*working!*—and I'll be in my bedroom—*working!*—and we'll be playing each other. I'd hear her shriek, right through the wall, whenever I got her a beauty.

Blinking furiously, I see that the game I'm playing with Vicki is open and she has sent through the word *sluts* for 22 points. Her message in the message window reads: *You and me, baby!*

She's intersected it with her previous effort—*nudes*—because getting naked with anyone, anywhere, is on her mind a lot.

I've got great letters, I could get her in a million different ways right now, but I flick out of the game we've got going on and tap into the one I'm playing with Mum. With a catch in my breathing, I see that it's still her turn. Nothing has changed.

Her last word was *peptide* and her message had been: *You're lucky I couldn't use my Z, darl.*

My screen is telling me to give her a *nudge* because it's been *two days!* So I do. I *nudge* my missing mother, heart in my throat. And I know it's completely irrational, but I actually hold my breath as I do it, in case she shoots something back. Which is crazy, right? Because she'd completely forget to come home, or even tell me where she is, but she'd keep on playing?

But there's nothing; even though I wait through an entire chunk of adverts then the news and weather bulletins on the radio, praying over my screen for the sparkly *bling* sound that will tell me she's sent me a word, that she's back.

Disgusted at myself for even looking, I flick to the last game I'm playing.

Changeling_29 has sent through: *qoph* for 46 points. Hebrew alphabet, 19th letter. Classy.

Nice. I message him. *But the day you beat me is the day the world ends, buddy.*

Unable to stop myself, I stab the word *teetered* into the screen for 78, using up all of my letters in one hit on all the good squares, together with one of his.

But he's right back with *qat* for 32.

I look at the clock. It's 6.09am.

When I'm on, he's always right there, ready to go, like he's been waiting for me. He never seems to sleep. I think that if I didn't live for our games so much, it would kind of freak me out: how much we play, how much time me and *Changeling_29* actually spend together, our thoughts bent on each other and total domination.

I crouch over the small pane of luminescence in my hand, studying my options. It's close this time, only nine points the difference. I wait for the taunt, the sledge, that any normal person would make. But it never comes, because *Changeling_29* never writes me messages. He just plays.

I don't know him. He's just some random who challenged me to a game a few days after I started at Collegiate and we haven't stopped playing since. We'll finish a game and one of us will call an immediate rematch, setting up the first killer word for an early advantage the way a decent chess player will always go for white over black: to set the pace; to niggle and press and destabilise. It's not that white is inherently better, you understand. It just always gets to go first.

The games with *Changeling_29* are always close. But it's been months, and he hasn't been able to crack a win against me, and I love that it must be killing him. I think of him as a *him*, because deep down I'm as desperate as Vicki is: even if it's just some lovelorn nerd-boy wanting to rub his consonants against me. I don't know how he found me, it's not like I have my gamer name—*Cenna*—tattooed onto my forehead, but I no longer care. He's my longest relationship, ever. And he plays bloke words like *pec* and *scrotum*, so QED, right?

Bastard, I write absently into the message box, before setting my phone down. What am I doing playing games with ghosts?

I suck in a horrified breath. *Take it back, take it back.*

I roll over the side of the bed, landing on my hands

and knees on the fat floor cushions lined up along the side. Mum laid those down for me herself the day we moved our belongings in. With the rocking, I often fall out of bed and she'd said: *Soft landings for you, my darling, always.* They're red and orange, like a sunset. Or a fire. It always comes back to that.

Eyes welling, I jump under the freezing shower water that tastes of iron, scrubbing myself a raw pink as the water warms up. By the end, it's always searing, and I give myself an extra five minutes because there is no one else to conserve the heat for.

I climb into the same passion-killing outfit from the night before, then shove my phone, wallet and Mum's journal into my pack that still smells of bananas. It's not yet 6.30, but it's a Saturday, and Paolo will be opening up at the bakery on Swanston Street that I've designated as my local.

I have a thing for Paolo, with his coffee-coloured skin, curly man-bun and dancer's body. Whenever I order a coffee and something loaded with custard, he makes me feel pretty, if only for the time it takes me to dig out the right change. That's our deal: a little light flirtation for $7.80. Just seeing him is better than the caffeine, and if I don't get my regular hit of him I get cranky.

I feel forward with my toes down three gloomy flights of stairs towards the pool of streetlight coming in through the glassed-in street door. After it slams behind me, I breathe out. A cloud that's white, like dragon's breath, against the dark sky.

'Good morning,' someone says beside me and I swear to God I leap two feet in the air. He's leaning against the red-brick wall beside the bean sprout company plaque and his nose doesn't look quirky or interesting in the streetlight; it looks broken.

'What are you *doing* here?' I hiss, already backing away. This must be an outer ring of purgatory, and somehow I'm stuck sharing it with Simon Thorn.

He's wearing a heavy plaid Bluey jacket and grey knitted beanie, and he keeps pace with me easily as I power down Little Bourke Street, cooking smells already staining the early-morning air.

'I'm sorry,' he says awkwardly, 'you know, last night? I didn't mean to say—'

But I hold up one hand as my phone rings, knowing very well what he meant to say.

'Avicenna speaking.' My voice is clipped, unfriendly, spikes in all directions.

I pull the zip up higher on my hoodie and turn left towards the Three Kings' Bakehouse as the man on the line says, surprised, 'Did I wake you? I just meant to leave a message.'

'Who *is* this?' I reply, brushing off Simon's outstretched

hand as I stub my sneakered toe in a tram track and almost go down face-first. *God*.

'Detective Senior Sergeant Stan Wurbik,' the man responds apologetically. 'We need you to come in to the St Kilda Road Police Complex this morning. Some questions. Need to talk options. Get more consents. And your laptop, we've looked at it. You can have it back. Expect you need it.'

Wurbik gives me directions as I duck into the bakery and breathe in the smells of super-refined flour loaded with lard, sugar and other goodies. Paolo sees me and waves from the back where he's de-bagging coffee beans, pouring them in a *tinking* steady stream into the grinder. Like mine, still damp from the shower, his hair is out, all down his back in dark waves.

As Paolo comes forward, I catch this look on his face—when he works out that Simon and I are together—that is a shade more elegant than surprise. Paolo raises a speculative eyebrow at me in a perfect arch, and I grimace back, telling Wurbik hurriedly that I'll be there by eleven: things to do first, won't be late, *see yuz*.

There's this feeling, tight in me as I hang up, that Wurbik's going to tell me something I won't want to hear.

I shove my phone into my pocket and Paolo stands facing me across the chrome and glass counter. We're exactly the same height, and I've told him before that it's a sign we were meant to be together. It always makes Paolo laugh when I mention it. But I can't seem to bring it up today, or even remember what it feels like to smile. It's like a nerve's been cut, somewhere in my brain. So I stand, slack-faced.

'*Bella*,' Paolo says in his thick, not-from-here accent that's so good you could bathe in it, 'today, we are like the lions,' giving his mane a shake for emphasis.

Then he comes around the counter and plants two kisses on me, one on either side of my face, the way he always does, even when there is a line behind me all the way to the door. As he does, his dark eyes never leave Simon. And it all feels a little off today, the flirting, because it's difficult to pretend that Simon's not Paolo's type. He likes a hard body.

Paolo drifts back behind the counter and picks up a set of tongs, clacking the arms together lightly like the fairy godmother of pastries as he moves towards the cake display that runs almost the whole length of the shop. He slides a couple of miniature chocolate *cannoli* into a white paper bag then fires up the coffee machine. 'Usual?' he says as an afterthought.

I nod, and he slides his eyes in Simon's direction. 'No thanks,' Simon replies, loud and nervous over the high-pressure hissing and squealing. 'Already wired.'

Paolo mock sniffs then pushes my long *macchiato*

across the counter at me, together with change from my tenner. 'Didn't I say you have the good taste in men?' he reminds me archly. 'But remember, I am the first.'

I jam the coins into my pocket, juggling the coffee and the little bag as I back up. 'The one and only, Paolo,' I say in a rush. 'You can have this one; I can't get rid of him fast enough.'

Paolo grins at the discomfort on Simon's face. I turn and say over my shoulder, the way I always do, as if this is a normal day, 'See you next week; have a good week.' But my voice sounds joyless and mechanical, even to my own ears.

Paolo reaches out and stops me, hand on my elasticised cuff. 'You tell your mother, the *occhi di bue* will be back on Monday, eh?' He gestures behind him at the pastry display. 'She was asking.'

My fingers go nerveless and I almost drop my coffee. Paolo can't know, because if he did it would be cruel to say what he's just said, and he's the kindest man I know.

'When?' I say breathlessly. '*When* was she asking?'

Paolo's head tilts right. 'Tuesday?' My insides loosen then tighten as he says, 'No, Wednesday. Yes.'

He can see I want more and his head tilts further. 'It was morning, not afternoon; she looked very tired. She bought the big one, not the regular.' He points at the two sample coffee cups taped to a corner of the counter-top. 'She *never* buys the big one, and never a latte, only espresso—double, no milk—but it was a latte, I'm sure, *two* sugars. I wonder to myself, *Will she finish it?* She is like the doll, your mother. And she wanted three *biscotti* —you know, with the apricot jam—but we sold out.' Paolo's eyes rake my frozen face. '*What?* What is it?'

I shake my head, unable to answer, and he says more kindly, 'You tell her; I will keep some. You tell her to come back, okay?'

I don't remember leaving the shop. All I know is that I suddenly find myself halfway up the hill towards the State Library, bawling down the front of my jumper while Simon holds my coffee and cake like a trained circus animal.

'Jesus Christ!' I howl, snatching them off him, throwing both in the bin so hard that the coffee cup bounces up off the steel rim and splashes me with hot liquid. Mum never snacked. She didn't like sweet stuff, and she ate like a bird.

She never had milk in her coffee.

'What are you going to do?' Simon says cautiously as I scrub angrily at my wet front, then at my face with the back of one sleeve.

'Finish having a small breakdown,' I mutter, too ashamed to look at him, 'and then I'm going to copy the entire freaking j-journal…' I wave my other arm uselessly in the direction of the balding, bird shit-infested lawns outside the State Library. 'Because I can't just leave it to people who don't know her to find her. Then I'm going to hand it in to the police. That's what I'm going to do and why do you *care?*'

It feels like there is a balloon just under my skin, slowly inflating. I stand here, clenching and unclenching my hands, struggling to get air into my lungs while the balloon goes up and up, squeezing me out of my body.

She told me everything: that was how things worked. Mum was a talker; you couldn't shut her up. But she never told me that *the eventuality* would end up claiming me, too.

I feel Simon slide my backpack off my rigid shoulders. He barely touches me, but it hurts my skin; that he should be here, seeing me like this.

'*Give me that,*' I say fearfully, scrabbling in the air for my pack. 'What are you doing?'

He leads me like a blind person to the pedestrian crossing, punching the button with one elbow. His voice is almost lost in the scattergun sound of the green man lighting up. 'I'm getting you there. Somebody has to, okay? Move it.'

❦

Inside his car, later, I'm surprised by lots of things. By the way he patiently positioned the journal while I was operating the copier. By the way he showed me the room where you can access old newspaper articles on the microfiche machine because *it might come in handy, later, you never know*. By the look and smell of his car.

I'm in Simon Thorn's *car*, travelling across Princes Bridge down St Kilda Road, thin sunlight kicking up sparkles on the surface of the murky river that bisects this city. It's a bomb, Simon's car, the kind of car *I* might one day drive: an early model Holden with peeling maroon paint and bubbly window tints, black plastic louvres across the back window. It looks like a low-rent drug dealer's ride on its second go round the odometer. On the inside, the car is OCD bandbox-neat the way Simon dresses—not a scrap of loose shit bouncing around anywhere. But it smells like stale hash browns. Like years of fried breakfasts eaten behind the wheel, with a throbbing bass note of male body odour.

I'd expected a late-model BMW with leather seats and chrome trims. And for Simon's ride to smell like he does: fresh, sandalwoody, expensive. But I find myself actually trying to breathe through my mouth.

Simon gives me a quick sideways look then cranks down his window with the kind of dinky manual handle you see in retro TV cop shows. 'It's kind of disgusting, isn't it?'

All I say, faintly, is, 'I appreciate the lift. But you aren't coming in with me.'

He shrugs and then says, 'Pick one.' He points at the poetry compendium, big as a brick, at my feet.

'*Are you dense or something?*' I say in an angry rush. 'I'm not *doing* it.'

'Just look at them,' he says patiently, slowing down and craning his neck up at the numbers on the passing buildings, big and concrete and sprawling. 'Looking does not indicate commitment to any further course of action.'

I lever the compendium up off the floor by its bent cover, turning to the single dog-eared page I myself inflicted on Simon's once-pristine book.

John Donne (1572–1631)

Beside the chapter heading, Simon's written in his anal, leaning script: *Military service for the Crown, Dean of St Paul's. Secret marriage (12 children!!) ended political career. Wife died of childbirth.*

'Well, that would be right,' I mutter, disgustedly, 'dying of childbirth. That's something to look forward to, as a woman. Why couldn't Dalgeish have given us Stevie Smith, or maybe Yeats or Auden or Whitman like some of the others? Even that guy who didn't punctuate enough and loved himself sick some alliteration...'

'Gerard Manley Hopkins?' Simon interjects dryly.

'Yeah, him. I could just about understand *him*. But she

always saves me the poems and plays written in *400-year-old* English. Crap. Not doing it.'

'She saves them for me, too, remember?' Simon says, easing his car into a service lane, still peering up at the buildings as we roll along slowly. 'Just read one out. That'll be the one, then we will—'

'*You will.*'

'—build the talk around it,' he finishes, sighing.

When I say nothing for an entire block, he tries again. 'There will be themes…'

'And shit.'

'*Themes* we…'

'*You.*'

'…can pull out of it—*you're very argumentative, did you know that?*—and maybe discuss in more depth.'

Conscious that I'm pouting like a toddler but I can't help myself, I stab my finger blindly into one of the pages and mutter:

> *If they be two, they are two so*
> *As stiffe twin compasses are two,*
> *Thy soule the fixt foot, makes no show*
> *To move, but doth, if the'other doe.*

'Oh, the metaphysical poets,' I snap. 'If someone compared me to a *compass*, I'd fucking drop them.'

Simon slows the car and turns to me. 'I would have

picked that one, too,' he replies evenly, and I can tell how hard he's trying to be patient because he's not patient— I've seen him in action reducing debating hard-arses like Catherine Dinh to tears. 'It's the best of the bunch, *A Valediction forbidding mourning.*'

'They're all about love,' I snarl, 'or God, or loving God. Not in the mood, quite frankly.'

'This one was probably about his wife,' Simon replies absently, pulling up the handbrake as the car shudders to a complete halt. 'I'll need to look into that. The whole secret marriage angle.'

'Angle?' I parrot, glancing out the window, distracted by the official signage and all the blank, black windows that allow only the looking out of, not the looking in. We're here. Then it suddenly strikes me; what I'm groping for, in my head.

'*Compass,*' I say.

Simon looks askance at me. 'Sorry, I thought we'd moved on from the whole compass thing.'

But I always play them, games of association: *This word leads to this word leads to this word.* Words are the only currency I have too much of. Simon has reminded me of my mother's battered tin box of compasses. She'd left all her almanacs behind—that chart the stars and planets in their manifold phases across the skies and years and decades and hemispheres—tattered and taped-up from daily use, cobbled from sources everywhere, indexed by country, by date. But in my multiple ransackings of home I never saw a single one of her compasses.

She's had them since childhood and sometimes even carried one around in the front pocket of her shirt; you'd see the silver tip poking through the weave, tiny but lethal, as she did the vacuuming, or picked at her dinner. Years after she stopped carrying me around, she still carried *them*.

She would only leave home with them if she was drawing a chart for someone *in situ*, in their own environment. In those cases, she had all the coordinates already mapped out in her head, memorised.

A parlour trick, she would call it, modestly, as she sketched out someone's celestially ordained life map before their rapt eyes. Over cups of tea, someone would have their own little universe rendered live on paper.

The compasses had to be *with* her. I wasn't sure if it was important, but I needed to tell Wurbik to maybe tell people, put it out on the wire, or whatever: that the crazy shaman lady had been packing her weapons. She had been on her way to see someone.

'I have to go,' I say breathlessly, chucking the heavy poetry book in Simon's lap before turning and hooking my backpack up off the back seat.

'Wait—' Simon shouts, but I'm already half out the door.

'That's just it,' I say, leaning in and actually looking him in the face, for once, in all sincerity. '*Don't* wait. Write your talk, win your prize, live your life, be successful, ride roughshod over the dead bodies of your enemies to get there, Simon—only, I'm not going to be one of them. None of it means anything to me without Mum. She took care of me, and I was going to take care of her. She *is* the point, the way I was hers. Now I'm without point; I am point-*less*.' I laugh, but my laughter sounds teary, edging hysteria. 'That poem could have been about *us*. Mum and I never made a move without each other. We were—are, *are!*—joined at the hip.' Simon has the grace to wince as I add gruffly, 'Only a mother could love this face, remember? Now *get*,' I tell him, slamming the door shut so hard the car rocks.

A group of police standing by the bushes near the front door stop speaking and move aside for me instinctively as I hunch my shoulders and enter the complex.

8

There is a laptop set up on a table at the front of the meeting room, with a Victoria Police logo etched into the desktop background. I'm bending over the keyboard when Wurbik—with his sharp-featured young man's face, old-guy hair—comes in with a black, leather-bound notepad and a couple of Mum's journals under one arm, my mangy laptop bag slung over his shoulder. He's followed by a lean Asian guy I've never seen before: in a grey suit and salmon tie with a thin navy stripe through it, clean-shaven, short back and sides. It's hard to tell his age or function and instantly all my antennae go up.

I blurt, 'Just because I'm a *mutt* doesn't mean I need an Asian liaison officer who looks like an accountant!'

Wurbik's eyes widen as he gives his colleague a sidelong glance. All my life, just about everywhere we've lived, I've been the token *whatever* in the room and I've hated it.

'Most people think I look Greek,' I add lamely. 'And I thought *you* were my liaison, Detective Wurbik.' I don't look at the other man. 'I appreciate the gesture, but if you speak slowly and loudly enough, we'll manage. It's all right; *he* doesn't have to stay.'

The Asian dude is smooth, because he doesn't even blink, or back up. He just says, 'Malcolm Cheung. I used to *be* an accountant, but I found there weren't enough stakeouts in Audit for my liking. I'm only here because Drayton got called to a job. Just treat me like wallpaper.'

He waves at me to sit down in one of the three chairs ranged loosely around the police-issue laptop then takes the one closest to the door. Crimson, I take the chair furthest from him, which leaves the seat in the middle to Wurbik, who sighs and inserts my computer bag into the space between our chairs. Stacking the notepad and journals behind the laptop, he looks at the other man and says, 'I guess I drive then,' folding himself into the narrow space we've left him. He squints at the icons, clicks open a folder.

My intake of breath is audible once the video gets going. Filmed from a fixed point somewhere above head height, Mum is looming into the shot holding that impossibly large cup of milky coffee Paolo mentioned. The fluorescent light shining down on her crown makes her long, loose hair look white and her eyes huge in her heart-shaped face. She seems nervous, unhappy? I recognise the place almost immediately, with its overtones of corporate, frosty blue. It's the bank. Mum's bank.

'It's her work!' I exclaim. 'The foyer outside her work. I've waited out there for her, like, a million times. She made it to *work*?'

Wurbik nods and points to a small string of numbers at the edge of the picture. 'That's the date and time stamp, Wednesday. Allowing that she stopped for a coffee on the way'—he gestures at the takeaway cup—'she walked straight to her place of work from home. But *look*.'

The piece of footage is in real-time, and I work out that less than a minute elapses before Mum looks both ways, hesitating, and then steps out of the foyer and back into the street. In a second she is gone, and the footage ends.

'That's it?' I exclaim. 'That's all you've found?'

It's the third day. I know, because I've been counting the hours. I feel a scream rising inside.

'Wait,' Malcolm says quietly. 'There's another one.'

While Wurbik trawls through the next folder, I tell them everything I learnt from Paolo: about the apricot jam biscuits she never ate and the milky coffee she never drank. 'And she took her box of compasses!'

The men look at each other.

'I went through the house so many times,' I babble, 'but they weren't there. Not a single one. The tin, you know, it's silver, flat, but rusty. Has a picture of a castle on it. No, no, a house, a big, grand, like, English house. And there's a dark-blue label thing, across the front of it, with white writing in capital letters that say: THE OXFORD SET OF MATHEMATICAL INSTRUMENTS. It has to mean something, right? That she took them.'

'Compasses?' Malcolm queries, brow furrowed.

Wurbik pulls one of Mum's old journals around the side of the laptop. 'She used them to make these, yeah?'

He flips the cover open and I see it straight away, taped to the inside front cover: a badly photocopied astrological chart for someone whose natal house is *Aries*. I drag my pack onto my lap and rummage around inside with shaking hands, drawing out the dark-red journal I found wedged inside my gym bag. I push the police laptop back a little and line the two books up, side-by-side. The charts are an exact match.

Wurbik pulls the journal towards himself and exclaims in a low voice, 'This the current one? The one she was working on when she…'

I nod.

'Where did you find it?'

I tell them as the two men flick through the contents,

glancing at each other again when they get to the old articles on Fleur Bawden.

Wurbik mutters, 'Mal, that the compasses are missing would tend to increase the chance of it being client-related, wouldn't you say?'

Malcolm Cheung nods before standing swiftly and, without warning, takes the journal out of the room. I made photocopies because I knew this would happen, but I still feel a pang that, just like that, Mum's book is out of my hands and is no longer mine.

As the door clicks shut, Wurbik says, 'That diagram was in all of the journals we recovered from your place. It's like some kind of key. There are cases where if a client's, ah, stars weren't compatible with that thing? She would scratch them. She wouldn't even start. We worked it out from the notes she left in the margins. There weren't many, but there were a handful.'

Malcolm returns, empty-handed. 'Is it hers, do you think? That chart?' he says, sitting back down and crossing his arms over his chest.

'She was a Scorpio,' I say dully. 'Well, at least that's what she always told me.' They can hear the hurt incomprehension in my voice. 'You know: intensely magnetic to others, passionate, painstaking. Scorpios are considered the detectives of the astrological world who feel everything deeply. They're supposed to be great at keeping secrets…'

My voice falters as I realise what I've just said. I push myself to continue. 'It's traditionally a house of great power and darkness. It speaks of profound transformation, death, the underworld. Pluto, you know, key planet.' I see that they don't understand; they have no idea what I'm talking about. I could be pulling all this out of my arse for my own amusement.

'But Pluto isn't even a planet these days,' Malcolm interjects. 'So how does *that* work?'

'Asked Mum the same question,' I say, shrugging. 'Just telling you what she told me.' I trace the outline of the photocopied chart. 'It could have been hers,' I mutter. 'I couldn't really—'

'Getting a birth certificate will sort that out,' Wurbik interrupts. 'Got some questions.' He writes Mum's star sign down in his notepad, putting a large question mark beside it.

'Shoot,' I say warily as Malcolm Cheung shifts in his chair.

I confirm Mum's full name, her birth month and mobile number; that she wasn't in any relationship I was aware of and hadn't been for centuries. I also confirm that, to my knowledge, we maintained the single joint bank account, details of which have already been provided.

'It hardly ever has much money in it,' I say, realising with a flash of horror that I haven't thought about money.

I wonder how much food is in the house and whether I'm going to make it through winter without a job. *Shit*.

'Maternal grandmother's name?' Wurbik says, breaking into my thoughts.

'Joyce Geraldine Crowe,' I answer, puzzled. 'She died before I was born. Sometime in the 1980s, I think.'

'Great-grandmother?' he presses. 'Just maternal. In order to establish…' There's a clear moment of hesitation and I wonder at it. '…identity.'

'Beverley something Crowe,' I reply, frowning as Wurbik asks, 'Also deceased?'

I nod. 'In the 60s, before Mum was born.' I look down, blinking. 'After Dad died, it was just me and Mum. Though she talked about them a lot, said she got "the knowledge"'—I do talking marks in the air—'from her mum and my gran learnt from hers. It came down through the girls. Beverley and Joyce actively made their living from it: private readings, funfairs, school fetes, whatever they could get. Mum was the first female Crowe in generations to hold down a "real" job as well, apparently. Said I was on track to be the first one *not* to earn a living from doing this stuff, that I was a "ground-breaker".'

I snort-sob into the back of one hand.

Malcolm leans forward now and looks around Wurbik, straight at me and my damp lashes. 'But you can do it, right? You've got it, too? This "knowledge"?'

I'm surprised when Wurbik and I both nod at the same time.

'But I don't, uh, practice,' I say, cautiously. 'I've always refused to. Mum never pushed it. It was *her* thing, not mine. But I can read them, her charts.'

'Draw one up?' Malcolm asks casually.

'If I had to.' They can hear the sudden, pathetic eagerness. 'I want to be part, of the, you know, investigation. I want to help in any way I can.'

Malcolm inclines his head, which isn't really any kind of answer. 'And your mum and dad,' he asks, 'they never married?'

I shake my head. 'She always wished they'd gotten around to it. But she said it didn't matter, anyway, because she felt married.'

'Where were they living?' Malcolm pushes gently. 'When you were born?'

I tell them Mum's Dimboola story and Malcolm gives a crooked smile and says, 'Got called *slant-eyes* once, walking up to uni, with accompanying visuals.' He lifts the outer corners of his eyes with his index fingers, lets them drop. 'I was born in Caulfield East,' he says in his broad accent, 'about twenty-five minutes from here. It's the only time I ever felt...'

He doesn't finish the sentence as Wurbik mutters, 'Try getting around a school full of skips with a name like Stanislaw Wurbik. Shall we show her the second one, Mal?'

There's even less footage this time. You get a bird's-eye view of a short stretch of concrete footpath, then a flash of bowed head going past, the plastic top of a takeaway coffee cup. Then there's maybe ten seconds of Mum's back, her shoulders hunched forward, slender legs outlined by slim-fitting trousers, the rounded edge of her tan handbag, receding out of the frame. At the very end, when she's a thin blob only slightly less pale than her surroundings, you see a dark compact van come in from right of screen. Then, after a moment, it's gone, and she's gone too.

All the time, people are passing her, oblivious that Mum is in the process of vanishing.

I find I am shivering and hugging myself tightly. 'You think she got into that van?' I say in a tiny voice. 'Do you know whose it is?'

'We're working on it,' Malcolm says quietly, 'because we want to find your mum as much as you do. But we need your consent to get that footage out. Someone might recognise her, or the vehicle.'

'We're not talking press conference,' Wurbik rumbles. 'Not yet. We just want to run the video through the usual media outlets. It's the only CCTV we've got at this stage, but it's good; clear. The second one was taken near the Flagstaff Gardens, on the edge of town. We think she entered at William Street, exited somewhere on King approaching Dudley Street. She was a long way off her usual route, and she's very...'

'...beautiful,' I finish for him, because it was always the first thing anyone ever noticed about her, even before the damage to her hand. 'So someone may remember.'

'Yes,' Malcolm replies.

'Consent granted.' My voice sounds weak, trembly, like it's not coming from me. 'Go for it, get it out.'

'Just be prepared,' Malcolm says, a touch of concern in his smooth voice. 'You'll get lots of questions, interest, from people who know you. Or her. Have some kind of standard response ready.'

'If you need to talk,' Wurbik adds, 'you just ring me. All hours.' He taps the front of his jacket and I hear a dull retort from the phone in his inner pocket. 'I mean it. I'm your liaison, remember? You insisted. So call.'

'Same goes.' Malcolm extends his hand and a card. Both men stand, and I realise that's all I'm going to get. I sling my laptop bag over one shoulder, my pack over the other, feeling awkward and bumbly and superfluous. Malcolm opens the door and says over his shoulder, 'We'll keep you informed, Avicenna, every step of the way. And thank you.' He goes right, disappears round a corner.

'I'll call the minute there's anything,' Wurbik adds. 'You'll be sick of me before the day's out.' Then he gives my arm a kind of squeezy-pinch thing meant to be comforting before disappearing up a different corridor.

I work out at that exact instant that Malcolm Cheung isn't Missing Persons Intelligence, he's *Homicide*. I don't even have to look at the business card in my hand to know, I just do.

But then I do. And seeing the word printed neatly under his name almost causes me to sit down on the floor right there, but a trim-looking policewoman in navy wool pants and a matching jumper with epaulets suddenly appears in the hallway, summoned as if by magic. She holds out a hand to me, palm up. Like an elderly woman, I take it, and soon find myself back outside, bereft under a sealed grey sky.

Something makes me look, I'm not sure why. I cross six lanes of traffic and Simon's car is still there, exactly where I left it over two hours ago. He is asleep behind the wheel, his beanie jammed down over his eyebrows, head thrown back against the driver's side headrest. He is wrapped up in a blue-and-white checked blanket that blends in so well with his plaid jacket that all I can see of him is his face. The purple bruise under his right eye is starting to go yellow around the edges. All the windows are rolled up tightly again, to keep the heat in, I suppose. And I suddenly get why his car smells like the inside of a fast-food outlet and a locker room, and it does something to my heart.

I go around the back of his car and pop open the crusty-looking boot. It's filled with books, sealed cups of *Suimin* that you just add hot water to, tied-up plastic bags, packs of wet wipes, loose towels, plastic bottles of water, a set of purple dumbbells, a toddler-sized pillow. All the usual shit you'd need to get through a day. If you, maybe, didn't have a house to keep them in.

My eyes fill and I dash at them angrily. I hear his car door open and then he's standing beside me, still wrapped in the checked blanket. I don't know what to say, and neither does he, and we don't look at each other. So we just stare down at his life for a while, then he puts his hand on the raised lid and slams it closed.

He turns and sits on the boot of his car. I do the same and we're facing down St Kilda Road towards the city, looking through the trees at all the cars driven by people whose lives are normal. He pulls his beanie off and twists it in his banged-up hands, while his massive genius brain tries to come up with an excuse.

I don't apologise for getting him so wrong, all this time, because if I don't talk about it then maybe the illusion that he's *The Guy Most Likely*—the one who really has his shiz together—will not crumble and fail him.

'I think there's lentil dhal on the menu at my place tonight,' I say in a low voice. 'You're welcome to share it. At least, until you piss me off, which might be all of five minutes; then you're out on your arse.'

I imagine him trying to fold himself along the back seat of the car, with that child-sized pillow jammed beneath the rough beginnings of dark stubble on his pale face, and have trouble swallowing.

Simon exhales. 'Deal,' he says unevenly. 'But only if we run through the talk. It's just a *talk*. Your mum wouldn't...' I tense up, but he doesn't finish his thought, instead saying softly, 'She raised you to be *strong*. You can tell that. Within a second of meeting you, I could...'

I scramble off the boot before he says anything he can't unsay, and bundle all my bags into the front seat, climbing in after them and closing the door.

9

Leaving Simon's car parked on the edge of the city, we pool our loose change and get a bamboo steamer's worth of *xiao long bao* and a small container of chilli-spiked soya sauce from the dumpling house two doors down.

Simon has a range of plastic bags from his car boot clutched in both fists. 'Just like a homeless guy,' he mutters as we head up the stairwell to the accompanying rustle. 'Thanks for the offer.'

I shrug apologetically as I unlock the front door. 'Smells like teen poverty. Don't thank me yet.'

Only hours ago, I would have killed to prevent him seeing this, but now it doesn't seem to matter. Snapping on the light in the front hall, I say casually, 'Just incidentally, if you reveal the location and condition of my crib, I will be forced to kill you.'

Simon's laughter turns into a small sound of surprise as I light up the place in increments. It's the bombsite I left it last night: everything hanging open; papers, books, cushions all over. As I pass through the living room, I turn on a lamp and fire up the ancient wall-unit gas heater. It hiccups a couple of times before roaring to life.

'Were you…?' Simon says hesitantly from behind me as I kick things aside on my way past Mum's room.

'Robbed?' I reply, not bothering to explain. 'No, I just like living like this. Bathroom's that way.'

I shut the door to my bedroom before pointing him down the corridor, and he disappears into the tropics with his bundles of bags, swiftly engaging the bolt.

While I'm wolfing down my half of the dumplings at the kitchen bench, I hear water starting through the pipes and the mental picture of what he's doing in there is enough to drive me outside. I head downstairs.

I can see Boon's profile through the glass. Usually he has at least one customer with him, or a graceful-looking assistant in a flowing pantsuit with the kind of straight black hair I would trade my wavy mud-brown mane for in a heartbeat. But it's late in the afternoon now, and he's alone, so I open the door that leads into his shop from our stairwell. A bell tinkles and the old man looks up in surprise, his face clearing when he sees it's just me.

'Avicenna,' he says kindly, before his expression goes complicated, anxious, and he half turns to look at something in the shelving.

Behind him are a couple of wooden stepladders giving access to rows of wooden shelves—separated into cubicles—that reach right up to the twelve-foot ceilings. Each cubicle is packed with lidded jars and tins with peeling paper labels. Propped in the gaps are calendars written in Chinese characters on paper thin as onion skin; incense holders; tiny shrines to unknown gods; characters out of Chinese mythology with long, flowing beards and wooden staves, cast out of shiny porcelain.

Boon runs one hand across the ends of his wild fringe of hair, before tugging the sleeves of his patterned pullover down. His gaze is enquiring, but wary.

'You knew them,' I state baldly, 'before I was born.'

Boon blinks. 'Yes,' he says, 'yes, I did. I remember the day Greyson first met your mother.' He smiles. 'At some, ah, alternative lifestyle exhibition. They were very big, you know, in the 90s; almost every weekend, something "spiritual". They had stalls next to each other. On their feet nine hours a day for three days straight. *Who wouldn't fall in love in such circumstances?* Greyson told me. *It was meant to be.*' Boon's smile fades. 'Greyson was the eldest son. The only son. His mother...'

The old man clears a small space, pushing pens and paperwork aside and sitting down on a battered metal stool behind the scratched, glass-fronted counter. He waves at me to come closer and I pull out a matching stool at the front of the counter, sitting on it gingerly. Up close, Boon's eyes are eerie. There's a distinct ring of blue around the dark irises, like his gaze is channelling an eclipse of the moon.

'She never talked about where she came from, your mother. She was a person without history, without family...' He gropes for the right words. 'Greyson's own mother suffered a lot to come here, and when she came, she still suffered. The language, you know; working in markets and restaurants all over town. Every day of the week, rising before dawn. She struggled to have Greyson. She was already old when he was born—she wanted him so much!—but her husband went to Sydney after, and he never... But by then, you know, she couldn't stop working; she didn't know any other way. She could never understand how her son would give it all up for someone so...'

His voice falters entirely to a stop.

'White?' I query finally.

Boon's mouth turns down at the corners. 'Different. We fear what we are not. *That* is something we all share.'

He sighs and gets back off his stool, pretending to straighten a couple of glass canisters on a shelf just behind him. 'Your grandma doesn't want to meet you,' he mutters gruffly. 'I'm sorry.'

'She knows I'm here?'

He nods. 'But she isn't. I mean, she doesn't live here anymore. She went back to Hong Kong a few years ago and she won't come back now. Not even for you. The pain...'

I look down at the countertop, which has grown blurry, understanding.

'Greyson was my godson and I loved him,' Boon says simply, his back still to me, 'the same way I loved your mother. When you were born, I knew. When Greyson...' His voice wobbles. 'I also knew. We were always in contact; your mum was good like that, always writing. When she said she was coming back to Melbourne after all these years, well, of course, you had to come back here and Ping—your grandma—she understood that. Your mother and father were happy here. It was already set up: just one new bed needed, a cleaner, not much work to do.' Boon turns and looks at me beseechingly. 'But Joanne insisted on taking the top floor this time. *No changes*, she said; I wasn't to do anything. I couldn't stop her.'

'I'm sorry,' I say, confused. 'I don't understand what you're talking about.'

Boon turns back and reaches into a wooden cubicle at head height, taking down a silver key on a short length of red string that had been hanging on a hook I hadn't even noticed was there. 'She borrows this sometimes. Just to sit. *For thinking*, she said. Your mother said you didn't need to know—I wasn't to show you, it wouldn't help, you wouldn't remember—but you should see it. It's part of *your* history.'

He takes his own set of keys out of his khaki trouser pockets and comes around the counter.

First flicking off a bank of lights, he locks the shop's main door from the inside and leads me into the stairwell that smells of decaying boxes, before locking up the shop from the outside. Pocketing his keys, he begins mounting the stairs. 'The *Mei Hua Bean Sprout Company*,' I say in sudden realisation. 'That was my *dad*?'

Boon's soft laughter precedes us both. 'It is your *grandma*. It should have been your dad's. Ping sold the business, years after he died, to someone who came out from the same village, on the same boat, in the late 1950s. She's very traditional. She only kept the business name. And this building.'

I go rigid in shock, but Boon doesn't see because he's already opening the mysterious door on the second floor that leads to the apartment only ever filled with silent voices. He swings the door wide and says apologetically, 'It's very dusty. It's been left exactly the way it was when they lived here, when you were born…'

Boon doesn't come past the threshold. He just presses the key on a string into my hand and tells me that I will know where to find him.

The light is fading, but I don't touch the switches, or any of the surfaces, which are covered in a furry pelt of dust. I stand in the doorway. The apartment is a carbon copy of ours upstairs, only nicer. It's dusty, sure, with a closed-up, musty smell. But it still looks like someone could be living here. Every magazine on the coffee table is stacked in a neat tower; the furniture is heavy, minimalist, matching, all in hues of black and grey and coffee. A man-cave, bach-pad; frozen in time for years.

But then I start seeing feminine touches. A couple of small framed Japanese woodcuts on the walls: of blossoms and geisha, 19th century-style; a couple of handcrafted throw pillows on the brown leather Chesterfield that have Mum written all over them. I recognise the quilting blocks she must have used, because years later she was still making the same ones out of the fabric from T-shirts I'd grown out of. There are pillows just like them, upstairs in our apartment.

She'd called the pattern *The Mariner's Compass*: a large, foregrounded, four-pointed star with a series of four rays set on the cross coming out from behind it, with a smaller, eight-pointed star sitting behind, for backgrounding. *Mum taught it to me*, she'd said once, piecing fabric together in front of the TV. *One day, darl, I'll teach it to you.* And I think I drawled something along the lines of: *I don't do craft and you can't bloody make me, so quit asking.*

The cushions have a Mariner's Compass set into the middle in an alternating pattern of blues and reds. I almost cross the rug and pick one of them up to hug it to me, to see if it smells of her—all warm vanilla and rose oil— but I force myself to stand still and just *look*.

This must have been where she came to commune with her dead. I can almost feel him, in here with me, the air heavy with presence.

There are two pairs of slippers by the side entry to the galley kitchen, in his-and-hers colours and sizes, and my eyes sting at how well suited they seem to each other, how they've been placed together with such care. It's clear from the way the dust has been disturbed that Mum only ever came here to think in one place, and I gingerly follow her tracks now, as if walking more heavily might somehow raise the dead.

I'm led to the windowless bedroom they must have shared. There is a neatly made up double bed with a navy-patterned duvet cover and matching pillowslips, the feather pillows gone lopsided from gravity. My gaze takes in the Moses basket on a stand in the corner of the room, made of some woven kind of off-white plastic, a hospital-issue blanket draped over the end of it.

But the footprints I'm following don't extend past a vintage armchair, set up at the foot of the bed that faces a retro-looking, empty wardrobe with two mirrored doors that swing outward from the centre. There are still hangers inside the wardrobe, pointing every which way, and both doors are wide open as if the thing has only just been hurriedly emptied.

Cautiously, I enter the dim bedroom and sit down in the chair, this tight and constant ache in my throat. I imagine Mum sitting here: then and now. I imagine her, then and now, listening for the front door to open; for the confident footsteps that will take him through the living room, down the hallway, to her. I imagine him placing a hand on her shoulder and the two of them looking at each other, reflected in the doors.

Only it's Simon Thorn with one hand on my shoulder and my mobile phone in the other, and my eyes are wide, my scar dark with fearful blood. 'What are you doing?' he asks me hoarsely, his face shadowy in the mirror.

My throat is still clamped tight from the shock of seeing him here. But seeing him has also made me notice something behind him on the wall, to the left of the door. And I point to it now. Simon turns to look, then turns back, puzzled.

The walls are a faded olive-green colour, save for a darker, rectangular patch just beside the light switch. On the wooden bureau below is an empty, glass-fronted photo frame, the warped cardboard backing lying abandoned beside it. I take my phone from Simon's outstretched hand and see Wurbik's number repeated in the screen of missed calls.

'Please turn around and go back outside,' I say quietly as I rise from the armchair and hit *call back*.

∽

I meet Wurbik on the ground floor. Boon's back inside his shop, talking to a customer, but I see his eyes slide sideways, taking in *the fuzz* gathering outside. 'Ask him,' I say urgently, 'what she took. Get him to tell you. Then tell me. Please? It's important I know what it was.'

Wurbik nods as we mount the stairs, a police photographer and a forensics guy following closely behind us.

When we stop on the first landing, Wurbik reminds me again: 'She'll be on the evening news; it's already on the net, just went live.' Then he opens the door to the apartment and the three of them fan out, making very little noise for such big men.

Upstairs, Simon—now freshly shaven, in a clean but dingy white T-shirt and grey trackpants with frayed cuffs—turns the TV up loud as I sweat the lentils with a spoonful of tinned curry powder and chopped onion, then drop two cans of tomatoes right over the top and leave it on a low flame to turn into sludge. Dinner sorted.

I get out of the kitchen in time for the lead story, which is Mum.

There is that cropped photo of her beaming, long hair hanging down across her shoulders, big blue eyes crinkled up at the corners, my tanned and disembodied arm slung around the base of her neck.

'Wow, she looks young,' Simon exclaims softly. 'You wouldn't—'

'Know we were related?' I say absently and he falls silent, listening.

I don't really take in the words that the pretty reporter lady is using, although some part of my brain must be ticking away, mulling them over, because later, a long while after we've turned off the TV, I remember she mentioned they found Mum's bank-issue name tag. It was in the gutter near one of the exits to the Flagstaff Gardens, the pin badly bent, like it had been hastily ripped off. Wurbik hadn't mentioned that bit, the same way Malcolm had omitted to mention that he was Homicide.

Simon's writing *our* talk—the one about John Donne and the secret wife—sitting on the floor at the coffee table, while I stare into space between running to answer the phone. It's been ringing off the hook, with especial surges after each newsbreak and late edition. Like every person who ever met Mum somehow caught the news and wants to share it with me. Old clients, mostly; sobbing about how extraordinary she was and wanting to know whether she'd be back, like I could answer that. The ones who are digging for information, I hang up on straightaway.

'It must be a terrible thing,' I say aloud to the water stains on the living-room ceiling, 'to be so *needed*.'

Simon ignores me, his lips moving silently as he reads parts of the talk to himself. It occurs to me that the two of us must be the two least-needed people in all the world.

After a while, I just hang up as soon as I hear crying down the line. It's easier for everyone concerned, seeing as I never got around to having that standard response ready.

'I'm going to leave the phone on message bank,' I say roughly, as Simon peers into his banged-up laptop screen with a pinched expression—the one I always call his *resting bitch face*—still ignoring me. I scoop up our dhal-encrusted dinner bowls bad-temperedly, along with all the partially drunk cups of instant coffee that have gone cold. Still his expression doesn't change. 'Going to bed?' I bark as he continues typing and deleting and ignoring. 'Hey, I *said*…'

'Yeah,' he replies, not looking up and not missing a beat, 'eventually. But not with *you* so stop asking and go, already. You make too much damned noise for someone who claims they aren't doing anything. It's distracting.'

Huffing away across the room, I drop all the crockery on the counter with a loud clatter that makes him sigh, before turning back to the phone and engaging the *recorded message* button. Mum never had it on record because she didn't like messages building up. She always said: *If it's important, they'll call back.*

But mediation is necessary tonight. And I know I've done the right thing when I'm soaking our dinner things in the sink and a couple of criers get through to the recorded machine voice and hang up abruptly, cut off mid-sob. I turn the volume on the ringer down, conscious that Simon will be out here later, sleeping on a couch two sizes too small for anyone. Except maybe Mum. But as I'm turning off the kitchen light, the phone goes again, and this time there's the *beep* and then it's just silence being recorded.

One cat and dog, I count automatically. *Two cat and dog.*

I get up to ten cats, ten dogs, and still there is only breathing. The constancy, the peculiar quality of the waiting, the watchfulness, seem familiar, and I remember all the hang-ups. I snatch up the handset, conscious that all this is being recorded.

Simon's humming to himself in the other room as I say sharply, 'Avicenna speaking.'

It might be my imagination, but the breathing seems to grow erratic, anticipatory. Usually at this point, whoever it is just puts the phone down. But tonight the silence stretches out further; the faintest electronic buzz in the background. And I want to leap into that buzzing void with questions and threats and fury, but the rational part of me is saying in Mum's voice: *Do not engage.* It was a lesson we learnt the hard way from Graham of Rainbow. But the void is still open between us, beckoning, and unable to stop myself I grate, 'Who *is* this? What do you *want*?'

The breathing stops altogether and it's unbearable: whether to hang up or hang on. Then across the line I hear a voice—hoarse and male—say: 'Slut got what was coming. And you'll get yours, too.'

I scream, dropping the handset like it's made of maggots, and hear Simon overturning the coffee table behind me as he surges to his feet.

PART 2

*Be prepared to journey to a place where
there's the likelihood of pain.*

10

Even though I don't know the faintest thing about him, Wurbik is the closest thing to a father I have at this point. His dry, no-nonsense voice is the first thing I hear in the mornings and the last one I hear before bed. And he hadn't lied. He'd been there when I'd rung him yesterday, near midnight—all my words sticking together in a writhing, ugly, fearful mass—and he'd told me calmly what to do next.

But he also passed on a surprise request, and I'd surprised myself by saying *yes* because it's what Mum would have done.

So Simon and I rock up to the St Kilda Road police complex at 7.30 on Sunday morning. Wurbik, in his trademark dark suit, meets us: me clutching my home telephone that's trailing wires all over the carpet in the empty reception area; Simon politely shaking Wurbik's hand after introducing himself.

I offer Wurbik the machine and he ducks away briefly to hand it to someone. 'You'll get to take that back as soon as this is over,' he says, and then he leads us back out of the building, taking us across the deserted six-lane road to a café just setting up for the day. It's a symphony of curved concrete with subdued interior lighting, white tablecloths, shiny silverware and bone-china plate: you can see that right away through the spotless floor-to-ceiling windows. Simon—in his Bluey jacket and beanie—hesitates at the threshold as he takes in the incomprehensible stone sculpture dominating the middle of the room that more than anything else says: *fancy people eat here*.

The look of uncertainty on Simon's face makes me reach out and give his elbow a tentative squeeze. As we languish by the door, feeling hot and stupid and out of place, Wurbik crosses the room and greets the head waiter, who seems to be expecting us. He's a young buzz-cut guy in black-framed nerd glasses and a three-piece suit. He shows the three of us to a table for four set up behind one part of a high concrete wave. It's utterly private back here, and quiet; a pendant shade casting moody light all over our table.

Wurbik dismisses the hovering waiter but none of us sits. To my look of enquiry, Wurbik replies, 'He demanded that we approach you to finish the job; chewed Mal's bosses' ears off till they said for Mal to make it just go away and he handballed it to me. The police force, you see, believes in astrology like it believes in the tooth fairy.' He sighs. 'I'm sure he'll be here in a minute.'

'I'll get out of your hair as soon as he does,' Simon offers. He'd insisted on coming with me, but being here has done something to the way he carries himself. He is hunched over, wary.

Wurbik, shooting the two of us a shrewd glance, sits himself down at the far end of the table with his notebook out like he's about to conduct a job interview. I slide into the seat beside him, my back against the concrete curve, regretting my sartorial choices—another polar fleece hoodie over a pair of denim-look leggings—as soon as a fit-looking old man in a navy blazer, pink jumper and pressed chinos, with thinning white hair and a pencil moustache, comes through the gap.

The waiter holds out a chair deferentially, but the older man comes straight around the table, towards me, and I am engulfed by a cloud of sharp, expensive-smelling cologne. To my right, Wurbik stands, and Simon starts backing towards the door. But I remain frozen in my chair, head tilted up at an awkward angle as the stranger holds his hand out and says smoothly, 'Avicenna? I'm *so sorry* to ask at a time like this, but it's very *important* to me. And I wanted it "on the record", so to speak.'

'Because evil never sleeps?' Wurbik enquires dryly from the other side of the table, and the stranger says, 'No, it doesn't,' without a pause, shaking my hand with a cool, firm grip.

Simon's almost made it out of our private area but the old man—still clasping my hand—looks at Simon with his alert blue eyes and says, 'Stay, *stay*, young man. I *insist*.'

The old man's speech is full of sharp emphases, like he's used to giving orders to idiots and having them instantly obey. Simon backtracks towards me, sliding his beanie off his head and into a pocket, while the old man takes the seat beside mine, opposite Wurbik. Simon takes the last one, across from me. I have to remind myself, as I look around the table at all the serious faces, that it's a Sunday morning, and this is the new normal.

Pulling my wad of photocopied notes from my backpack, I place them on the table even though I won't need to refer to them. After I hung up from Wurbik last night, I spent hours analysing Mum's handwritten notes, the finished chart, doing a progressed one of my own, just to check. And I wonder again, just like Simon did, why on earth anyone would want to *know* the date and way they were going to die.

Elias Kircher—the first client in Mum's current journal—takes out a slim silver voice recorder and places it on the table, pressing the *record* button. Then he folds his hands together and rests them in his lap. Wurbik looks at the tiny machine then surprises me by sliding out one of his own and placing it beside Kircher's. It starts with a tiny *whirr* when Wurbik states his name and rank, the date, place and time.

'We're here today for a number of reasons,' Wurbik continues smoothly, like he's rehearsed it. 'We called you, sir, because your details cropped up as part of a current investigation. Independently of that call, you rang the hotline, yesterday, after seeing an online news article regarding Joanne Nielsen Crowe.'

Mr Kircher inclines his head once and says, 'I called straight away. I was shocked. I'd been expecting her to call *me* for days, you see, so she was very much *top-of-mind*.'

He looks at me then, and it feels like I'm in a play where I don't know my lines. There's this sensation, like I'm about to step out into the abyss and there's no safety net, and I will freefall.

'For the record,' Wurbik adds, 'you have been ruled out as a suspect in Joanne Nielsen Crowe's disappearance and this meeting with her daughter, Avicenna Crowe, also attended by Simon Thorn'—Simon widens his grey-green eyes at me across the table—'has been instigated at your insistence, Mr Kircher, and doesn't form part of the official investigation.'

Kircher's blue eyes bore into mine as he states, simply, 'Nevertheless, there are answers, and I want them.' Then everyone looks at me expectantly.

I clear my throat, a surge of acid in my stomach. 'I've never done this before,' I say gruffly.

'But you *can*, Avicenna,' Kircher replies, placing his hands on the table in front of him, 'and that's the *vital* thing. The detectives assured me that you possessed your mother's...talents. Please begin.'

I push the fancy table settings in front of me to one side so that I am facing him down an expanse of snowy-white cloth. 'You asked for a horary reading.' My voice is slow and hesitant. 'Elias Herman Kircher. You wanted to know the date you are ordained to die.' I pause to swallow. 'And you want to know *how*.'

Elias Kircher leans forward in his chair, replying softly, but clearly, for the benefit of the voice recorder, 'Yes. Yes, I do.' His face is eager, alight with interest, and his eyes are fixed on me like there is no one else around.

'Uh, okay,' I continue, discomfited. 'So your natal chart indicates that you're a, ah, Capricorn, and your progressed aspects between Jupiter and Neptune—the uh, what did Mum call it? "Millionaire Aspect"—and between Jupiter and Saturn are really very exceptional and bear out your luxurious, um, lifestyle, and ability to get and maintain enormous wealth. But there's a repeated pattern of afflictions in your fifth and seventh houses—to do with love and marriage, the moon and Venus, you know—which indicates a strong attraction to the, ah, female sex, but a general lack of harmony and support in your relationships. So I'm seeing multiple marriages, lots of divorces. You also have extraordinarily powerful aspects for accumulating property, but as Uranus rules your ninth house, and you see how Jupiter sits right *here...?*'

I point to the photocopied chart. Wurbik half stands and pushes the page across the pristine tablecloth to Kircher, who receives it without even glancing at it.

'This indicates constant travel in connection with the maintenance of your wealth and a level of upheaval and risk-taking that—'

'Yes, *yes*,' Kircher's voice is impatient now. 'That's all very well, but it's really very *simple*. All I want to know are *two* things. I don't want the helicopter-level, tourist's version of my life. I am *living* it. I just want to know *when* and *how.*'

I feel the blood *whoosh* up into my face. 'I suck at this, I'm sorry,' I mumble. Mum would have known that this guy took his bad news straight up, no preamble. 'But Mum's not here,' I remind him, 'and I'm not *her.* She would know how to tell you. She just had this way with people.

I've spent my entire life *avoiding* these kinds of moments.'

I find myself emphasising my words just like Kircher does, so that the idiot might somehow understand how much he is asking of me.

'And you shouldn't ask these kinds of questions,' I add beseechingly. 'You're probably *really* rich and *really* important and *really* smart, so you will understand me when I say that these things are *self-fulfilling*. I've seen it, like, a million times before—Mum tells someone what's going to happen and then it happens. No matter how many times she told them: "These are just planetary conditions, you have the power to influence the outcome, free will, blah, blah, blah." Whatever she warned them of *would just happen*. People behave like sitting ducks. Knowing what's around the corner has the power to make you freeze in place and then it just *gets* you; the future you're so scared of. I don't want to tell you, Mr Kircher. I'm *afraid* for you.'

The whole café seems very quiet after I finish talking, as if even the waitstaff, the short-order cooks in their exposed, gleaming, million-dollar kitchen are all listening with bated breath. I'm sweating so furiously that I swipe my forehead, inelegantly, with the back of one hand and it comes away glistening.

It's true, I'm afraid for him. I've *never* seen stars like his.

'Nevertheless,' Kircher says, quiet but adamant. 'I want

to know.' The only sign of nervous anticipation? A single fingerstroke across his neat moustache.

We stare at each other for a long time before I gesture at Kircher to return the sheet of paper. He looks down, before jabbing his forefinger into the page, and pushing it back across the table. There are smudged notes in lead pencil on the back, scribble only I can read, though I spent hours on it, working long after Simon turned the lights off in the living room. I'd gathered all of Mum's almanacs around me, with the internet locked and loaded for backup. All in all, I managed maybe a couple of hours' sleep, tops, before my alarm went off, but I know—like I know my own name—that I'm right. *We're* right, me and Mum.

I'd written:

> *Unnatural death signified at the hand of <u>open enemies</u>. Sun, moon, ascendant and ruling sign, fourth, fifth, seventh and eighth houses, all afflicted with no mitigating benefic aspects. Multiple eclipses. Multiple malefic angles and planets (both Mars <u>and</u> Saturn). Confirmed by natal vertex rising, conjoined with Neptune.*

I'd only managed to sketch out a shaky-looking chart, because Mum really did take every compass in the house with her and I'd been forced to use my school-issue plastic protractor. But the glyphs are in the right places, progressed by several degrees from Mum's own, like a dial has been turned, or a focus magnified, because everything moves inexorably forward, time cannot be stopped. And what they say, those glyphs—when read alongside the chart in Mum's journal—are undeniable. Reading the two charts together is like a slow-motion death-scene tracking shot in a horror movie. The first chart foreshadows the badness to come. But the second?

I swallow. Taking a deep breath, I hold up Mum's chart to Kircher's gaze. 'An astrologer creates one of these on the basis of the time the question the subject of the horary reading is *received* and *understood*. This is the answer Mum came up with based on the meeting she had with you.' I flip the piece of paper around to show my workings on the back. 'This is mine. I received and understood "the questions" last night, at 11.13pm, based on my discussions with Detective Wurbik here.'

Wurbik chimes in with, 'We actually agreed the time over the phone, both of us looking at our watches. For the, ah, record.' His voice is faintly sceptical.

Kircher inclines his head again, in acknowledgment.

I clear my throat. 'I have to tell you that the two charts are entirely consistent. I also have to tell you that it is usually very hard to predict a person's exact date of death with certainty. Astrologers can do it for themselves, obviously, because of their ability to understand the themes present at their own birth, and then read the flowering of that potential in subsequent progressions of their own natal chart.'

'So?' Kircher says eagerly. 'Spit it out, child! I'm more than ready to *receive* the answers. As you might gather, conventional methods have so far *failed* me.'

I know every word of what I've written off by heart, but I find that I can't raise my eyes from the page. I'm a terrible coward, because I read aloud the second part first, the *how* versus the *when*.

'Death of subject indicated,' I blurt. 'Sudden, violent and unnatural death indicated involving spouse and/or some other person related to subject through close business or professional connections. Travel and water indicated, asset of great value indicated that is not fixed. Afflictions associated with the blood indicated. Afflictions associated with swallowing, digestion and lungs also indicated.'

I pause for breath and Kircher snaps, 'When? *When?*' His eyes are very wide, as if he has recognised something in my words that holds no meaning for me. The three men around the table are leaning forward in their chairs.

I put my piece of paper down and place my shaking hands flat upon my own words, hiding their awfulness.

'You have a short window,' I say weakly, 'maybe a week, eight days at most? Before the conditions change. But I'd say that, uh, any time now would appear to be a ripe time to die. *Act accordingly.*'

I cover my mouth with my hands, knowing I have uttered some kind of death sentence for this man. But Elias Kircher beams at me as if I've just told him he's won the lottery. He presses the *stop* button on his voice recorder with a flourish, calling out to the hovering waiter, 'Ben? *Ben?* I think a spot of breakfast is in order.'

✦

Wurbik and Simon flanked me silently as we crossed back towards the police complex. None of us had felt like eating, so we left the waitstaff fawning over Kircher and his morbid celebratory brunch.

Wurbik tells Simon and me to wait for him in an empty meeting room that looks and smells almost identical to the one from yesterday. As I fumble my way into one of the swivel chairs, Simon's voice breaks into my thoughts. 'Why don't you do what Kircher suggested? You know, do a, uh, reading for your mum? Maybe it could help? It wouldn't, like, hurt.'

He slumps down into the chair beside me, and I see that tug-of-war between belief and disbelief in his expression, too. He's leaning away from me like he's almost...afraid.

Instead of feeling triumph—imagine, Simon Thorn, afraid of *me!*—I feel sadness. Mum got the same reaction, all the time. Like there was an invisible forcefield between her and the rest of the population. It made her want to reach out even more. She would talk to anyone, anytime. It embarrassed me so much I would often pretend we were not out walking together.

I swivel to face him. 'We are men of *science*, Simo,' I reply tiredly. 'How could it possibly *help*? You saw Kircher's reaction: he just read whatever he wanted to read into what I told him, and now he's going to go fall into a six-star swimming pool in Bali, or whatever, and drown because he's convinced himself that's the way he's going to go. I'm interested in finding my mum. I'm not interested in *theory*. Besides,' I whisper, picking at some loose stitching on the edge of my chair, 'I don't even know when or where she was born; she made sure of that.'

And I don't want to do it. Reduce her to symbols. Hold her entire life in my hands. It's too much. I don't say that part out loud.

'Oh,' Simon replies, surprised. 'Well.'

Wurbik comes back into the room with my home telephone. 'Appreciate what you just did,' he says, taking a seat and sliding the machine across the table to me. 'Kircher's been hassling us independently for weeks. Issues with extended family. Thinks they're after his money, all out to get him. So when he heard your mum had come up with a finished chart and you could read it? Well, he wouldn't take *no* for an answer. Who'd want to be rich, eh? Whole different set of problems.'

I look at Simon and he looks away, face shuttered.

Wurbik leans forward in his chair, his expression suddenly grave. 'We're making progress, Avicenna. We've got her mobile phone moving through a tollgate to the north-west of the city on the day in question. It pings off a few more towers before going off the grid, but we're following that up as a matter of urgency, trying to work out exactly where she ended up, how she got there. Keep you informed, of course, every step of the way.'

The room seems to waver in and out. Wurbik and Simon both put a hand out hurriedly, when it looks like I might pitch forward, face-first. I shake my head weakly to indicate I'm fine, I'm still listening, hair falling all over my face as I jam the base of one palm into my eyes.

'Three other quick things,' Wurbik says when I finally look up. 'Good news is you're not going to starve. That bank account you gave us details for has just over $40,000 in it. You're cleared to use it again, but let us know if you notice any discrepancies between transactions. Strange things coming in or out, that sort of thing.'

I blink. Mum's monthly take was less than $2000. Even accounting for this month's wage, the number he's just named is astronomical: *five* figures. I've never seen five figures on one of our withdrawal slips, ever. A couple of weeks ago, we had $324.62 to our names, and Mum had warned me sharply to *make it last*.

'But that's a fortune!' Simon turns to me accusingly. 'You could buy, like, three new *cars* with that.'

Wurbik says quietly, 'Looking into that, too. Recent transactions include one large deposit by cheque and a couple of other odd amounts by direct wire. What did she charge?'

I look at him in confusion, thinking of all the porcelain giftware littering our rooms, how you could even put a value on that. 'First consult was free,' I say finally. 'Nominally, she charged $135 per hour, but based on her time, and whether or not the person could pay, it could be anything.'

'That might explain at least one of the transactions,' Wurbik muses. 'And that place with the funny-sounding description…'

'*The Ark of A–Z*,' Simon butts in, with his perfect recall.

Wurbik shoots him a measuring glance before returning his pale-blue gaze to mine. 'Yeah, that place. It was closed when we sent an officer over yesterday, but it's open Mondays to Wednesdays between 12 and 3pm. Strange hours. Some kind of rare-antiques dealer. You'll get an update as soon as we find out what that's all about.'

I'm still thinking about the money when I remind him weakly, 'And the third thing, Detective? You said there were *three* things. That's only two.'

Wurbik sits straighter and his face is suddenly so kind that I know I'm not going to like what he's about to say.

'Reason we had so much trouble establishing identity,' he says carefully, 'was that your mum's legal name is Joanne Crowe *Nielsen*. Even her work didn't realise her surnames were around the wrong way. Caused us plenty of confusion, let me tell you.'

'But,' I interrupt hotly, primed to refute and deny, 'that can't be right! We're all *Crowes*: Bev, Joyce, Jo and me. An unbroken line of women with "the knowledge". She used to boast about it. How starcraft was in our blood, *la-di la*. I don't understand.'

Wurbik slides his chair forward on its castors and his voice is gentle. 'It may or may not have something to do with that phone call you got last night…'

'What?' I say, confusedly. 'The mouth-breather? What's he got to do with Mum?'

'A man called Erik Nielsen called our hotline yesterday,' Wurbik continues doggedly, 'mostly to cover his arse. Insists he's got nothing to do with her disappearance. But did claim he and your mother were legally married until she ran away with "a Chinaman" (his words, not mine) in '96 and he hasn't heard about her since. Till now.' Something feels wrong with my face when Wurbik adds, 'And her middle name isn't *Nielsen*. It's *Melissa*.'

It takes me a while to arrange the words in the right

order: *Joanne Melissa Crowe Nielsen*. Okay, got it. Won't forget it, now that I know. Beside me, I glimpse Simon closing his eyes, like he's praying for me.

11

'So, unlike John Donne's children, who were merely not formally recognised by their maternal grandfather for several years until he got over his annoyance at his daughter marrying a recusant Papist,' I mutter as Simon and I exit the police complex, 'I am actually *illegitimate*, from several new standpoints.'

'You're taking it surprisingly well,' Simon murmurs as he scrolls through a text that has just come in on his phone. It's long and rambling, and I watch something in his face sharpen. 'It's from Mum,' he says suddenly, shoving the phone into a back pocket of his jeans. 'She needs help. I have to go. You'll be right to get home?'

Then he's gone, taking two lanes against the lights in

his long stride before I can even draw breath to reply. I don't even make it to the pedestrian crossing on the corner before he is back in his car-slash-mobile-home and already three-quarters of his way through a U-turn.

I watch him roar up St Kilda Road, back towards the city—in the exact direction I want to go, the bastard. 'No,' I say aloud to myself at the deserted tram stop. 'Actually, *you're* the bastard. A proper one. Get used to it.'

I board the next tram, still cradling my home phone against my chest like it's a pet that startles easily. The tram is crowded with interstate footy fans, irritated locals and tourists. I end up strap-hanging over this thin woman with sleek hair in gradated shades of brown, cut short in a kind of gravity-defying, rich art-dealer kind of bob. She glances down, annoyed, as our feet tangle together, toes touching. The woman is dressed in a sleek scarlet suit and black, open-toed stilettos with red soles, and her mouth is surrounded by those vertical lines you get from too much lip pursing and cigarettes.

My pack is crouched on my back like a giant carbuncle, and I wish to God I'd put the answering machine away before I got on, the plastic now slick in my one-handed grip. The tram sways back up the road towards the city, more people getting on than getting off, and it's close inside, stuffy, smelling of wool and polyester and un-washed people. As I scan all the faces, I wonder if he could be one of them—Erik Nielsen, Mum's *husband*, shit—and whether I've ever passed him on the street, looked him in the eye, and not known. Without warning, the bobbed woman stands and spears me in the foot with one of her stiletto heels. It's jammed down squarely between my flesh and the side of my runner as she swings a designer leather tote off the floor.

'*Owwwwwww,*' I howl, because it bloody hurts.

Her heel is still inside my shoe, grinding down on the edge of my left foot as she snarls, 'Well, *move* then,' and my eyes fill with tears at her unkindness, at all the random unkindnesses of strangers.

Mum wasn't called a *chink-lover* in Dimboola, I realise suddenly. Dimboola was just a story—no, a cypher—she used to illustrate a point. It must have happened here, when she was out walking with Dad, in the city where I was *born*. Maybe it was this woman, or someone just like her, who ground her forefinger into my pregnant mother's breastbone and made her want to leave, starting the chain of everything that has led right back to now.

For a heartbeat, the woman and I seem suspended in time. She isn't even looking at me, face averted in distaste, although the entire packed tram seems to be staring at us, waiting to see what I'll do, the two of us standing in the middle of a giant, sucked-in breath of anticipation. Then time restarts the moment the woman rips her high heel out of my shoe and shoves her way forward, through the sea of eyes and faces.

She's going to get away with it, I realise. And I know I will return to this moment again and again for the rest of my life, with regret and anger and sorrow; this moment where I did nothing, and said nothing, and was made nothing because of it.

My home phone drops out of my hands onto the floor with a hard *thunk* and before I've thought it through, I'm lunging forward, reaching out and grabbing the woman by her narrow shoulders, fingers digging hard into the slim shoulder pads of her suit jacket. I spin her around, so that she will see *me*. And her bright red lips fall open, eyes widening fearfully, when she catches sight of my face; my flaming, melted skin.

In the packed tram, people have cleared the space around us as if by magic, and I'm bawling at the top of my lungs, 'I. AM. NOT. MY. *MOTHER*.' Only, by the time I get to the word *mother*, I'm actually roaring like a lion, the word just devolving into this long scream of sound, and the woman jerks out of my grasp, stumbling to get away from me. The tram doors are only half-open, but she's leapt right off the step. I watch her running on the tips of her ridiculous heels through the crowd waiting to get on and realise that the forcefield between me and the rest of the world is up, it's *on*, because all I see are shocked faces turned my way, bodies leaning sideways to avoid me touching them.

I pick my telephone up off the floor, and walk slowly towards the exit and it's like I'm the filthy, crazy, muttering person on the tram that no one wants to be near. I might as well be stinking of urine and raving about Armageddon, the way everyone's looking at me. But you know what? I *did* something. I reacted. If time is a concertina, then I will *never* return to this memory with a feeling of shame.

Embarrassment, maybe. But not shame.

As I get off the tram a block past the Three Kings' Bakehouse, I think I hear someone applauding. Or maybe it's just my heart, beating, steady as a drum.

I've almost reached the Little Bourke Street exit to the arcade opposite my building when something strange happens. A man leaning against the wall beside the TattsLotto shop gives a start as I pass by, and then speed-dials a number on his mobile. It's not my imagination; the two things are connected, Action A leading to Action B. When I look back, his eyes drop down to a little black notebook he's holding in his other hand, but I swear I hear him mutter my name.

Mum named me after a famous Persian astronomer from the 11th century: *No Bevs or Joyces for my girl*, she would say grimly when I complained about someone giving me stick again, at my latest school. No one ever says *Avicenna*, just in passing. It's not a place, it's not a thing, and it's got four syllables. So I notice, when it happens.

The guy's tall and gaunt and weather-beaten with short, iron-grey hair slicked close to his skull. He's decked out in fancy lace-up black brogues and tan slacks, and a collared shirt worn under a heavy blue jumper. Doesn't look or smell homeless; never seen him before in my life.

I take it all in in a millisecond, picking up speed, almost tripping over the power cord to the answering machine as I make it out into Chinatown. I've exhausted my confrontation quotient for the day. Hell, I've exhausted my talking-to-strange-old-guys quotient for the day.

I look back over my shoulder and the man looks away, still talking about me, I just know it.

I'm so *close*.

The *Mei Hua Bean Sprout Company* sign is winking at me from across the road in the brilliant sunlight. Somehow it turned into a beautiful day. I'm only twenty metres from my door but instead of crossing over, the way I want to, I go right. Continue up the hill from my place, towards the two-storey Yum Cha palace with the bright-red pagoda façade at the front, intending to go around the block and come back from a different direction, just in case.

Because, as Mum used to say grimly: *People possessed with ovaries can never be too careful, pet.*

'Hey!' someone calls out from behind me. 'You, there. *Girl*. Stop!'

I just walk faster, darting a quick look backwards as the lights change on the corner. Behind me, the front passenger door is starting to open on an early-model Mercedes the size of a boat: royal blue, well preserved, car wax gleaming in the sun. Can't tell who's coming out. Male? Female? I feel my adrenaline spike and keep rising.

As I'm looking back, the man from the arcade runs out into the street, throwing a hand up in the air. He starts hurrying up the footpath behind me, eyes intent, dodging pedestrians and couriers pushing trolleys stacked with boxes of bottled spirits. I'm jogging now, begging people to get out of my way under my breath. The man starts jogging, too. I'm almost running crab-ways up the street trying to see how much distance we've got between us when I see him cross Russell Street against the lights at a full run, long legs pumping, horns blaring. He's closing the gap.

Everything's moving: breath sobbing in and out of my body, pack bumping from side to side against my shoulder-blades, boobs, pot belly, all jiggling around under all the sweaty layers. I trip repeatedly over the telephone cord, getting it caught between my knees and around my legs, but it doesn't stop me taking the Exhibition Street crossing at a full run, too, until I barrel into someone standing on the other side.

The man rocks backwards, then grips me by the upper arms. I'm beating at his chest with the telephone, while at the same time trying to twist out of his grasp. The sun's in my eyes as the man growls, 'Avicenna! Avi-*cen*-na!' He's really shaking me now. 'Pull yourself together.'

All I can make are animal noises of distress. 'It's Boon, *Boon*,' he adds, voice sharp with concern. 'What's *wrong* with you, girl?'

I focus on him with difficulty. 'Le-me-go, le-me-go,' I finally wheeze out in terror, still trying to pull away. I've got kilograms and inches on Boon, but he is as immovable as a tree. 'There's a man,' I blurt, 'following me and I don't know why. *I have to go.*'

Boon looks over my shoulder and his expression shifts. Before I understand what's happening, he has propelled me down a narrow cobblestone alleyway and into… a commercial kitchen.

'*Dai Gor*,' someone yells out in surprise as Boon and I skid across the slick tiled floor. All around are clouds of steam rising from pans and woks that smell of braised meats; stainless-steel bowls filled with yellow noodles, glassy vermicelli, mounds of cut, pre-washed green vegetables. Men in cook's whites and check pants that have gone dingy from repeat washing look up in surprise as we pass by. Over the sound of running water and sizzling woks, Boon continually calls out in greeting, but we're through to another alleyway at the back of the restaurant before I can draw breath.

Here it is quiet, reeking of rotting food and beer; exhaust fumes from the commercial car park that runs alongside it. There's no one in sight, but Boon keeps going, taking us in through the back screen door of another old building off the alley on the opposite side. The kitchen we're in now is dimly lit, and at first I think there's no one in here until I spot, through a bank of steel shelving, the burly figure of a bald old man in rolled-up blue shirt-sleeves and jeans consulting a wall chart.

Boon takes us up the central kitchen walkway, island benches on either side, calling out confidently, 'Newlands! My apologies. Just passing through, my friend.'

This place smells like baked-on, caked-on apricot chicken and meatloaf, goulash, hash browns and boiled vegetables with an overlay of hospital-strength disinfectant. It smells like The Caf at school. Newlands turns his head in angry surprise until he sees who it is and comes forward to shake Boon's hand. He eyes me interestedly. 'Of course, and you'll have good reason,' he says calmly.

'There's a man following my goddaughter,' Boon

replies with an ease that, for a second, makes me wish it were for real. To be someone's daughter again. Newlands' expression sharpens under his bushy white eyebrows.

Boon adds, 'This is *Greyson's* child.'

Newlands' face brightens, then falls immediately, like the two old men have discussed my father's sad demise many times over cups of coffee.

'I don't know what to say,' is Newlands' simple response. He squeezes my free hand in greeting, or sympathy. 'What would you like for me to do, Boon?'

Boon shakes his head. 'She can wait at the museum while I check our building. Nothing for you to do, old friend. As I said, just passing through.'

'Offer stands,' Newlands responds mildly, leading us out of the quiet kitchen and into a suffocatingly dark space on the other side of it. He puts one of his hands under my elbow in a way that isn't creepy, just solicitous, like he's known me forever.

In the darkness, linked between the two old men, I feel the consistency of the floor suddenly change beneath my feet: from the dull feel of burnished concrete, to the warped and pitted wood of old floorboards. Our footsteps have a hollow echo now, as if the space has grown cavernous, and I ask, suspicious, 'What *is* this place?'

Newlands suddenly stops. The wood-floored room we are standing in is bounded on the far side by what appears to be a heavy curtain, a thin chink of pale daylight coming through it. My eyes are beginning to adjust. On the far side of the space, in the corner by the back wall, is a faint glow, too. Subterranean. Maybe stairs.

Newlands lets go of my arm and I sway momentarily in the darkness. I hear him tripping and cursing, feeling about on the wall. Then he flicks up some kind of metal lever and the narrow band of light through the curtain grows bright, dazzling, artificial.

Newlands moves forward to tug one edge of the velvet curtain open, and I see old-style footlights, like glowing white teeth, outlining the edge of a stage. Behind me is a faded theatre set made up of trees and swings, a hint of bucolic lawn, protruding out a little way from the wings on either side. We emerge onto the lip of the stage, blinking, as if we have just emerged from a fairytale wood.

Before me, the shadowed room rises up steeply in tiers of fixed bench seats and tables; it's shaped like a small amphitheatre. Everything is painted black, and the huge crystal chandelier in the ceiling looms unlit; so high off the ground that it hurts me to look up at it.

'Oldest operational theatre restaurant in Melbourne,' Newlands says proudly, helping me down off the side of the stage. 'Featuring one of the few surviving star traps in Australia.'

Newlands points up at an octagonal shape set into

the floor at centre stage. We're standing at eye level to the thing, which has eight separate hinges, one for each section of the asterisk that bisects the octagon. I imagine the lines breaking up, springing open like a vicious, toothed flower made of wood, disgorging tomfoolery and hijinks from below.

'It was a hit when we did a run of vampire shows in the 70s; people couldn't get enough of it. Dry ice, flames, you name it, and suddenly the baddie's right there, amongst it. *How'd he get there?* Everyone screaming their heads off. It was a sensation. But we don't use it now because the mechanism jams and there's no surprise in it these days. The last person who shot up out of "Hell" to terrorise the living had a nasty shock.' The old man's eyes go distant and opaque. 'Nearly broke us.'

We follow Newlands up a steep set of stairs at the left of the auditorium towards street level, passing a deserted bar and ticket booth. He pauses with us by the front door, just inside the scuffed-looking foyer that still smells of the cigarettes of yesteryear.

'I'm here every day, except Mondays, till late, just remember,' Newlands tells me, his voice grave, his fingers still curled beneath my elbow. 'Family have wanted me retired for years, but retired is another word for dead in my book.'

He lets go of me then, and pulls open the heavily carved

wooden front door, holding it slightly ajar. 'Perverts all over these days,' he says, swinging the door wider and nudging us out onto the threshold. 'Can't be too careful, lovey.'

There are faded black-and-white theatre shots plastered to the windows on either side of the entrance—people in feather boas and lederhosen and crazy headgear, exaggerated face paint—and a colony of dead flies lying around on the sills underneath with curled-up legs and dull wings. Newlands urges, 'Ask for Uncle Des, understand? Always welcome. Greyson was like a son to me.' His voice is sombre. 'Watched him grow up around the place.'

Then he shuts the heavy door in our faces.

With a sweeping gaze that takes in the Sichuan noodle house and sushi train joint on either side, the entrance to the commercial car park just beyond them and the down-at-heel hotel across the road, Boon turns us left and walks briskly past a bottle shop, a mini-mart and a travel agent before we cross towards a faded building on the corner that proclaims itself *Her Majesty's Theatre*. We cut back into the top end of Little Bourke Street, still blocks away from home. Boon steers me under a ceremonial stone gateway, between a matched pair of snarling stone lions with curved fangs, bulbous eyes and clawed feet.

We walk up a ramp at the far end of a small stone square and enter a set of wooden swing doors. The young Asian woman at the cash register at the far end of the foyer looks up enquiringly before breaking into a smile of recognition. Boon waves airily and simply proceeds up a set of stairs without payment, although the sign near the register sets out all the prices quite clearly. 'Something to show you,' he says as we climb.

As I look in on each floor, I see ceremonial dragons, masks, ancient artefacts. It's the museum Boon spoke of to Newlands, but it's a *Chinese* museum.

I scowl fiercely. 'Propaganda!' I mutter, unsure why we're here, as we emerge into a light, airy exhibition space on the top floor. 'Now is *not* the time for me to get back in touch with my ancestral roots, or whatever. Couldn't I just wait somewhere else while you run recon...?'

'Just see,' Boon says calmly.

The hall-like upstairs room we enter is filled solely with photographs. By the door are pictures of kids from the 1950s, 1960s, 1970s in all the bad fashions and shocker hair-styles: quiffs, bowl cuts, shags, mullets, flicks and perms. They're all Chinese, or variations on; caught forever in black-and-white or lurid technicolour. I bend and look at some of the names: Goon and Louey and all the weird bastardisations wrought by the Gods of Immigration, legalised forever. There's a Peter Gok Kar and a Shirley Wing Loon; a whole dynasty of Quong Gongs, poor souls: Shirleys and Maureens and Denises, big toothy girls with long limbs and long faces, milk-fed skin.

Neither here nor there, just like me.

'How long do I have to stay here looking, feeling, *belonging*?' I demand accusingly. 'Until it's safe to go home?'

'Look around for as little or as long as you like,' Boon says mildly. 'Just stop by my shop first, before you head on upstairs to your place? I'll check the building; make sure there are no more surprises.'

He pats me on the shoulder, about to turn on his heel, when he seems to recall something. He takes my home telephone out of my hands and tucks it into my backpack, doing up the zip so firmly that I'm almost lifted off the ground. 'You wanted to know,' he says from behind me, 'what was missing from your parents' apartment? That detective asked me to tell you, but I can *show* you.'

Suddenly, I'm conscious of this sick, breathless feeling inside me, my pulse hammering in my inner ear. Boon crosses the carpet and I trail after him, surrounded by a diorama of grinning Asian faces: babies, toddlers, youths. We pass a section devoted to Chinese boys in matching football jerseys, posing in the classic, butch, arms-crossed way, tallest at the back, shortest at the front. Teams from the 50s straight through to the early 90s. 'Ethnics' versus 'locals'. I can imagine the backchat and niggling at the sidelines. Must have been awesome.

Boon jabs a forefinger into one of the frames in passing

and says, 'That's your dad, front row, centre. He was short until he turned fifteen, but he was *fast*. His trick was to keep running: ran all the bigger boys into the ground until they were too tired to kick straight or hold the ball.'

I bend, peering at the tiny image, heart in my mouth. So it *is* true; I do have his eyes. We lost all our photos in the fire and, even in dreams, I can't recall his face. This is the first concrete proof I've ever seen that he even existed.

'He's in this one, too,' Boon says, passing a school formal photo, all the boys in dodgy 80s tuxes, a scattering of frilled shirts; all the girls in horrid bright colours like emerald and scarlet and amethyst, with crimped hair and straight bangs, hideous corsages made of carnations. 'Dance at the Melbourne Town Hall. Big deal at the time. To your dad, anyway.'

Dad's a lot taller in this photo, stiff-looking in a black tuxedo, white shirt and ruby-red cummerbund, with a bogan haircut: spiky on top, short sides, long, mullety back. Haircut aside, I am shocked at his lean, tanned handsomeness. I look like neither of them, it's true.

Some new animal.

Boon shoots me a quick look. 'But you wanted to know about the missing photo?' he reminds me.

He stops before a picture in the far back corner: of an olive-skinned little boy with a broad face, gappy teeth and the kind of terrible haircut that indicates an actual

157

mixing bowl might have been involved. The boy has smiling dark eyes and a sprinkling of freckles across his nose, and is, inexplicably, dressed in a green Peter Pan costume with green stockings, hands fisted on his hips in a classic Errol Flynn-style pose. He can't be more than six or seven, chubby and adorable, posed against a backdrop of powder-blue photographic curtain made up to look like a cloud-filled sky.

'This is just a copy, of course,' Boon murmurs. 'The original was inside the frame. But this is it. This was what was taken off the wall in the apartment.'

Long after Boon's footsteps on the wooden stairs have faded away, I stand under a shaft of late afternoon sunlight, just staring at my father as a child.

12

When I'm politely chased out of the museum at closing time, I emerge to find night has fallen and the female restaurant touts are out on the street, in their slinky, faux-silk *cheongsams* and Uggs, waving menus at anything living that goes by. As I trail past the shop with all the Taiwanese-style, pastel-coloured cream cakes lined up in rows in the window, I'm reminded again that I've eaten nothing since an awkward bowl of muesli with Simon Thorn. Wherever the hell he's got to.

Boon had told me to check in first, so I do. The bell over the street-facing door jingles as I enter his shop. 'Avicenna,' he calls out in warning, but it's too late, because the tall, thin guy from the arcade, the one who gave me chase clear up three blocks, is leaning against the door in the far wall that opens out into my stairwell.

I yank my mobile phone out, intent on calling Wurbik. But my fingers aren't working and, in my panic, I drop the phone onto the hardwood floor. In a red haze of fear I scrabble for it, but it's like the phone's alive: it is slippery, impossible to catch. It pops through my slick grasp, once, twice, and I'm almost sobbing.

'Avicenna,' someone says gently.

I look up, startled to see an elderly woman I hadn't even noticed perched on the stool in front of Boon's counter. She's slight, bird-boned, and a little bent over, but from the neck down she could be a twenty-year-old art student in a chunky, grey marle cardigan over slim, indigo jeans and black leather ankle boots. Her long grey hair is pulled back in an elegant knot at the nape of her neck and, under her wrinkles, the structure of her face is lovely. And kind of familiar, even though I know I've never seen her before.

'I'm sorry we gave you a scare,' she says quietly, 'but it was imperative we try to catch you. To ask, you see.'

I sit back on my haunches to better see her face, which is really quite beautiful. Ruined, but arresting. There are deep grooves between her nose and mouth, and her forehead is a patchwork of crisscrossing lines, up and down above the bridge, long parallel scores, like knife scars, across her forehead. Her eyes appear sunken, like she no longer sleeps; the skin below them purple as bruises.

'Just to talk,' the old woman adds quickly. 'To put our case across.'

I look up at the gaunt-looking man by the door and his dirty-green, yellow-flecked eyes slide away. My brain slowly puts together that the two of them are a package deal and that I was being *fetched*. I take in the diamond studs in the old lady's ears, the heavy, antique rings on her bony hands that breathe *old money, exquisite taste*. She must have been the one getting out of the front seat of the Mercedes.

'Who *are* you people?' I rasp, rising from the floor. I scoop my mobile up, too, the screen lit-up, ready for use if I need it.

Boon's eyes are apologetic as he brings out his own stool and plants it beside the old woman. He pats the surface of it before leaving the shop through the stairwell entrance. The tall man sidesteps to let him pass, then moves right back into place, darting a look at me before refocusing on his shoes.

'*Please,*' the old woman says, indicating the rickety steel stool beside her. I perch on it reluctantly, my backpack jammed between me and the glass counter, the hard shape of my home phone digging into my lower back.

'This is Don Sturt,' she adds, 'my companion. Who makes sure I take my pills, and gets me where I need to go,' indicating the man by the door. I seem to drop back into my body from a great height, understanding all at once.

I turn to the old woman immediately. 'You're the mother,' I say in a weird rush, recognising Fleur under all the wrinkles and lines and slackness. 'Mrs Bawden.'

The woman gives a little laugh that doesn't hold any amusement. 'Oh, there hasn't been a Mr Bawden for many years, dear. I go by Eleanor Charters these days. It deters the sightseers and amateur investigators. Cranks. They've given up trying to track me down for anniversary interviews. Don's put a stop to that.'

Looking at him now, I see Don is at least a decade younger than the old woman. By his deferential body language, I don't think he's a *companion* in the biblical sense, but you never know. She could be the world's oldest cougar.

'You didn't have to *run*,' Don says gruffly, glancing at me then away. 'I wasn't going to hurt you.'

Eleanor Charters grasps both my hands tightly in hers. 'I'm so sorry about your mother. It's the very worst time to be asking a favour, but I've waited so long. And when Don told me that you could read these things, just like her, I needed to know...'

She reminds me of Kircher. Her need, all-consuming, so much greater than mine. I withdraw my hands, wriggling out of my backpack before opening it up and rifling through it.

I show her the pages I photocopied out of Mum's journal. 'This is all there was,' I say, pointing at the names and dates, birthplaces and times in Mum's writing, the note to call Don Sturt for more details. 'She hadn't started. There's nothing to really tell you.'

Something happens to Eleanor Charters' face as she absorbs this. 'Don?' she queries in a funny, high voice. 'You're the private investigator. What do you suggest we do now? I had been led to believe that there were charts, *results*.'

Sturt clears his throat and says, still not really looking at me, 'So we had an initial meeting with your mum, right? El and me, and she says she can do it. Produce, you know, a *hoary...*'

'Horary,' I say dryly.

'Yeah, hoary reading,' Sturt ploughs on, 'for these four fellas. It's a cold case, see, coming up on thirty years...'

Eleanor's eyes drop to her knees. 'And no one's ever been charged,' she whispers. 'Dozens—*dozens*—were interviewed. This was in the days before DNA testing was commonplace, you understand, so although physical evidence was taken from, from, her body'—Eleanor swallows but doesn't look up—'corresponding...material was not taken from all of the men who were interviewed, not until much later. But by then the original evidence was misplaced; people had died, fled overseas, changed their names...'

She gives a small, crooked smile and I catch Don looking at us, a quick sideways thing with his eyes, before he looks down again.

'Hopeless,' she finishes raggedly. 'Nothing left to do but consult the heavens. Which saw and would know… everything. The only true witness to *events*.' Her voice rises and cracks on the last word and her eyes flick back up to mine. 'Based on years of interviews and research by kind people like Don here, we think these are the four men "most likely" due to strange alibis, responses, inconsistencies. Tendencies. Things that can't be explained. And gut feeling.'

Don clears his throat, takes over talking. 'Dirt on these ones,' he says, 'there's plenty. All we want is some kind of' —the look he shoots Eleanor is hard to read—'impartial corroboration. But we didn't want to burden your mum with all the research it took to get us here. We didn't want to predispose her mindset, so to speak. So, as we knew the material best, we gave her the bare fac—'

Eleanor cuts in. 'I just want to know if it's possible.' Her voice is husky with emotion. 'Possible to tell if one of these men was born bad enough to do *this thing*. That's all.'

'She took a down payment,' Don adds, sounding strained, 'your mum. We'd understood that she would call as soon as she had the, you know, hoary readings ready.'

'And then the police call me,' Eleanor wails, clasping

her hands together at chest height, 'asking if I knew anything about why she might be missing. And then Don tells me he *saw* you with Elias Kircher, whose issues with family are the stuff of legend, so naturally I hoped…'

Chilled, I glance in Don's direction but he won't look at me, and Boon chooses that moment to re-enter his shop. I can tell by the gentle lift of his eyebrows that it's fine to go back upstairs; I'd worked myself up over nothing.

These people hadn't meant you any actual harm were what Boon's eyebrows were saying. *All they want from you is the name of a killer.*

Eleanor bends forward and puts her small, bejewelled hands on my knees. 'People come into your life for a *reason*.' Her voice is beseeching as she looks into my face. 'I am asking you to finish what she agreed to do. It may mean nothing, but all I want to know is whether it is possible…'

'To tell if someone was born bad enough to…?' I repeat tentatively.

'Rape and murder my daughter, yes,' Eleanor says fiercely. 'Once I have that knowledge, you leave the rest up to me. You are done, you are finished, and I will never bother you again.'

☙

As Boon escorts me up the internal staircase after Eleanor Charters and her private investigator have gone, he says suddenly, 'These things are dangerous.'

'What? Horoscopes?' I answer, surprised.

He nods, adding solemnly. 'You don't—how do you say—tempt fate.'

'I know, I know,' I reply. 'I agree. I violently agree. People are so suggestible. It's the last thing I want to do. But Mum took their money. I'm honour-bound to finish what she started. She would have wanted that.'

Sounding faintly hysterical, Boon says, 'I warned her. I told her many, many times, do not muck around, this is not joking here.'

'You're just being superstitious!' I snort. 'Plus, you're freaking me out. It's just a bunch of flat diagrams on a page that the subjects will never even know about. And maybe if Eleanor gets what she thinks she wants, it will lessen her pain, I don't know; anything to help that poor woman.'

But I knew what Eleanor asked of me wouldn't lessen her pain. Now I had an inkling of what it must feel like to be her: with this indefinable thing sitting below the heart and stealing your breath away at the slightest provocation. A song, a smell, the back of some stranger's head could push on that phantom pain, making it blossom. The wild, lost look in Eleanor's eyes reminded me of *me*.

Mum said once, hugging me fiercely, that the worst

thing in the world would be to lose a child. But to lose a mother? I'm too young to have these feelings, and I make a small, gobbling noise of grief, which I somehow turn into a cough. But Boon shoots me a look of concern, like he knows exactly what I am doing. I'm a crap actress.

As we pass the closed doorway to my parents' old apartment, Boon mutters, 'I could not make your mum understand that three things govern all forecasts. I told her: you must only proceed on that basis, and then only with extreme caution.'

He sticks a pointer finger upright in the air for emphasis, so that I am forced to look at him.

'One: Nothing is accident, Avicenna. Every effect has a cause, and every effect gives birth to another. *Every outcome is already ordained.* This we disagreed about the most. She tells them they have a "choice", but they do not. Their fate is already written; she merely, how do you say, delivers the message. Your mother's disappearance is a direct consequence of some link in this chain. Find this link, this cause, and you will find your mother.'

'Right,' I snap back. 'That sounds easy enough. I'll make sure to tell Detective Wurbik.'

'Don't be disrespectful,' Boon answers sharply. 'These are our beliefs.' He makes a sideways Victory-sign with his hand. 'Second: Nothing occurs on its own; everything is connected. So, if you finish what your mother started, whatever touched her will touch you.'

I feel a chill at that word, *touched*. My beautiful mother, with her alabaster skin.

Boon and I pause outside my door as I dig wearily in the side pockets of my pack for the key. He adds with a sense of finality, 'Everything that has happened before will happen again.'

'Sorry?' I say sharply, glaring into his troubled face. 'What's happened before happens again? That's the third "thing"?'

He nods, without elaborating, and I snap, 'Well, that makes absolutely no sense whatsoever. My father and mother met. Then he died, and she vanished. The dying and the vanishing are terrible once-offs, Boon, in a straight linear progression from boy-meets-girl. See any second chances there? No? Because there are none.'

'Nevertheless,' Boon replies as I shove my front door open and flick on the hallway light, 'this is what we believe. Time is infinite, all life moves in cycles. Bad things that happen will happen again. She didn't believe me either, and see where it got her?'

After I let him out, still muttering about fate and divination, I kick off my runners. Half-heartedly, I fold up all the blankets I'd dragged out for Simon, setting them in an untidy pile on the couch. The moment I plug the phone back into the wall socket in the kitchen, it starts ringing. But with the volume turned down low the sound is almost comforting. It means I'm not completely alone. Someone's thoughts are bent on me. The last thing I hear as I disappear into my bedroom with a bowl of microwaved dhal is a man's deep voice whispering into the voice recorder: *Do you shave your legs, girl? Well, do you?*

Fucking psychos. Something like this draws them all out, like writhing worms disgorged from the earth after a rain.

On my bed, I construct an unsteady fort out of piles of Mum's threadbare almanacs and sit in the middle of it, pulling Don Sturt's list of four names, birthdates and birthplaces towards me.

For a long time, I just eat and stare, afraid to begin. Mostly I think I am afraid that, despite my best efforts, I might be *becoming* her. Finally, setting aside the bowl, on a blank page of a jotter pad I write:

> *Mallory Fielder Bloch, Shanghai, China.*
> *9 September 1946. 9.47pm.*

On the next I write:

> *Geoffrey Andrew Kidston, Melbourne, Australia.*
> *17 July 1965. 7.21pm.*

Then I headline the following two pages with:

Lewis Griffinn Boardman, Sydney, Australia.
5 December 1957. 7.21pm.

Christopher John Ferwerder, Edinburgh,
Scotland. 29 May 1927. 5.06am.

And I begin to chart, bearing in mind the specific question received and understood by me at precisely 5.56pm today:

> *Did you, on 9 July 1984, between the hours of*
> *9.30pm and 11.59pm, rape and murder Fleur*
> *Lucille Bawden?*

Hours later, my mobile gives off a muffled *ping* and I look up to see it is 4.13 in the morning. Out of instinct, I check to see whether anyone's played me a word. Vicki's still stuck on *sluts*, because I never played anything back. She hates waiting and is going to be supremely pissed, but I have no appropriate comeback handy at this juncture. I'm so tired that I am devoid of meaningful language, only symbol.

I see that *Changeling_29* has intersected the *t* of his last word, *qat*, with a new word: *death*. I tell myself sternly that it is *not* a sign; that it means nothing and is merely the coming together of a randomly thrown-up, system-generated conglomeration of letters.

I look at the last game, the game with Mum. It takes

me a whole, consciousness-altering second to work out that it's my turn. *My* turn.

Appalled, barely able to locate the word on the teeming electronic gameboard, I see there really *is* a new word waiting for me. I'm not deceiving myself. Mere wishing has not made it so.

There's no accompanying message, nothing to say if it's really from her. Just the word. It was played on Saturday, at 12.24 in the morning. With a pang, tears streaming down my face, I see that the word is: *always*.

13

I call Wurbik before it's decently light, trying to tell him about the word—*My God, she played me a word!* But he tells me to *hold that thought*, saying he'll meet me outside Collegiate High at home time with updates. 'Because you're going to school today,' he says. 'You don't put your education on hold for anything.'

'Even homicide?' I query, fear and curiosity piqued. 'Does it mean she's still alive if she's playing words?'

'*Go to school*,' Wurbik insists. 'If I had a kid I would be telling her the same thing.'

Before I can say anything else, he hangs up.

Next I make a call to Don Sturt's mobile and go straight to his message bank, which is only mildly annoying because there's something about the man that gives me the willies. The way he can't look me in the eye.

I had spent hours on the charts before I'd noticed the anomaly—my heart sinking because the first two were almost done. 'Are you absolutely sure,' I say now, slowly and loudly into the dead air of Don's voicemail, 'that the two Australian-born suspects were born at exactly the same time? There are *a lot* of minutes in a day. I mean, it seems a bit weird, but not entirely out of the question. Call me back, okay?'

In my ear, as I'm pulling on my clothes in the bathroom, I hear Mum murmur: *Every minute counts, Avi.* And I feel a spurt of acid in my heart that she could honestly believe that all that separates the psychopaths from the rest of us are mere minutes, mere revolutions. But here I am, doing it, following in her footsteps: giving comfort to the desperate and gullible and deranged.

The morning is icy, but sunny. Unwilling to face another packed tram of bald-faced, staring people, I pull my beanie down low over my ears and unbound hair, beginning the long uphill walk to school against a slicing wind.

On autopilot, I almost trudge past Little La Trobe Street. But somehow I find myself turning in, already looking out for numbers.

Specifically, 232A. A part of me is actually expecting to see a giant wooden boat marooned somewhere in the middle of the street by the right hand of God, but of course there isn't one. Instead I come across a dim, Victorian-era shopfront.

On the windows, outlined in faded gilt, I read:

THE ARK OF

WUNDERKAMMER & EMPORIUM

Behind the grubby glass, there are mysterious-looking brass scientific instruments on display; a full-sized human skeleton on a stand wearing a feathered, tricorn hat; stuffed birds and animals under bell jars; shells; corals; weirdly shaped pieces of tusk and horn; lumps of rock; found objects; liver-spotted nature lithographs in dusty, unmatched frames.

I wrinkle my nose, thinking, *Ugly junk*, unable to imagine what more Mum could possibly have wanted to add to our already festering collection. The place looks neglected, but eccentric. Expensive, too.

But then I remember the $40,000 sitting in our bank account and crowd closer to the window. There's a crooked *Closed* sign hanging in the top glass pane of the locked front door. I'm about to turn away when I see a flash of movement behind the dirty glass.

The shop is unlit. But I get an impression of long silver hair trailing down over a black-clad shoulder; a high forehead and stern, straight nose. Someone is leaning over the countertop at the far end of the shop, studying something on the white blotter pad before him. Most of his face is hidden, just the palely gleaming crown of his head, but it's a man, I'm sure of it: tall and broad-shouldered, almost blending in with the overflowing case of antiquarian books behind him.

It is hours before the official opening time. But he's here, and I'm here, so I tap on the door, peering around the sign, but the man doesn't look up from what he's doing. I tap some more, sure he can hear me, sure that he's just being phenomenally rude, but he still doesn't look up. His gaze is intent. As if he's memorising something out of the thing that's open before him.

Pressing my nose right up to the glass I see that it's a thick book, bound in black, as black as his clothes. The man's long-fingered hands are marble-white against the covers. He looks up, suddenly, straightening behind the counter, still holding the book open, a frown pleating his brow. And I see that his eyes are sharp on me, as blue as the daytime sky. Despite the fall of silver hair over the man's shoulders, his face is young, sharply planed. It's possibly the most arresting face I have ever seen.

I look above the lintel at the name edged in faded gold,

surprised that someone as ordinary-sounding as *R. Preston, prop.* could have a face like that.

He's a giant of a man, I'm guessing even taller than Simon. As we stare at each other across the crowded, dusty expanse of the shop, I see a look of recognition, or maybe consternation, cross the man's face.

His gaze on me never wavers as I now pound on the door in earnest. He doesn't look away or make a move forward. He just continues to hold the large, open book in his hands, weighing me up steadily through the dirty glass as if I'm a particularly noisome bug.

'Please!' I yell, pushing on the fixed handle of the front door, which I see with a jolt of revulsion is shaped like a long human femur, cast into unyielding bronze. 'What do you know?' I cry, shouldering the door. 'What do you know about my mother? *Please!*'

I'm sure he can hear me, because the man shakes his head sharply, closing then placing his book down on the countertop. With a suddenness that shocks me, he turns and vanishes through a door set into a gap in the back wall that I hadn't known was there.

He doesn't return, though I wait and wait until I'm sure I'll miss the first bell at school, even if I sprint the whole way to get there.

༄

'Everyone's talking about it,' Vicki confides from the corner of her mouth with relish. 'They're just too afraid to bring it up. Honestly, it's like you've got actual leprosy.'

All morning, the personal forcefield we Crowes carry around with us has been up, sizzling away; Vicki the only person proof to it. Even the school principal and the school counsellor couldn't get at me with their long, sad faces and offers of help because, as Wurbik himself had said resignedly: 'You can't *make* a person do something they don't wanna do, right?'

I'm aware of the *awareness* about me. Everywhere I go, spaces open up; people draw together in groups of two and three, the air filling with sibilant waves of: *That's her, there she is, she's the one.*

I overhear Glenn Tippett confidently telling Miranda Cornish as I pass right by that: *She sure got hit with the ugly stick, hey?* I turn on him immediately and he actually shrinks back—all pimply, flaky-skinned, sandy-hued, six feet of him—even though he meant for me to hear.

'Hey, double consonant,' I snarl. 'Glen with two *n*s. Where's Simo? You know, *Lucky-as.* Where *is* he? Seen him?' I don't know why I'm asking, but I am. And from Vicki's startled body language, I can see she isn't sure why, either.

Glenn, recovering himself and standing up straighter, shakes his head, tight-lipped. I turn on Miranda with her size-six ballerina's body, doe eyes and long caramel hair. '*You* know?' Miranda looks at me with something approaching hatred and pulls Glenn away by the sleeve.

Vicki murmurs, 'And she scores, with another delicious instance of foot-in-mouth. Rumour has it that Simon Thorn dropped the divine Miss M last week because she couldn't *spell*, can you believe it? I give them three weeks, max. Glenn always takes Simon's slops, and it *always* ends badly. The parties concerned should all know better.'

Vicki takes me by the arm and steers me in the direction of Maths Methods, through a sea of rounded eyes and mouths. 'If Thorny stays away long enough, will you split the Tichborne with me?' she says, laughing.

But I think of cups of just-add-water instant noodles, towels gone grey and frayed from the repeat ministrations of coin-operated tumble dryers, and I don't reply.

After school, plenty of people see me getting into the bright blue unmarked police car (that screams *police car*) with the grim-faced, grey-haired man at the wheel. They point and stare. A few hold up their mobiles and take pictures. Mum has been everywhere. Every news concession stand I pass, every newsbreak, features that heartbreaking photo of my big-eyed, grinning mother in which my tanned right arm makes a cameo.

'Let's give them something to go with, hey?' Wurbik says under his breath as he fires up the red-and-blue flashers on the dashboard and the siren, giving it a few more loud *whoops* until we reach Royal Parade and turn right into city-bound traffic, before switching it off. 'People can be *shits*,' he says into the sudden impression of silence. 'Just hold your head up, the way you're doing. She would be proud.'

My skin prickles because he's using the past tense again, but maybe I'm just being too goddamned sensitive. 'So, "updates"?' I say, trying to sound upbeat, chatty.

'First things first,' Wurbik says, letting the siren have its head again until we cut up through Elizabeth Street into La Trobe. 'Need you to make sense of something for me.'

I recall *R. Preston, prop.* 'Did you speak with him?' I say eagerly as Wurbik turns into Little La Trobe Street: a stub-end more than a thoroughfare, really, of crouching, mismatched buildings.

Wurbik nods, braking. 'A very helpful man. He's agreed to stay open just to speak with you.'

I frown in the act of getting out of the car. 'But he wouldn't even let me in this morning!' I grumble. 'And we were both right here. I was throwing myself at the door like a lemming. Could have saved himself the trouble.'

Wurbik shrugs as he points his key at the car. There's

a *deet*, *deet* and blink of headlights. 'Mr Preston has been very sick, still is. Doing us a favour, from what I can see.'

The *Closed* sign is still up on the door, but Wurbik curls his fingers confidently around the femur-shaped door handle and gives it a push. The lights are on this time: three dim pendant lights—beautiful, antique Moroccan lamps in shades of rose and emerald green and old gold— and I look for the tall man with the long, silver hair and blue, blue eyes. But I'm confused when a small, elderly man in a white shirt and gold-framed glasses greets me from the back of the shop with a raised hand.

I stop dead before I've even taken three more steps. There's a Mariner's Compass set into the centre of the marble floor, in veined shades of variegated blues and reds, outlined in thin bands of gold. Its outlines are interrupted by stacks of old newspapers and protruding bookcases set at weird angles, but for a moment I feel like the ground's pulling away from me.

Wurbik grabs me by the arm and says, 'Steady on.'

'Do you see it?' I murmur helplessly. 'The Mariner's Compass?'

He nods. 'Is that what it's called? It was one of the things I wanted to ask you—whether she made those pillows because she saw this first, or whether it was just a coincidence. Some New Agey thing I'm not aware of.'

'Those pillows aren't new,' I say breathlessly, lurching

forward again in the direction of the small shopkeeper whose expression is now concerned, rather than welcoming. 'She hasn't worked on anything like them, all the time we've been living here. It's just an old design. People have been making them for centuries, Mum said.'

Wurbik and I come up to the counter and I see the black book set neatly to one side, its spine tantalisingly out of view, mottled, unevenly cut pages facing me.

'R. Preston?' I query, my voice sharpened by a weird anxiety I can't name. 'Mr Preston?'

The old man is shorter than I am; his grey skin, with a sweaty sheen to it, slack over his facial bones. I can see his flaking scalp straight through his sparse white comb-over.

The old man nods. 'Call me Robert,' he says huskily, spittle shining at the corners of his mouth. 'And you must be Avicenna.'

He hesitates next, as if he'd like to shake my hand, but I take an infinitesimal step back and his own hands drop flat onto the white blotter I recognise from this morning. 'I'm very sorry,' he says slowly, perspiration shining old gold under the light overhead. 'If I can help in any way?'

The act of speaking makes him cough and cough.

'If you could show her the entry?' Wurbik queries after the man has stopped dabbing at his face with the back of one shaky hand. 'She might be able to explain it to me in, ah, layman's terms.'

I glance sideways at Wurbik as the old man brings up a blue, leather-bound journal from under the countertop. He turns to a page marked with a gold ribbon and I see it's some kind of ledger, filled with book-keeping entries in blue fountain pen, flowing copperplate handwriting.

'Here it is,' Robert Preston says, frowning. 'It's in my hand, certainly, but I can't understand how I would have sold her that particular one. If—as you say—she was a professional astrologer, this one would have been nigh well useless to her. It's a bit of a mystery. I'm sorry, but I don't recall…' The rest of his sentence is cut off by a fit of coughing.

The entry says, as far as I can make out:

Sold—the Kairwan-school (mistake) Astrolabe.
$2200 (excl. GST).

'Mum bought an *astrolabe?*' I exclaim. She'd shown me an encyclopaedia entry once, years ago, of what an astrolabe was, and what it could do. Used for determining latitude on land, it was essentially some kind of manual calculator or *star taker*; that was literally what it meant. If you knew how to read it, the thing you held in your hand could predict the positions of celestial bodies: determine time, latitude, the future. We'd never been able to afford one.

I explain all that to Wurbik as Preston comes around his counter to fetch one out of the front window for us to look at. It's made of brass: a flat, disc-like thing on a sturdy fob chain, slightly bigger than my palm. It looks kind of like a manually manipulated compass—the kind that shows magnetic north, not Mum's kind, with the arms—with a rotating bar or ruler in the centre that moves over an ornately designed, stylised map of what looks like an ecliptic plane. With a pointer finger misshapen by terrible arthritis, Preston shows us how the map itself can be rotated over an underlying plate engraved with clusters of circles, like a web.

Layers on layers; all moving and circling. I see immediately the elegance of it, the genius. How, years before computers were invented, you could use one to take the measure of your place in the universe, provided the map, and the pointers, reflected your slice of the horizon.

'She's always wanted one,' I say aloud, tentatively touching the face of the thing Preston is holding out to us. It swings a little on its chain, when I push it. It's surprisingly heavy for its size.

'But the one she purchased was useless,' Preston wheezes, laying the astrolabe flat on the white blotter. He peers over his glasses at it. 'It was never properly assembled. I mean, the *tympan*'—he points at the flat plate with etched circles on it that lies beneath the two moving layers—'is of no known azimuth or altitude. The celestial sphere it represents certainly doesn't correspond to *our* horizon. And the stars that are the subject of the pointers on the *rete* are completely unrecognisable, at least to me...'

Preston twirls the ornate upper layer of metal that lies beneath the movable ruler-like arm. 'I bought it cheap out of a private collection, on that basis: that it was some kind of elaborate 18th-century fake. It's certainly old, but almost a *joke* astrolabe. A mistake. That's what I called it, you see here?' He points again at the journal entry, from about a month back. 'It's Tunisian in origin—of the Kairwan school—cast metal, antique, rare; but a joke, nevertheless. Just someone's interpretation of a sky I have never seen. Probably worthless but, because of its age, and the delicacy of its manufacture...'

Wurbik thanks Preston for his time and the old man nods, clearing his throat before saying, 'Any time, Detective, any time. If I can be of any further assistance...'

The old man starts turning off the lights as we head back towards the door, but I stop and turn, remembering the tall man in black with the gleaming hair and skin like marble, who was reading the old book that still sits to one side of the blotter. There's no giant now, though the book's here, it's as solid as I am. If I don't ask, I will never know.

'Do you have any assistants, Mr Preston,' I call out, 'who might have seen my mum or maybe talked to her? You don't remember selling her that astrolabe, but there was a man here this morning...' I describe him, and it's Robert Preston's turn to look startled. I see his right hand pause over the book beside the blotter, then come to rest protectively on it.

He shakes his head. 'No, it's just me these days. It's not a going concern of much consequence, you understand,' he rasps. 'And since I started my last course of treatment, well...' He shrugs.

Baffled, I point at the book under his palm. 'But he was reading *that* book,' I say. 'And then he turned and left by the back door.' I indicate a spot to the left of the bookcase, unable now to spot the egress through the dim of the shop.

The old man looks down sharply at the leather-bound book and turns it over. '*This* book?' he queries, again surprised. 'I confess I've been dipping into it lately, as I've been much...preoccupied with the things it speaks of: death, time, love, God.'

I feel a cold trickle down my spine as he murmurs, 'Donne's *Songs and Sonnets* of 1635. A rare edition, hand-cut pages; I would never dream of selling it or letting anyone handle it. You must be mistaken,' he adds, patting the shelving behind him with pale and twisted fingers that almost shine in the gloom. 'There's no back door here; never was. These are handmade shelves; solid jarrah. I had them put in back in 1978; cost me almost as much as my car in those days. Behind them? There's a wall of rendered double brick. And behind that? A block of flats, some trendy warehouse conversion. The side door'—he points to a spot just behind my right shoulder—'leads to Boundary Lane. It's where I park…'

His voice trails off, baffled, and turns into coughing that sounds draining, fatal. I reach out blindly to Wurbik, who I'm sure can feel strong tremors in the hand that's resting on his sleeve.

'Thanks again!' the detective calls out as the door with the leg bone for a handle swings shut behind us.

14

'What was *that* all about?' Wurbik says as he steers the car back into Exhibition Street.

We're only minutes from home, so I babble through my recollections of the morning. 'I know what I saw,' I insist fiercely. 'He had to have been at least seven feet tall. He was standing there like you're sitting there, reading that black book. Then he disappeared through a *wall*.'

'Grief does strange things to people,' Wurbik mutters, firing up the siren long enough for us to get past a turning bus.

'I know what I saw,' I repeat numbly. 'He was real. He looked at me and he *shook his head*.'

Wurbik stops the car outside my building in a *No*

Standing zone, because he can, and I suddenly remember the word Mum played: *always*. Thinking about it again sends a shiver straight across the skin of my belly and I clutch at it as if I have just been knifed. Eagerly, I hold up my mobile to Wurbik's scrutiny. He peers intently at the screen, then pulls his notebook out of a side pocket in the car door, jotting down the word; the time and date it was sent.

'I passed on my turn,' I say shakily, 'in the hope that she'd play something back straight away, but she didn't.'

'It could be a spasm in the system,' Wurbik says cautiously, handing my mobile back. 'Word was maybe sent a lot earlier, but it came through on delay. My wife plays this,' he adds, sounding resigned. 'Gets locked out all the time; up to a day, even two. She's always getting invited to play phantom games with strangers who resign without making a single move, days later. Drives her bananas. The system seems to just, I dunno, generate things.'

But he can see the whites of my eyes, feel my desperation, and says hastily, 'But we'll double, triple check, okay? It's important, and I'm glad you told me. But it'll depend on where the server is. If it's run out of another jurisdiction we'll have trouble getting a straight answer. But someone will be on it right away.'

I nod, shoving my phone back into the pack at my feet. 'Well, thanks for the lift. Saved me walking.'

I'm pulling on the car door with fingers that won't work

properly when Wurbik says from behind me, 'They're organising a line search for tomorrow, Avicenna. Nothing definite yet, but I'll call you the second we know anything.'

I turn back to face him. 'That's the update?' I whisper.

He nods, his eyes never leaving mine. 'Mount Warning National Park.'

I look at him blankly. Never heard of it; never been there. I would remember, I know I would.

'It's in New South Wales, near the Queensland border. They'll start at first light. Her phone goes offline inside its boundaries just before 9pm on the Friday. Your dad, you know, the anniversary of the fire, would have been the Saturday. But if the place had any special significance to her, we're struggling to find it. She was'—he stares out the windscreen for a second, then back at me—'a long way from home. That's all I want to say at this point. I'll tell you more when I know more.'

I do the math like I'm standing underwater with concrete shoes on.

Friday was three days ago. Although it was sent on Saturday—*the anniversary of the fire?*—I saw her word *today*. Any way you look at it, by the time it reached me, the word was already a lie.

It didn't mean *always*, as in *love always, be home soon*.

It meant *gone for always*, *dead for always*.

I find myself shrieking, pounding on Wurbik's chest.

'You need to work on your *delivery*! Your delivery *sucks*!'

Then I slam my way out of his neon-bright car and into my building, a raging, noisy, tearful bull, blundering up the stairs in the dim afternoon light, bouncing off the turns and railings like a pinball. I don't notice the young man leaning against the wall outside my front door until I'm almost on top of him. But the sight of him chokes me silent. I stare at him appalled, face smeared, tears still clumping my eyelashes together, as he pushes off the wall, crossing his arms like the explanation I've got for him had better be *good*.

He is honestly…breathtaking. I see that right away. It's unavoidable, how good-looking he is, like a hand seizing you around the throat.

My gaze snaps away from his face, then back again. I can hardly stand to look at him, having to take tiny, incredulous, up-from-under-the-eyelashes peeks. People like this actually *exist*? It's an insult to the rest of us.

The guy is tall, and built along these perfect lines. Early twenties, I'm guessing. Dark-blond, tousled, collar-length waves, great shoulders, great bones; slim-fit jeans with torn knees under a dark-grey flannel shirt open at the collar and rolled up tight at the elbows to reveal forearms corded with veins and lean muscles. Artfully maintained two-day growth shadows his jawline and he wears a shark tooth pendant around his neck. A leather satchel with a black jacket and grey-toned scarf draped over it sits near one boot-shod foot.

I blink as the stranger begins moving towards me with a languor that doesn't quite match the fury in his dark eyes. I figure he must have blundered his way into my stairwell by mistake until he demands harshly, 'Who are *you*? Where's Joanne?'

A sneer curls his beautiful mouth as he looks me up and down, his eyes narrowing momentarily on my scars. 'She told me to come back today for my *reading*, so I came, preparing to be *read* to, and no one was here. Do you know how long I've *waited*?'

An awful thought is forming.

Ish Hee-yoooooo.

I'd completely forgotten about him. What had I promised him the other night, to make him go away? My hands rise up to my face in horror and I shrink back in the direction of the stairs as he draws closer, snarling, 'You're crooks, aren't you? Scammers? It was *you* the other night, in the bathroom, wasn't it? Not Joanne. I thought she sounded funny, different.'

I'm shaking my head as he spits, 'Where is it? My so-called "fortune"? She hasn't done it, has she?' He pushes his hair back off his forehead. 'What you people don't understand,' he adds slowly, like I'm stupid, 'is that I'm not your usual brain-dead spiritualist who's easy to put off and *con*. Unless I see every cent of my money back, I'm going to report you charlatans to the *police*.'

The shouted word reverberates, hanging there in the still, cold air of the stairwell, and for a churning instant—when he extends his hand in accusation—I think he's going to touch me. Or hit me.

Then there's a sudden clatter of shoes on the stairs and I back straight into a hard male chest, my scream freezing in my throat as a large hand falls on my shoulder and gives it a squeeze. I slump where I stand, recognising the tobacco-raddled scent of the man's aftershave.

'The police are already here,' Wurbik says laconically from behind me, causing the young man to blink and straighten in surprise. 'What seems to be the issue, Sport?'

೭

Inside my apartment, Wurbik refuses to hand me back the bag I'd left in his car until he has established to his own satisfaction who it is he's looking at. But when he realises that he's actually in the presence of the last client named in Mum's journal—in the flesh—not a single muscle moves in his face. I can almost hear him thinking: *Well, that's all of them then, come forward. Kircher, Bawden, de Crespigny.*

While Wurbik's distracted, I grab my pack out of his big callused hand and kick it under the overhanging lip of the kitchen bench, giving him a speaking look with one eyebrow that says: *Thanks,* Dad, *I can take it from here with the angry hot guy.*

But Wurbik steps around me and opens my fridge door. He peers at a bowl of collapsed and weeping tomatoes with every appearance of interest, saying casually, 'So, Mr de Crespigny, you haven't seen or heard *any* of the blanket media coverage regarding Joanne Nielsen Crowe's disappearance last week?'

Beside me, Hugh de Crespigny visibly hesitates. 'Disappearance?' He looks to me for confirmation, but a sudden wave of pain makes me look down. As the silence lengthens, Hugh blusters, 'I've been in Tasmania all week.' He draws himself up, saying like it matters, 'At the opening of an *arts festival*, if you must know.'

'They get the news in Tasmania, too, last I heard,' Wurbik replies evenly, giving Hugh a sideways glance, before slamming the fridge door shut. 'But it does go some way towards explaining why you haven't returned a single one of our calls.'

'Look,' Hugh says in a more conciliatory tone, 'I got back late on Friday and this *girl* here'—he jerks a thumb in my direction—'promised me a reading if I came back on *Monday*. That's all this is. I'm here for a *reading*. And if she can't do it, I will settle for my money back and be on my way.'

'He was *drunk*,' I tell Wurbik beseechingly when his pale gaze alights on me. 'He came with a couple of mates while I was locked in my bathroom.' Wurbik frowns and I dart Hugh a venomous look, which he declines to acknowledge. 'I was scared.'

The detective comes out of my galley kitchen and leans against the bench, studying the younger man expressionlessly. 'You one of the Ballanchine Road, Toorak, de Crespignys?' he says, and I can tell by Hugh's sudden stillness that he's been caught off guard. 'The judge's boy? Justice Alaric de Crespigny? Look like him.'

The younger man's brows draw together. 'He's my uncle,' he responds warily. 'What's that got to do with anything?'

'Ah,' is all Wurbik says.

Hugh's eyes widen. 'Surely, you don't think I had anything to do with, with…' His voice rises incredulously.

'Can you give a good account of your recent movements, Mr de Crespigny? We'll be needing a statement from you in short order,' Wurbik says, deadpan. I know Wurbik is shit-stirring, but it still shakes me, to hear the words, how official they sound, the weight of them.

Hugh's frozen expression suddenly dissolves. 'I have been out of the *state*,' he enunciates bitingly. 'Happy to give you the names of all the people I *slept* with over the course of the last few days, *Officer*.'

For some reason known only to my traitorous subconscious, I flush a hot beet-red right up to the roots of my hair.

'Well, I'll be off then,' Wurbik replies.

Ducking forward awkwardly, I open the door, and it is Wurbik's turn to hesitate when he realises the furious younger man—watching us with arms crossed—is actually intending to stay. 'You don't have to do it,' Wurbik urges, his deep voice going quiet and gravelly with concern. 'I know Eleanor Charters made contact, asking for answers. Lovely woman, but her judgment's skewed. She's desperate, tried everything, is willing to believe. I can understand why it would make sense for you to see Elias Kircher—I mean, Mal and I talked long and hard about it but decided there was no harm because his chart was already done—but you don't have to deal with *him*'—he tosses his wiry, clipped head of grey hair in Hugh's direction—'or get involved in "finding" Fleur Bawden's murderer. The $250,000 reward Eleanor posted in 1985—that's a quarter of a mill in *1985 dollars*, Avicenna—has not yet been touched. The best police minds in the country haven't been able to pin it down to a single man. There's just not enough to go on and no star chart's going to do it. You can just say *no*, okay?'

Behind me, Hugh is very still, very silent. But I'm tough enough and ugly enough, I tell myself sternly, to handle a rich boy who wants to know how his rich life is going to pan out; piece of cake.

Wurbik and I continue to glare at each other, both refusing to be the one to look away first, but I feel something in my face softening. He would have made a great dad. A scary, gun-toting, hard-arse—but great—dad. 'I know, I know,' I say finally, 'if you had a kid, you would be telling her the same thing. But even if Mum's journal doesn't hold any answers, I owe it to her to finish, don't you see? *No loose ends* was one of her favourite sayings. *All loose ends*, I used to say right back. Meeting her halfway, for a change.' The laugh I give sounds harsh, like a bark.

Wurbik blinks. 'Well, you call me if this clown gives you any trouble, understand? And the duty to provide updates is an entirely mutual one, unlimited by normal office hours. If I don't hear from you, Avicenna, you'll be hearing from me, right?'

Wurbik scans Hugh de Crespigny's face again, as though searching for visible signs of a flawed character, saying in his direction, 'And you'll be hearing from us,' before pulling the door shut behind him.

As the detective clatters away back down the stairs, Hugh says, almost like he's thinking out loud, 'I could have that man *seriously* inconvenienced.'

It takes a good second for the meaning of his words to filter in. I swing on him, revolted. 'What did you pay her?' I demand, stepping around him and heading straight for the meals table covered in its plasticky, faux lace.

But he doesn't answer. I am simultaneously drawn to Hugh and terrified by him, and that makes me angry. I pull out a chair and wave a hand at it before hurrying into my bedroom for my laptop and Mum's almanacs, some paper and my pencil case and protractor. When I come out, Hugh is still standing in the same spot, looking around with that faintly sneering lip. 'I didn't imagine it,' he adds for no one's benefit. 'This place *is* an unrelieved dump. How did Rosso talk me into *doing* this?'

I drop the whole teetering mess I'm cradling on the table and pull out my own chair at the head, exactly where Mum would have sat, banging it down. *'What did you pay her?'* I repeat. It would give me some idea of how much time I would lawfully have to spend with this bozo.

Hugh's dark eyes snap to mine and he stalks over before sprawling in the chair opposite, the whole length of the table away. 'Enough,' he snaps. 'Rosso's mother is an incredibly superstitious woman who swears by these things. I lost a bet.' Hugh's voice suddenly hardens, as does his face. 'So here I am. *Hit me.*'

I glare at him over the collapsed mound of books and paper between us. 'Don't tempt me,' I reply. 'Hugh Athelrede de Crespigny?' He inclines his head curtly. 'Birthdate: 19 October, 1992. Birthplace: London, United Kingdom. Time?'

The time of his birth hadn't been in Mum's journal or

on the back of that envelope he'd left me. Without it, the chart I was about to draw for him would read like a greeting card: *Hugh has lovely people skills; is a great self-starter and party host.* I swallow down a snort of derision. Jerk.

'What?' Hugh replies, gaze challenging, sensing my amusement. 'Why do you need to know *that*?'

'*Time*,' I repeat, like he's the slow one. 'It's quite vital.'

Hugh eyes me coolly then leans down and draws a slender mobile phone out of a pocket of his designer bag. He hits a pre-programmed number while he studies me across the table.

'How'd you get that scar?' he says before suddenly drawling in a completely different voice, 'Mother, dear, at what exact moment was I *born*?' He laughs, and it is a warm and natural sound.

There is a muffled flurry of surprised noise at the other end, then silence. My colour rises again as Hugh says, the phone still held to his ear, 'What sort of name is *Avicenna*, anyway?' before bending in to hear her response.

As he slides the phone back into the front pocket of his shirt, he purrs, '4.52am, darling. Take it away. Do your worst.'

He knows I want to. Dislike and suspicion hang over the table like warring storm fronts. According to Mum's notes, all Hugh asked for was a simple radix. Emphasis: *wealth, health, love.* No progressions were required, no

answers to specific questions. Just platitudes and gener-
alisations. Cake.

But I can't stop my scalp from prickling as I start chart-
ing. Every time I look up, Hugh is watching me intently.
He's a looker: one of those people with so much confi-
dence and entitlement that he is without shame, without
embarrassment. There is a cool and absolute stillness about
his indolent frame that's almost preternatural. He's a big
guy—all legs and arms and hard shoulders—but while
I consult books and websites, shuffling pieces of paper
and rulers around nervously, he doesn't fidget. It's like
he's breaking me down into little pieces, just with his eyes,
as I try to do my worst.

But glyph after glyph, the building picture tells the same
story: excellent general prospects for money and success,
love and physical health, no adverse aspects or major afflictions involving either of the luminaries, his midheaven or
his ascendant sign. In all probability, throughout his life
he'll be loved and have children, friends, community; every
material thing he could wish for. These are good stars;
you would want to have been born under stars like these.
Without going beyond Mum's brief, without progressing
his chart forwards, I will not find *the twist*: the one that
could unmake him; derail his assured and munificent
future.

So in a monotone I tell Hugh that the universe was

both kind and bountiful when he was born, that he will have love, wealth, health, in spades—*The signs in your fifth house regarding offspring are particularly fruitful*, I find myself droning—but I don't pull any punches as I go, overcome by the desire to hurt, but also by desire itself.

'You're a perfectionist who can't stand to be alone,' I say gravely, hands on my knees under the table so he won't see them shaking. 'This may stem from issues with your father, who may be cold or distant? Absent?'

Hugh actually shifts in his chair when I say that, but he doesn't speak. There's something troubling about the stars in his fourth house signifying the male parent, but nothing definitive. Lots of people are raised by a single parent; I mean, look at me, no biggie, right? Hugh's face has tightened but he doesn't ask me to elaborate, so I continue with: 'You're highly sociable, hypercritical, judgmental, intelligent. Analytical, touchy. Vain.'

I let that word linger a little before adding: 'And you're also a hedonist with a constant craving to be needed, desired, loved, which—thankfully for you—is largely reciprocated by all who meet you—though you have a strong tendency to be overly possessive, obsessive, jealous. You don't so much love people as smother them. And if you don't like someone? Then they are dead to you.

'You abhor everything that is ugly or mundane,' I say finally, knowing that I must fall somewhere into this sub-category of *ugly things* with all my surface flaws. 'And the indications are that you will always have your wealth.' I can't resist finishing with, 'So, congratulations, yeah?'

Hugh is silent as I scribble all this down beneath his roughed-out astrological chart. And he is still silent as I date and sign it the way Mum always did.

A good astrologer, I remember her saying once, as she autographed someone's chart with a flourish, *always takes pride in, and stands by, her work. Those with the knowledge are here to be tested.*

But I go against Crowe protocol and don't bother keeping a copy of the radix for myself because I don't expect this prick to ever darken my doorstep again. The thought of it actually hurts me—that this is the only time our two lives will ever intersect—but there it is.

I push the piece of paper over the table to him and get to my feet, marching across the room and throwing open the front door. *Awareness*—of him, the shabbiness of the room, the unfairness of it all—is making it hard to breathe. Still, job done, right? Easy money.

Suddenly I find myself blinking away tears, actually tilting my head back against the door to hold them in; a feeling in the back of my throat like razor blades that I can't swallow down. If the year at Collegiate High never ended up panning out, I could always become the fortune-teller Sergeant Docherty accused Mum of being. Maybe she'd been onto something, my mother. Maybe she'd always meant for this to be some kind of lucrative fallback for her plain, ungainly daughter: because people are always going to be credulous slobs, having 'the knowledge' would mean I'd never starve.

Good one, Mum. Thanks. Always thinking about me.

Hugh hasn't moved. He just stares down blindly at the piece of paper I gave him like it's toxic. For a second I feel almost guilty because I've seen that look before. Somehow every word I uttered has seemed to him to have held some essential truth.

It's the nature of our art, I almost tell him. *To raise hopes, or destroy them. Don't let it affect you too badly.* But there's no duty to offer comfort, so I don't.

I look on silently as Hugh finally rises from the reading table, knotting his elegant scarf around his neck before shrugging into his jacket and slinging his leather satchel over his head. He hesitates above the piece of annotated paper, then folds it in half, then into quarters, before shoving the small square into a pocket. *Why is it*, I find myself thinking, *that the worst arseholes have faces like angels?*

But if that were really true, it would make me one of the kindest people on the planet, and I'm not. I know the reading I just gave was deliberately harsh, mean-spirited. There were so many other ways I could have phrased things, but I chose the low road. Mum would be appalled.

Hugh draws alongside, muttering, 'Looks like you have me all worked out. I haven't turned out to be a very nice person, have I?'

There is that *awareness*. I don't know if he can feel it, but it's almost an atmosphere in the room, stifling.

'Oh, I don't know,' I say vaguely, crossing my arms, staring at a point past the guy's broad shoulder; wanting my dinner, wanting to cry, wanting him over with and crossed off, just like Wurbik's crossed him off. Really pretty people have this effect on me—something goes wrong with the muscles in my neck and I can't hold my head up properly or look them in the eye for any length of time. It's a defensive reflex I've developed against the possibility of judgment, or hurt.

With Hugh, I think it is the worst it's ever been. He's both magnetic and intensely repellent. Very push-pull. And I have to remind myself that the only reason he's in my life in the first place is because Mum isn't.

He's standing so close now, I almost have to lean backward or we'll touch. But there's nowhere to go and even the air I'm breathing smells of him. 'You forgot one thing, though,' he says.

That makes me look at him, stung. 'I don't forget,' I say hotly. 'I don't *forget* anything. You got what you paid for and, buddy, it's *accurate*. You know it is.' Hugh's gaze on me is watchful; his irises so dark I can't see into his soul. And I want, desperately, to look away. But I can't. Instead I flick my fingers in the direction of his pocket to distract and confuse because I'm good at deflection, at attack. At the heart of all attack is defence. I live by that credo.

I jabber, 'That radix is you in a nutshell, right? Am I right?'

I *know* I'm right, but my left hand slips up nervously into the loose ends of my hair anyway, pulling it into a thick rope that I tug down tightly over my ruined ear. Around him, I am a bag of nervous tics, and it's disgusting.

Hugh is staring at me like he could melt me with his eyes. Maybe it's the ugliness thing, and I offend him. *Snake and mouse, mouse and snake*, I think.

Then Hugh gives me a sudden, crooked smile that does something painful to the muscles of my diaphragm. As I flush beneath his steady scrutiny, his smile broadens, actually reaching his eyes, making all the interesting lines of his face more prominent.

'You *forgot* to say,' Hugh emphasises quietly, 'that I hate mysteries; that I won't leave them alone until I get bored...' He steps forward until I'm pressed into the grain of the door, trying to keep some air between us. 'Or I get answers. You've given me a lot to think about, Avicenna. I think I was wrong about you, and I *hate* being wrong. You missed that, too.'

Then he laughs—a laugh of genuine amusement—and says, 'Later,' in the kind of light, Prince Charming voice that only serves to remind me of our last encounter before this one; the innate violence of him, drunk, beating at my door.

My hands are still shaking as I draw the safety chain across. And I listen with my good ear pressed up against the wood, not breathing out until I hear the door at the bottom of the stairs slam shut behind him.

15

I wake with a start to a room bathed in red-gold light, and to Mum bending and whispering in my ear, her long hair hanging down, all red-gold, too. *All readings, like all people, are inherently contradictory. But find the pattern? And you will find the person. You will know them absolutely.*

For a second, I'm paralysed by joy and relief; that she came back.

But then I wake in earnest to a pitch-black bedroom and panic makes me lash out for the lamp switch, sending the whole thing crashing to the floor off the bedside table. My mobile phone begins to shrill.

Crawling amongst the soft-hard debris on the floor, I finally locate my backpack near the foot of the bed and crack open my bedroom door to let in the watery day. Back against the doorframe, I look down at a number I've never seen before and breathe out my name. The person on the other end inhales shakily, as if they might speak, then hangs up. Seconds later, I almost drop the phone when it starts ringing again in my open palm.

It's Wurbik, crisp, best policeman voice. 'Just checking you're still alive, kiddo. I take this liaising business seriously.'

I give him the upshot of the reading I did for Hugh de Crespigny; though I don't tell Wurbik about how mean I was, because I actually care about what he thinks of me. The act of talking begins to slow my racing heart.

When Wurbik doesn't respond right away, I tell him I'm planning on calling Don Sturt later in the day with the results of the horary readings I'm doing on the Bawden suspects. 'As far as I can tell, they're all loaded.'

'It's your funeral,' Wurbik replies, sounding distracted, like he's suddenly got someone in his other ear.

'Has there'—I swallow, wanting to know, but also wanting to hide under my bed with my hands over my ears forever—'been, uh, any word, yet, about Mum?'

'Too early.' Wurbik's voice is almost curt. 'Give us a chance. And you stay away from that boy's mob—they all love a recreational drug. All sex addicts, too, the judge especially; he's had to work hard to keep it out of the papers, his weakness for the rough stuff. Big breeders. Tentacles in politics, law, racing, fashion, *philanthropy*.' Wurbik's voice is heavy with sarcasm. 'Too fast for you; you've done your bit. Call you when I hear. Hang tight.'

Wurbik cuts the connection and it takes me a while to put my phone away and scrape myself up off the carpet. The apartment is redolent with the bitter smell of burnt toast, which is what I ate for dinner last night. I'm ashamed by how much I crave the sound of another human voice. It's like a sickness.

It is the sameness that gets to me, every day the same; the Mum-shaped hole in the fabric of things. I wake, and there is a split second of the way life was: *What's on for today? What do I have to wear that's, maybe, clean?* Then it all comes crashing down—the lack of her, like a rock settling on my chest. And I have to get up and haul that rock—while I eat, while I brush my teeth, while I interact with the rest of the human race.

The morning rapidly turns into a re-run of the one before, right down to the choice of outfit (jeans, runners, polar fleece), the icy, sunny weather, and me taking a special detour up Little La Trobe Street, past *The Ark of A–Z*.

This time, when I get there and press my forehead up against the glass, there isn't a silver-haired giant standing at the counter behind the *Closed* sign. There is nothing to see except dust and eclectica inside a faded, empty store. Even the old black book has been put away. I could have imagined everything.

'But I know what I saw.' My breath makes a circle of fog on the dirty upper pane of the front door as I address the dim glass. 'And I saw *you*.'

The footsteps of a lone passerby drawing closer cause me to pull my beanie down lower over my forehead and hurry back the way I came. Everyone I ask looks at me strangely, but at school no one has seen or heard from Simon Thorn, who has never taken a sick day in living memory.

But Dalgeish lights up when she spots me going into my form room and hurries over, leaning into me with a bony elbow. 'You're doing the talk with or without him,' she hisses through lipstick-stained front teeth. 'Your situation's been noted. All you need to do is stand up and *say something*. I've told Ednah Daniels this is the year one of my kids takes out the Tichborne, not hers, so don't let me down.'

'No pressure.' I find Vicki at my elbow after Dalgeish's lurid purple and yellow calf-length sweater-and-skirt set has flounced out of view. 'Catch you in the Common Room after first period?' she says as we slide into our usual places up the back, for rollcall.

I shake my head, knowing it'll be too hard to explain

what I'm doing; my reputation's bizarre enough as it is. 'Double spare. Something I need to finish in the library. Catch you when I catch you.'

The implication is to leave me alone; we both hear it.

Vicki pouts, her dark eyes suddenly dangerous beneath her curly fringe. 'I'm still *waiting*,' she says pointedly.

She means the word game we're in the middle of playing and how the word *sluts* needs, urgently, to be addressed. But I also see that she's asking about when it's going to get back to normal: me and her, the big-haired, bosomy twins who get around being ballsy, loud and notorious; everyone's favourite general pains-in-the-arse who are guaranteed to shout out from the back of the room.

I want to tell Vicki that I've somehow left *normal* far behind, as if it's a country and I've stowed away on the wrong boat, and it's sailed. Instead, I smile tightly and bellow—*Here!*—in a hearty voice when Clarkey calls out my name. When the bell rings, I rise to my feet and leave the room without a backward glance, feeling Vicki's eyes—all their eyes—doing things to my back.

In the library, there is a round of double takes when I walk in. I invoke the forcefield so successfully that, when the dust settles, mine is the only table for four without a single extra person crammed up against it. Everyone leaves me alone near the shelves dedicated to warfare and catastrophes of the Far East, and this time I'm not obscurely hurt. It means I can spread out my workings for Mallory Bloch, Geoffrey Kidston, Lewis Boardman and Christopher Ferwerder without some sightseeing ghoul trying to get a handle on what I'm up to.

Putting the finishing touches to the fourth and final chart a moment later, I am struck by one thing. If the charts are to be believed, none of these four men was responsible for raping and murdering Fleur Bawden that day.

I look up when the bell goes for recess. But I can't face the avidity, the questions, so I go over all of the charts again, house by house, segment by segment, from start to finish; first checking the radix, then the wheel representing the progressions, then the outermost wheel, where the triggering, focusing transits are arrayed in a less-than-perfect circle.

I wasn't joking when I told Wurbik all four men appear to be loaded. Collectively and individually, their second house and fourth house stars for wealth and assets are off the charts and their first house indicators (delineating abilities, looks, energy) and tenth house stars (professional standing) are uniformly phenomenal. A couple of them look to have lost and regained their fortunes a few times, but all seem to be self-made men with money to burn. Jupiter in good aspect is in evidence in all of the progressions.

But on the day in question there are no squares between

progressed sun and moon in the men's charts, no significant afflictions affecting progressed moon and Venus, or signs of the malefic planets—Mars and Saturn—being in prominence or in harsh opposition from the angles, or afflicted by the signs of violence—Capricorn, Aries, Scorpio. Progressed Pluto, signifying death, makes no significant connection with the men's progressed moon that day, nor is it transiting the seventh house—which traditionally indicates *other people*. And none of the charts contain aspects for bereavement, misfortune or intense violence for the date in question. Even if any of them knew Fleur Bawden, she meant nothing to them.

The library is empty now, so I pull out my phone, wishing I knew Simon's number, or he would maybe call and tell me what had been so urgent he'd just left me standing there in the street. Then I dial Don Sturt. After two quick rings I get, '*Don.*' His voice is dry as dust, cautious.

I find myself furtively racing through a summary of the men's charts before someone overhears me talking like a witch, in a public place.

'Okay, so Bloch's in his late sixties now, and he's got this explosive temper and an apparent lifelong dislike of women. But according to his chart, he's almost pathologically obsessed with cleanliness and hygiene—I don't see him messily bludgeoning anyone to death, wouldn't want it on his hands—and he wasn't even *there* the night Fleur was killed. According to his stars, he was travelling that day, moving around; because the man has never been able to stay still. Bloch was born in a situation of transit, and that pattern has continued throughout his life.'

'Okay,' Don says, sounding muffled now because he's probably struggling to write all of this down in that tiny private investigator notebook of his.

'Kidston—who's almost fifty now, right?—is an intellectual snob who loves cultivating friends in high places. He's got loads of unresolved daddy issues. And he's really highly strung, super emotional, so there appear to have been a few mental breakdowns in his past? But nothing around the date of Fleur's death. There are no indications for physical confrontation regarding his ruling sign or progressed ascendant for that day. At the time Fleur died, Kidston was in the middle of a good period for physical and mental health.'

'Go on,' Don rasps curtly. He's barely said a word the entire time I've been firing away at him about the predilections of strange men.

'Boardman—the other Australian-born suspect, now in his mid-fifties—is some kind of charismatic, smooth operator with a wide circle of friends and great business sense. His seventh house stars for marriage and long-term relationships are unbelievably bad—in the sense there's heaps of movement, but maybe he likes that, being a *playa*—but he's never been seriously ill or suffered any serious form of bad luck, violence or affliction, whether physical or mental. There are indications for sex and pleasure on the night that Fleur died, but nothing resembling an accidental or purposeful involvement in the violent death of another. Maybe he saw her or knew her? But it's hard to say, nothing is definite.'

'Mmmm,' is all Don says as I look out the window and see people returning to the main building, flooding in through all the doors off the sodden playing fields. I'm suddenly talking so fast, I'm almost impossible to understand, my voice dropping to a whisper because people are filtering back into the library and glancing over at me in undisguised interest, with all my papers and books spread out everywhere.

'Ferwerder, the Scottish guy, is nearing ninety now. But on 9 July 1984 he would have been a man in his late fifties and entirely capable of murdering someone. But again, I've got nothing, Don. Happily partnered-up at the time; though he's a highly social, touchy-feely, flirty kind of guy with a short attention span who was likely to have been in town on the night in question. But the stars indicate no acts of extreme rage or violence for the time frame you've indicated. There's nothing of note for that day. *Nothing.*'

Don digests all this in silence. 'Does it change anything,'

he finally says, 'if Kidston, the nervy, high-strung guy, was born at noon? We're still talking Melbourne, but 12pm exactly.'

I feel the blood rush up into my face as Wez Ellery wanders right past—close enough to touch—with his hand shoved down the back pocket of Mila Abramovich's jeans. Both of them have no reason to be over here, craning their necks to get a look at what I'm doing. I actually hiss at them, while I scoop piles of papers together untidily and start shoving them into my pack.

Don's tone is apologetic. 'You were right, the birthtimes for the two Aussies weren't the same. Transposition error on my part, sorry. Don't know how it happened. Does that change anything?'

Of course it does, you idiot. It changes the entire thing, I almost say, knowing I'll have to start Kidston's chart all over again from scratch.

'It will,' I murmur tightly as Ozzie Palomares and his massive fro approach my table. I look up as he levers his vast frame unapologetically into the seat opposite mine, nylon-clad arse cheeks squeaking against the vinyl. He raises his monobrow at me as if to say: *This okay?* I shrug, trying to seem cool with it.

'Look,' I say tightly, 'if I re-run Kidston's again, am I off the hook? I'm not a public service, you know. It has to end somewhere.'

'Look,' Don counters right back, and I hear a faint *swish* of passing cars down the line and realise he's actually driving, he's on the road. 'Eleanor will want to hear all of this in person. Can you rejig the Kidston reading and I'll...' There's a long pause. '*I'll* pick you up outside your school at, what, *three?* And take you straight to her. I'm coming back from her place up country at the moment—she wanted me to fetch a few things from the vineyard—but I'll try and make it across town so that she gets the wash-up straight from you. El's going to be disappointed. But at least now she knows we've tried... everything.'

I think of being trapped in a car with Don Sturt and his nervous, yellow-flecked eyes and gangly teenage awkwardness that sit so at odds with his old-guy body. 'Do I have a choice?' I reply as Ozzie pretends, laboriously, to read. He's either checking out my rack again at close quarters, or running interference for Vicki; because all the Greek kids at Collegiate have each other's backs. It's an unspoken rule. I turn my back on Oz, leaning up against the edge of the table so that all he sees is a big expanse of dark-purple polar fleece and maybe half an inch of my squashed-down backside.

'Please,' Don rasps. 'You do this for Eleanor and I promise you're out, you've done your bit. Some things—as tragic as they are—they don't have answers. I told her that—that having some person do a bunch of horoscopes wouldn't prove a bloody thing.'

I want to say: *I could've told you that.*

But instead I say brusquely, 'I'm already late for Chem. Meet me outside the Catholic hospice two doors down from school at 3.30. And you have one hour of my time, right? If you don't make it, Don, you don't make it; there aren't any re-runs and I'm not waiting. My mother is *missing*, don't you people understand?'

I'm almost in tears as I cut the call, and I'm sure Ozzie can hear it in my voice, so I don't meet his eyes, or anyone else's, as I careen out of the library. I just head to Chemistry like nothing's happened, and all Dr Terrasson says dryly is: 'Well, look who's decided to grace us with her presence today,' and then it's business as usual from his perspective, no special favours, which I'm grateful for.

Though, again, there's that weight of eyes. And no one will partner with me until the Doc forces Candice Ong to do it and she insists on doing everything herself like I'm injured or retarded: gathering up all the materials with her own tweezers, doing all the measurements, firing the Bunsen burner up so that the flame blazes between us like a boundary that may not be crossed; all in silence. It's like I turned up at school with no hands, rather than with no mother, but I don't make a fuss.

As Candice burns shit and I look on helplessly, I think:

Right now, Cenna, right now, there are people out there in the bush looking for her, thousands of kilometres away.

In the meantime, all I can do is put my head down, pick up my ballpoint pen and swim. Swim for the distant shores of *normal*—even though I know I may never make it back again.

Something about Don Sturt makes me sit very straight on the edge of my seat, my pack between my knees, hands on my kneecaps, wishing like hell that the car ride was over. I've never been this close to the guy. It's not that he's a talker—he's not, he's silent and hunched-over—but there's just…something. It's like his body is emanating some weird, screamy vibe so supersonic I should be able to read it. It's possible that he's even more uncomfortable about the whole situation than I am. The phone call earlier was bad enough, but this? A whole other level of *awkward*. Maybe he doesn't like girls, I dunno. When I sneak glances at him between the stops, I sense he doesn't like me. It's in the pinched lines of his gaunt face. He wants me away from him somehow, even though he suggested the ride, and the knowledge makes me almost want to leap out of the car while it's still moving. Even his driving seems erratic, twitchy; the car drifting across lane boundaries and skidding on the tram tracks when he accelerates at the lights.

When we leave the known universe that is bounded to the south by St Kilda Road and the Shrine of Remembrance, turning off to points leafy and even more traffic-jammed, I'm officially lost. We're not far from town, I know that much. But the inner-city suburbs that surround Collegiate High do not remotely resemble what we are driving through now. It's like we've entered that part of the map that some higher power has designated: *the better part*. Once we leave the ritzy strip shops, art galleries and tram-clogged main road behind, the side streets are broad and alien, with houses and accompanying grounds that are enormous, almost unfeasible, surrounded by high walls or spear-topped iron fences that seem to go on for miles.

Up a wide, hilly street graced with massive old-growth elms on either side, we come to a ten-foot-high red-brick wall covered in balding winter-grade ivy. As the blank steel gates swing open, I see that it's the kind of estate that comes with its own double-storey gatehouse, CCTV security system and central flagpole. Huge cast-iron lamp-posts are strung out all along the sweeping gravel driveway and the trees are all towering, bare-branched things I can't name, each one big enough to take down a house if it ever fell in a storm.

Don pulls up with a spray of gravel, muttering, 'Wait there.' Pointing through the windscreen, he indicates the return veranda of a sprawling, single-storey Victorian-era mansion built out of the same dark brick as the gatehouse, with leafless canes of wisteria threaded through the intricate iron fretwork.

As I get out of the car and head towards the bluestone front steps, Don drives the early-model Mercedes into a four-car carport with clear glass doors. I watch him park the gleaming car between a compact grey delivery van—the kind with double swing doors at the back—and a boxy white Range Rover, both with heavily mud-encrusted tyres and plates.

While Don's still crossing the driveway, the front door opens above me and Eleanor steps out onto the mosaic-tiled veranda. She's wearing another oversized jumper and blue jeans, looking elfin, with an expression on her ruined face that isn't *hope* exactly—more a willingness to be taken by surprise.

And I curse Don Sturt for the coward he is. I can tell he told her I was coming to see her this afternoon, but none of the rest.

'I'm so grateful,' is all Eleanor says as she shuts the heavy front door behind us. We move down a long central corridor bounded by rainbows thrown by stained-glass windows. The Persian hall runner under my feet is thick and soft and muted, and the walls are crowded with etchings, mirrors, wall sconces and artwork in heavy gold frames. I'm a major art dyslexic, but even *I* recognise some of the names in the lower right-hand corners of the paintings. They aren't prints—I can actually see individual brush strokes and surface cracking—which means Eleanor is just as loaded as those four men whose charts are stuffed inside my backpack. Fleur would have been, too, had she lived. She would have been one of those mythical girls with everything: wealth, love, elegance, beauty.

The air smells like tea roses and clean linen, baking cookies, and I suddenly understand, in a way I didn't before, that those four men must be people just like Eleanor Charters. Once her friends, or the children of her friends, her neighbours; they are intricately bound to her in some way. The thought makes me rub the backs of my arms, as if I'm cold.

Eleanor leads me into a large, high-ceilinged room that must have once functioned as a formal dining room. But the twelve-seater Victorian dining suite in the centre of the carpeted space, lit by a matched pair of crystal chandeliers, is now a repository for books and papers and manila folders, computer equipment, crime-scene photographs and tomes on true crime and police procedure. There's a repeating pattern of *fleur-de-lis* picked out in gold thread running across the dark-blue carpet, and heavy, marble-topped mahogany sideboards against the walls; that feature flocked wallpaper and gilt mirrors.

It is a beautiful room, with heavy curtains thrown open at the floor-to-ceiling sash windows that are now a faded salmon colour from never having been drawn for years. As Eleanor settles into a sagging velvet wing armchair standing next to a carved white marble fireplace dominating one wall, I gather this is her nerve centre, the place where she spends most of her days, sifting for answers that will not come.

Eleanor indicates the matching armchair across the marble hearth and I lower myself tentatively into its collapsed depths, feeling the displaced springs shift and protest beneath my weight.

Seconds later, a matronly woman with silvery short hair in a dark skirt and dark blouse brings in a silver tray set with an antique silver pot and three paper-thin matching china cups on saucers. The tray also holds a plate of tiny scones and dainty biscuits with oozy, jammy centres, a dish of cream and another holding the same yellow-gold jam that's inside the biscuits. When the woman places the tray down on a low, marble-topped mahogany table standing between Eleanor's chair and mine, I shake my head apologetically. 'I'm more of a coffee person, sorry, and I don't really like, uh, jam. Mum never had it in the house.'

Eleanor's housekeeper murmurs, 'Your mother did mention that when she was here, so I've made coffee. But the preserve is Don's particular weakness; so there's something for everyone.' The elderly woman flushes at the expression of shock on my face, leaving the room quickly as Eleanor dismisses her with barely suppressed eagerness.

Removing her leather slippers, Eleanor now tucks her small, bare feet up under her like a kid and says, 'Well, *well*? What did you find?'

Flustered, I dig around in my bag, about to answer, when Don Sturt lopes into the room, pulling up a dining chair beside Eleanor's armchair. She pours him a cup of coffee, placing a jam biscuit on the saucer accompanying his cup before handing it to him. 'Cook made your favourites,' she murmurs as Don's eyes drop to the surface of the hot liquid. He pours a long slug of milk from a pretty porcelain jug into its ebony depths, stirring in two teaspoons of sugar from the pretty silver pot on the tray. He takes a sip, the jam biscuit disappearing in two bites before he takes another, all without looking up.

'So? Tell her the upshot,' Don says, in a faux-airy voice that makes me want to reach across the afternoon tea things and strangle him.

Putting my papers in order, I clear my throat and begin to speak.

16

As I run through the results for Mallory Bloch, Eleanor's eyes grow cloudy, distant. When I reach the end of my notes on the man, Don turns to her and says, 'He was a long-shot anyway, remember? Just because no one remembered seeing him at the house party in Mount Eliza didn't mean he wasn't there, or coming back from there, the way he insisted. Even though the man's an abusive, officious prick, and there was never any proof, I never thought he was a *liar*.'

Eleanor picks at one of her cuticles and says nothing as I push on with the reading for Ferwerder.

Vanilla, vanilla, vanilla.

As I shuffle the notes for Ferwerder to the back of

the pack, Eleanor insists unhappily, 'But Chris Ferwerder *knows* something. He couldn't look me in the eye back then, and he still can't. I have seen him leave a function, just to avoid me.'

'He might know something,' I answer gently, 'but it's not something I can tell you from the question you asked me to address. There's just nothing in his stars.'

'She was supposed to be at a party at his place,' Eleanor whispers. She places a miniature scone absently onto the edge of Don's saucer and I watch as he saws it in two with a butter knife before slathering it in jam and eating the thing whole; flushing slightly when he catches me watching. 'Geoff Kidston used to drive her everywhere,' Eleanor continues with quiet anguish. 'I trusted him to do it because he was *Margaret's son*. He and Lew Boardman used to take her around, like she was their mascot: drive her to school, pick her up from parties, never a hint of trouble. They were supposed to be *good boys*; *fine young men*. I knew them when they were *children*.'

I exchange a helpless look with Don, who is busying himself pouring another coffee.

The moment I tell Eleanor Charters that Lewis Boardman possesses the stars of a serial sex fiend and womaniser—*but that he didn't do it*—she pushes herself out of her chair, hands over her mouth, and leaves the room. After a second's hesitation, Don walks out, too, and I'm reminded that I still don't get the vibe around these two, why they are even together; how this gaunt, hard-worn, stick of a man became a kind of general dog's body, driver-cum-servant, to a haunted rich lady.

When Don returns a moment later, he is alone.

'I'm sorry,' I tell him as he dips an entire scone into the dish of jam, cross-contaminating the cream with it, before stuffing the whole catastrophe into his mouth. 'These are what their charts say.'

'Well, what about Kidston's?' he counters, wiping self-consciously at the corners of his lips with the knuckles of one hand.

'Yes,' Eleanor begs as she sweeps back into the room. 'What about *his*?'

Her eyes are very red, but she sits back down in her chair, her posture rigid. I give Don a hard look, and he tells Eleanor sheepishly about the transposition error he made with Kidston's birthtime. I read out my original summary and Eleanor tilts her head to one side, saying, 'And now? How does this one mistake change anything?'

I tell her that taking Kidston's birthtime backward by several hours intensifies the apparently secretive, selfish side of his nature, and his phenomenal sensitivity. 'I'm seeing a lot more arrogance and snobbery, ego, the pursuit of people and things that make him look good, or befit his perception of himself.'

'Fleur would have fit right into that category,' Don says musingly.

'Fleur treated him like an annoying older brother,' Eleanor snaps back. 'Fleur was a young fifteen. She wasn't even thinking about boys or...'

Her eyes go shinier, and Don and I exchange furtive glances as Eleanor blinks rapidly and looks down. I know that when I was fifteen I was thinking about boys and cars and riding around in cars with boys. But I was never a young fifteen, after all, with this rack, and this face, and I don't say anything because it won't help.

After a while, Eleanor looks back up at me and murmurs, 'Did he or didn't he do it?'

I hesitate before shaking my head, and she covers her mouth with her hands and rocks forward, wordlessly, in her seat. 'But,' I say tentatively over her bowed head, grey hair swept into its signature, elegant chignon at the nape of her slender neck, 'there *is* something in Kidston's progressed chart. Something the others don't have.'

She raises her eyes to mine like a threatened animal, and I say quickly, glossing over the finer detail because it would make no sense to someone like her, 'That night? The way Kidston's ascendant was conjunct progressed Neptune indicates that he was brewing some weird plan or deception. Looking at where Uranus sits with regard to his natal moon, and how Mercury is moving into square with Mars, all this signifies some kind of conflict or fight, some issue to do with travel or...*delivery*? Is that making any sense to you?'

Eleanor's eyes have grown very wide, and she shakes her head, mystified, while Don struggles to write it all down in his little notebook between bouts of nervous eating. 'If you look at the way Saturn is transiting through here.' I indicate a portion of the rough handwritten chart I threw together between PE and the final bell. 'The interrelationship between Mercury, Mars and Saturn indicates a conflict with someone he considered an authority figure. Someone he was afraid of, or maybe wanted to impress? It can also mean a forced farewell of some kind.'

Eleanor actually inhales with horror at my words, and begins crying in earnest, plucking at the front of her sweater, rocking and shuddering in her chair.

I actually jump out of my own seat then and hold out my notes to Don, wanting to be free of these people and their horrific burden. 'I'm sorry,' I babble. 'I'm so sorry, that's the best I could do. You asked me to do it; I didn't want to.'

Don takes the untidy sheaf of notes and diagrams out of my clenched fist. He looks at Eleanor, but she's gone to that place beyond speaking. I see him hesitate before reaching out and placing his free hand—thin, sun-damaged, hairy-backed—onto her frail and shaking shoulder.

The juxtaposition between his hand on her, and the elegant, jewel-coloured room—lit with rainbows from sunlight hitting all the glass—brings on something like hot panic, or nausea, and my own hands rise to my face in horror.

Some things have no answers. God, let that not be true.

I swing my pack onto my shoulder, already backing away from the two of them, seated in awful tableau. The roaring in my ears seems to grow louder. Jesus, I don't even know where I *am*. I'm so far out of my narrow comfort zone, it's like I'm in a parallel universe. 'If you could just tell me what tram or bus I need to take?' I plead. 'To get home? It's kind of late. I just need to get there. *I need to go home.*'

Don looks up, an arrested, almost pained, expression on his face. And it strikes me again how wasted and out-of-place he looks, despite his expensive clothes, his expensive surroundings. He's like a grey, weathered tree—uprooted from the side of a dusty bush track somewhere—that's been replanted in a hothouse.

Don's eyes slide away even as he mutters, 'I'm to see you home. It's all been fixed.'

And I nod once, sharply, before fleeing the room, and the howling old woman in her bright, jewel-box house, who will never find peace. It's like looking into my own future.

While Don brings the car around to where I'm standing like I'm too delicate or posh to walk the short distance to the carport, I check my phone and see at least a dozen missed calls. A couple of the early ones are from Wurbik, but there's one from a mystery landline, one from the mystery mobile caller of this morning—*the inhaler*, I've taken to calling that one—and the rest are from Malcolm Cheung.

Malcolm Cheung: who's Homicide.

I climb numbly into the front passenger seat of the royal blue Mercedes, agonising over which of them to call first—Malcolm or Wurbik.

The light is fading.

Where they are, the searchers, the light would be fading, too. Most likely they'd all be reporting in after a long day of bush-bashing. Suddenly, it doesn't matter that Don's driving and that I'm stuck driving with him. Don could be wallpaper. Don doesn't matter. As he shifts the big car into gear and we sail out of Eleanor's grounds straight into peak-hour traffic, like a coward I speed-dial Wurbik first. Wurbik is a known entity. While I continue to deal with Wurbik, it will continue to be just a *missing persons* case.

That's all, I tell myself, *she's just missing and they're just checking in.*

But Wurbik's unmistakably cagey; unwilling or unable to give anything away. 'You need to hear it from Mal, who's been trying to reach you for hours. Where have you been?'

I tell him I've been to afternoon tea at Eleanor's place—me and Eleanor and Don—and Wurbik makes this unhappy noise that could be exasperation, or sympathy. 'Call Mal before you do, see or hear anything else,' he insists. 'Got that? You need it all put into context.'

'Context?' I parrot dumbly.

'Just call him,' Wurbik says with a harshness I recognise as checked emotion, 'especially if you don't already know.'

'Know what?' I mumble, staring out blindly at shiny shop windows that proclaim: *Versace, Miyake, Provence, Saldi, Boss.*

'Do it *now*,' Wurbik replies by way of not replying, and hangs up.

'At least Eleanor had a body to bury,' I find myself saying in a dazed voice and I swear I see Don wince out of the corner of my eye.

I'm still dumbly staring down at my phone when the thing rings in my hand—how I freaking *hate* when that happens—and I freeze.

But it's the mystery landline number that's flashing up at me, not Malcolm Cheung's, of Homicide. And it's not an anonymous number (the kind favoured by dickless sickos who like to make calls to young girls) so I answer it.

'Hello? Am I speaking with Simon Thorn?' says a woman—brisk, efficient, harassed. Immediately I sit up straighter because this is something I can handle; it's not about me.

'No, but he's just in the bathroom…'

I see Don's eyes dart sideways before hastily refocusing on the red light we are waiting at. Thank God he didn't decide to put on the radio.

'…and I can give Simon a message as soon as he gets out,' I finish smoothly.

'He's not answering the primary number he gave us,' the woman says, 'and he needs to make a decision. I'm sorry, but we need it today. And there are forms to fill out, if he's really serious about what he agreed verbally with Dr Gurung. He needs to come back in and speak with the specialists in charge because things need to move quickly from here—if he's serious. Can he come in right away?'

I have no idea, but I say, 'Yeah, sure. I'll let him know. Sorry, tell me again, where were you calling from?'

The woman tells me *Royal Melbourne Hospital* and I ask for directions, and she tells me, suspiciously, 'Intensive Care Unit. His mum's situation's worsened. Tell him it's critical that he comes back in, as soon as possible. Her organs…'

She thanks me, and I thank her and hang up while we're passing some snobby boys' school all decked out in bluestone and ivy and broad skirts of emerald-green playing field. I turn to Don and tell him quite calmly that if it's all right with him, could he drop me outside the Emergency Department at the Royal Melbourne instead of taking me home?

Don doesn't actually answer. But instead of cutting right at Flinders Street Station, he turns left and does a sharp U-turn into Elizabeth Street, sending up a flock of dirty pigeons. While he negotiates the giant nightmare roundabout just before Parkville with five hundred other angry drivers, I send a quick message to the mystery mobile caller who keeps calling me, but doesn't leave messages.

You need to go back to the hospital NOW and make a decision. They said something about her organs. I'm very sorry.

I'm not dumb. I can put two and two together. He wants to talk but he can't. I get that.

The mystery guy may be one of the raft of random mouth-breathers I seem to have attracted in the days since Mum's story got out. But I don't think so. What had Eleanor said? *Gut feeling.* Even the sound of him drawing breath has become familiar to me, and necessary.

A moment later Don's pulling into the hospital's front courtyard and I'm out of there without a backward glance, asking for directions to the ICU ward.

Looking through the ward doors, I see that the ICU is full. I don't recognise any of the still and shadowy shapes strapped to rhythmically beeping machines as having anything to do with Simon Thorn. And because I'm nothing to him, or to the ill and the dying in that room, the nurses won't let me past the night desk.

There is nothing left to do now except call Malcolm Cheung from a quiet place. But I can't make myself do it. Unsure what I'm even doing here, I head in the opposite direction to *quiet*, backtracking towards the public cafeteria, which is lit up like a bad dream and packed with people. I'll need to be with someone, anyone, when I hear what I'm supposed to hear in its proper *context*.

The air smells of hot pies. Something by The Carpenters is playing and it's like a sign. Mum loved The Carpenters; loved that tragic, anorexic singer with the voice like liquid caramel. I join the queue at the window for hot food and the woman behind me says out loud, nudging me, as if we're in the middle of a conversation: 'Isn't it sad? Such a beautiful smile. Such a beautiful woman.'

I turn and look at her and her tight, grey perm and lilac velour tracksuit, tan comfort shoes. 'Sorry?'

The woman takes a step back when she clocks my face but she points up, gamely, above the counter, at a TV screen. It has white, computery text running along the bottom of the picture which I recognise as tele-text for deaf people. Put on especially for those cafeteria patrons who like to watch their news while enjoying The Carpenters singing of *rainy days and Mondays*; even though it's a Tuesday today, and fine out. The text says:

> —*blood-stains found in a clearing, several kilometres from the main hiking trail close to the summit.*

I see people in orange jumpsuits, boots and hard hats with miner's lamps emerging from the trees with the characters *SES* emblazoned across the front on a glowing white band positioned at chest level. A slightly out-of-focus man in a police-issue jumpsuit holds up a plastic bag with something white inside. The words continue:

> —*and emergency workers with assistance from the Queensland police cadaver dog squad recovered what appears to be an item of clothing. Homicide detectives are pursuing several lines of enquiry—*

The text makes way for the newsreader saying brightly, 'In other news...' and my eye is drawn to the photograph behind the newsreader's shoulder: a head and shoulders shot of an elderly businessman in a navy suit. He looks younger in this photo because the neat pencil moustache is not yet completely white. It's the kind of photo you'd see on the wall of an office building, or in an official report. No red-eye, a snowy white background; the subject deliberately angled towards you in a firm, reassuring stance. *Your money is in good hands.*

The photo is followed by images of several rescue boats motoring around the partially submerged hull of a big yacht. Blue water; open water; waves. The sea under bright sunlight, dazzling: like the eyes of the giant, in the curiosity shop. Police divers in sleek wetsuits and face masks.

'Excuse me,' the old woman nudges me again, less friendly this time. 'Were you going to *order?*'

I can feel myself beginning to tremble, already starting to gasp, so I step to one side so the woman can get at her pre-heated pastry items without delay. Face tilted towards the screen, I keep reading, the blood roaring in my ears:

> *Mr Kircher, a non-executive director of several ASX top 100-listed companies and founder of biotech powerhouse Emer-Tech, is survived by six adult children from several marriages, and five grandchildren–*
> *Foul play–*
> *Homicide–*
> *Contract hit gone wrong–*

17

I think I might have screamed, or maybe my knees buckled. Many hands push and pull me to a table in the corner near a stand full of packaged chips and someone shoves my head down between my knees and people are saying:

> *Take a deep breath!*
> *Take it easy, love.*
> *Settle down, it'll soon pass.*
> *Can I call your mum for you?*

All on top of each other: so that it's a mess of instructions, a mess of well-meaning voices. A cruelty of kindnesses. I almost dig out my phone and thrust it at them, wanting to scream: *You try! You try calling my mum because I can't seem to get through to her.*

But I place my head on the table instead, the surface pressing into my cheek. There are hard crumbs still on it, which are hurting my scars and mixing with the tears leaking out of my eyes. And I could just about close them tight and sleep here, shut them and never wake up, never make the call, when I hear someone say—in a voice I recognise, but sort of don't, because it's thick and awkward and tight, not smooth and assured—'I'll take care of her from here, thanks. Nothing to see.'

Someone pulls out the chair at the head of my table, sits down heavily, and there's the grumble of people talking in low voices moving away. I can feel him trying very hard not to touch me because he's not a toucher, and neither am I, not really, and it would be—

'This is fucked,' is all he says. Knowing as well as I do that saying *sorry* actually doesn't cut it in cases like ours. Neither of us caused it. Neither of us can take it back, or change the outcome. For a second I get what Boon was saying about how everything is connected and this, we two, are just links in a chain of awfulness that stretches on forever. Atoms bashing against each other in a vast vat of bashing atoms.

'Put Malcolm out of his misery and call him,' Simon says in that tight, scratchy voice I recognise as the voice that comes after too much crying. 'He's even called *me* looking for you, which is desperate.'

'What, the way the hospital called *me* looking for *you*?'
I shoot back, taking my head off the table and actually
squealing because Simon's face is a pulpy-looking mess:
grey-green eyes, small and puffy, set in a mass of bruises
over a split lower lip with a jewel of bright blood hanging
right in the centre. There is an open gash across the bridge
of his already broken nose and purple bruises in the shape
of thumb marks on either side of his windpipe.

'What happened to your *face*?' I breathe and Simon
laughs, wiping the blood away, although it's clear it hurts
him to laugh. 'Not telling,' he says, 'until you tell me what
happened to yours because you never did say...'

My tears dissolve into a smile that dissolves back into
tears. I bury my face in my fleecy sleeves and tell him how
I just saw the submerged hull of Elias Herman Kircher's
luxury yacht sticking up out of the water. On the television.

'Death of subject indicated,' I whisper. 'Sudden, violent
and unnatural death indicated involving spouse and/or
some other person related to subject through close business
or professional connections. Travel and water indicated,
asset of great value indicated that is not "fixed". Afflictions
associated with the blood indicated. Afflictions associated
with swallowing, digestion and lungs also indicated.'

Simon, too appalled to answer, says nothing.

'But that's not the worst part,' I sob, my words so hard
to make out that he is forced to lean forward. I know,

because his breath is stirring my hair. 'I think they found something of *hers*!' I wail, recognising for the first time what my conscious mind had refused to countenance: searchers emerging from thick scrub, a dense, old-growth forest, at sunset. 'They used *cadaver dogs*.' I'd never heard of them before, but the words need no explanation.

Simon does touch me then, just a warm, lean hand on my shoulder. And I do something that's brave, even for me. I twist a little in my seat and grab that hand, which causes him to give a yelp.

It's not the reaction I was expecting, and I loosen my grip, looking down at his grazed and oozing knuckles resting across my palm, understanding something at last: that Simon never worked out with punching bags at some designer gym. He *was* the punching bag. No one sleeps in their car for fun. Something must have come to a head; some critical, terrible thing that has ended with his mother lying motionless in a hospital ward, rapidly shutting down.

'I've been so wrong about you,' I say in a low voice.

Simon doesn't draw away, saying awkwardly, 'You should have seen the other guy. The *de facto human being* who supplied her, and bashed her, and called it *love*. If he decides to press assault charges maybe they'll just cancel each other out?' He gives this rattly laugh that might be a sob.

For once I don't rush in fearing the silences. I let him

talk: about how every window in the house was broken and there was actual human shit on the carpets; how his mum weighed less than a fourteen-year-old girl because she'd forget to eat, but never to shoot up; how her corneas were still good enough to donate, though the doctors would have to get in, to know for sure, about the rest. But she'd be okay with that. Underneath, she'd been a good person. She just loved these dangerous men she could never walk away from.

He looks up into my eyes, pleading, 'How do you make someone want to *live*?'

'You can't,' I say, getting a catch in my breathing as the awareness suddenly blossoms between us that *we are holding hands*. I can feel it through the skin of his palm, the new tension. So I withdraw mine gently first, because defence is always the best form of attack, right? 'You can't make anyone do anything,' I whisper, hot and confused, the thoughts struggling to come. 'You can't really ever know them; only what they choose to show you.'

I am talking about his mum, but I'm also speaking of mine.

'Call him,' Simon urges over my bowed head.

I look around then: at the three nuns in top-to-toe white at a table across the room; at the old man and his wife squabbling over a bag of lolly-coloured pharmaceuticals they've got spread out between them; at a sad-faced teen and his exhausted-looking mum having a silent, solemn early dinner.

'Good a place as any,' I agree.

Malcolm picks up almost as soon as I put the call through. I don't need to actually say anything because he's had a statement prepared for hours in anticipation of just this moment. They need to run tests, of course, but they think they got her blouse and I will, at some stage, have to come in to formally identify it. 'It's making its way back by police chopper right now,' he tells me.

My mother, without her stupid, foofy blouse, on a two-degree night.

I don't really take in what Malcolm says next about the operation of tollway gantries and the mechanics of SIM card analysis, how police technicians have been working around the clock to try and narrow down the vehicle she must have travelled in to get to Mount Warning. Someone swears they saw her crying at a petrol station on the New South Wales–Victorian border. It was her long, pale hair that caught the woman's attention, her obvious distress. Even when the Caucasian driver of the dark-coloured van—Black? Grey? Navy?—ducked out to do something the servo cameras didn't catch, Mum never got out of the front passenger seat of the van. She didn't appear to be restrained, but you never know.

'The Queensland bomb squad's actually looking at

whether someone planted explosives on board Kircher's yacht,' I hear Malcolm add from a long way away. 'I'm only telling you this because I've got a recording of your voice here that says you saw it coming. You caught the news? How they recovered three bodies? Kircher, the wife *and* her lover. That was unexpected. Like a bad movie. If it was supposed to look like an accident, someone cocked that up badly.'

I can't make my throat work. After a humane pause, Malcolm clears his own and says kindly, 'It's a lot to process, Avicenna. Call me back if you can think of any questions, okay? I'm right here.'

Then he hangs up and I look down at Simon's battered hand, which has somehow made its way back into mine. I can see individual hairs and freckles; make out the snaking blue of his veins in the parts that aren't too messed-up.

My voice, when it finally comes, sounds faded. 'Part of me has been hoping—even though it's the worst kind of thing to hope, you know?—that she just went crazy, couldn't take it anymore, and walked out. I could almost stand that—that maybe the pressure of our life got to her, and she just left.'

I cradle Simon's hand in mine for a moment longer before depositing it gently back on the table. He looks down at it for a second, as if he's unsure whether it belongs to him.

'They're looking for the van, running the criminal records of the owners of vehicles that went through the tollway that night. There's a contender registered to a builder in Glenroy and another to a rural property in Macedon; a meat transport vehicle with dirty plates belonging to an abattoir in Footscray. But they're still working on it.'

I'm proud of how calm I'm sounding. Later, maybe, when I am home, and in my pyjamas, I will break into pieces; but not yet.

'You need to get upstairs.' I phrase it like a question, in case Simon needs the hand-holding returned. But he shakes his head, already rising from the table, his thoughts already moving outward—the way they always do when he decides to do something—as he strides out of the room.

I wish I had that ability of his: to inject iron into my soul; temporarily slough off my troubled life, as if it were a dirty coat.

Where do I go from here? I think. *Where do I go?*

Boon's shop is in darkness as I let myself into the gloomy stairwell to my apartment. A single voice floats down from above; there is desultory laughter, the rumble of a one-way conversation. Some weirdo talking to himself on the landing outside my door.

For a moment, frozen below stairs, I consider leaving again. But I'm exhausted, and I have a direct line to the Victoria Police, so I force myself to keep moving upward, my tread deliberately heavy. I transfer my mobile into the pocket of my hoodie just in case, and take my slender silver Maglite torch out of my pack. I close my right hand around the base of it, so that the thing is protruding out of my clenched fist. If I have to, I will drive it into the soft tissues of the neck or the face, the way Mum taught me, when we lived near Rainbow.

A voice floats down. '*Avicenna?* It's Hugh.'

And I hesitate again, mid-step, my skin going hot, remembering how he was so beautiful to look at that I couldn't do it properly, I lost all nerve. Being in the guy's presence was like a kind of suffering. I'd wanted to grab him and… I don't know. It's all technical stuff I've read about in books from there. The mind digresses.

But a tiny, unreasonable part of me is telling me a happy ending is still achievable. Even in the face of whatever's happened to Mum, I can't squash it down and I can't kill it. Every so often it will rear up—the way it's doing now—and proclaim, like one of those cheesy motivational posters with a flying eagle on it: *Believe in the power of you.*

The inner voice—my eagle voice—had taken one look

at Hugh the last time and said: *There's your dream guy, Cenna, just grab him. How often does the dream guy come along? This is the guy. Do something, fast.*

It's saying now what Eleanor had told me inside Boon's store: *People come into your life for a reason.*

I imagine that chirpy, positive voice; how it would look if it were, say, a pink butterfly instead of an eagle. Then I imagine myself grinding the pink butterfly into the concrete stair tread and call up, sharply, from the landing below mine, 'I'm officially retired, Hugh, as of today. Shop's shut.'

He doesn't reply.

I lean against Mum and Dad's old apartment door for support, bellowing, 'I told an old man on Sunday that he was going to die sometime during the next eight days. And you know what, Hugh? He just did. His yacht exploded. I'm not safe to be around.'

There's shuffling on the floorboards upstairs, but Hugh still doesn't respond.

I force myself to keep walking, but as I come to the last flight of stairs, Hugh's standing at the top of them with a second guy who is dark, fine-featured, preppy. Handsome: but with a stocky frame, logos all over his clothes. He's a lot softer-looking, a lot shorter. It must kill him to have a friend who looks like Hugh. Both of them are standing there, lit up all ghostly from the mobile phones in their hands. I flick my own Maglite on.

'Is this *her*?' There is laughter in the shorter man's voice, and my skin seems to shrink back as I recognise it instantly. *Rosso*. When Hugh still doesn't say anything, Rosso says snidely, '*She's* "the last in a long line of soothsayers with whom Death walks"? You have to be kidding me. You think *she* has the power to settle our longstanding bet, once and for all?'

I have no idea what Rosso's talking about. But the way he's looking at me actually makes me want to cover my body in a *burqa*, or hide.

'If it's a question of payment,' Rosso drawls, his eyes never leaving me, running up and down me like spiders, 'we've got plenty of *money*, right Hughey?'

Both men have the grace to back up when I mount the stairs towards them. Hugh actually seems apologetic as he holds out a clear plastic slip cover full of papers. I look down at it in his hand, but I don't take it.

'We talked to Jacqueline…' he says, running his free hand through the fringe of hair hanging over his face.

'My sainted mother,' Rosso interjects sardonically.

'And she gave us a little background on *your* mum and your family and how—'

'She's devastated, by the way,' Rosso interrupts again, 'my mother. Took to her bed this afternoon when she heard the news. She raved about your mother, *raved*.'

I gaze at him, bewildered, the pain rising up and rising up, until Hugh catches the look on my face and says roughly, 'Shut *up*, Rosso, let me *speak*.'

'What I want to know,' Hugh continues in a wild rush, shaking the plastic slip cover, 'is whether one of these men is a killer. I mean, could you tell if one of them might actually have killed someone?' He corrects himself sharply, '*Murdered* someone.' Rosso shoots him a hard look.

I glance at the packet of papers Hugh is holding, still not understanding a word that's coming out of his mouth. 'What…bet?' I say weakly.

He pushes the documents at me and I finally take them. The top page has two sets of birthdates, birthtimes and birthplaces scrawled across the top of it in Hugh's bold hand in black permanent marker. No names.

Hugh shoves that lock of hair back again off his face. It's weird, but he seems almost nervous.

'You want me,' I finally reply, 'to do a horary reading for each of these…men?'

Hugh nods while Rosso just watches me with his silver eyes, mouth quirked up hatefully at the corners.

Okay, so the two subjects are men.

Even though I don't intend to actually follow through on Hugh's request, part of me is trying to understand the question I'm receiving right here, right now. I look down at my watch automatically, making note of the time: 8.03pm.

'You want me to tell you if one or both of these men deliberately…murdered someone?'

Hugh nods. I do the mental arithmetic on the birth-dates and come up with both men being in their early sixties. There's a roughly two-year age gap between them; that's all I can glean.

'Just look at everything that's there and then call me?' Hugh says, almost pleadingly. 'My number's in there. As Rosso said'—he gives Rosso a hard hip and shoulder from the side—'we can pay; that's not a problem. It's just that what you said the other day, about my father, got me think-ing about—'

Rosso goes, 'No names, Hughey, *shit*,' and Hugh actually grabs him by his shirt and half lifts him off his feet, pushing Rosso into motion so that he stumbles forward towards the stairs.

'Call me?' Hugh says. 'Once you've read everything. I hope you'll do it. It's, it's…' He closes his glorious eyes briefly. 'It's stuffed up my entire life, not knowing.'

Still confused, I watch the two guys manhandle each other down and around the corner and out of sight before lowering my Maglite. I must have looked like a crazy person, standing there with my jammed-down beanie and unbound, witchy hair, lit torch in my raised hand, like a stake. I can still hear their feet on the stairs below when something suddenly occurs to me.

'Who?' I scream down the stairwell. '*Who* are these men supposed to have killed?'

'That's classified,' Rosso shouts up, straight away. 'You don't need to know that.'

'But it's not *enough*,' I say furiously. 'I need something more: a date, a place. Was it a woman? A man?'

There's a scuffle of sound from below, murmured voices, low and angry.

'Do you want to know or *not*?' I hear Hugh snarl.

'If he finds out you've been airing very private dirty laundry with a cheap *palm reader*, he will kill you *himself*,' Rosso snaps back. 'And I will stand back and let him. I can't believe you're actually going through with this.'

More scuffling, then: 'The 9th of July, 1984,' Hugh shouts, as the street door opens and slams.

I go weak, momentarily unable to fit my key into the lock. My hand is shaking too hard because I know that date.

I *know* that date.

PART 3

Don't allow the past to poison the present. Fight it.

18

Now that I am home, and in my pyjamas, the tears won't come.

The rock I am hauling seems heavier than ever, but I lift it effortlessly as I unplug my home phone before taking cans of creamed corn and stock out of the kitchen cupboards, dumping their contents into a saucepan. Then I microwave a hunk of frozen chicken until it's hot on the outside, but still frozen in the middle, chopping it up haphazardly and throwing it in until I have something resembling soup going. I season the whole mess and stir an egg through it so that the white flares out into streamers resembling drowned blossoms, before turning the flame down and washing up. The whole time I tell myself I must be a bad daughter because I do not cry.

The tears still do not come as I lay out blankets and pillows on the couch avoiding the squat, blank shape of the TV in the corner. The worst has already happened; there's no need for the relevant footage, or an accompanying voice over; blow-by-blow coverage:

> *SES volunteers found her bloodied shirt, hanging*
> *in the lower branches of a tree–*
> *Disturbed undergrowth–*
> *Strange circular impressions in the topsoil–*
> *Police sources say the blood trail went for almost*
> *six hundred metres up the mountainside before*
> *abruptly ceasing.*

While I'm cleaning my teeth and trying to brush out the worst knots in my hair, my mobile goes off on the vanity unit beside me. It's Simon, with a two-word text that says only: *I'm outside.*

Ignoring the reams of missed calls and messages—Wurbik and Vicki amongst them—I let Simon in. Neither of us speaks. We are both bad children, for our eyes are dry. I know that nothing could ever surprise us again. We will be impervious.

He sways a little on the spot and I put my arm around his waist gingerly—conscious of all his wounds, both visible and invisible—and lead him to the made-up couch in the living room. He lets me hold him lightly for a second, then his plastic bags slide out of his fingers and he lays down with his back to me, fully clothed. I douse all the lights except for the lamp that turns everything in its vicinity a soft orange. Even from the darkened kitchen I can see his outline, shaking. There's the soup, of course, but nobody wants it. So I turn off the gas and put the covered pot in the fridge.

As quietly as I can, I slide Hugh's packet of papers off the kitchen bench and take it and my phone into my bedroom, closing the door behind me. I'm not doing these readings for Hugh, I tell myself fiercely, who is nothing, and can never be anything to me. I am doing it for the person who was *murdered*—it wasn't an accident, Hugh made that clear enough—on 9 July more than a decade before I was born.

Already the problem has arisen of what I should do if the answer, in the case of either man, is: *Yes*. But I park that for later because I'm good at compartmentalising. Grief has taught me that: how to batten down the hatches; seal off the affected areas.

Setting aside the two sets of handwritten details, I fan the rest of the papers out across my nubbly bedspread. There's a URL crawling along the bottom of each page from an obscure astrology website I've never heard of; research from the internet that Hugh thought was important for me to read, as background.

What had Mum said once? *They show you the darndest things, Avi.*

And they do. I've had more windows into my mother's life than I could ever wish for, and yet she remains mysterious, out-of-reach, unknowable. When I think of her now, she comes bathed in that soft, red-gold light of my dream, as remote as the stars.

There are computer-generated astrological charts interspersed amongst the pages Hugh provided, the symbols coloured in baby pinks and blues and greens. Curious, I backtrack until I find the last relevant subheading, helpfully outlined in green highlighter:

Case Study 3
The Descendants of Beverley Eunice Crowe, Astrologer (Australia)

Every hair on my body standing on end, I read:

Beverley Eunice Crowe was the first in a recorded matrilineal line of soothsayers with whom Death was reputed to 'walk'. She was said to have told one querent that Death had blue eyes and a calm and cultured demeanour, who 'is a great personal comfort'. When her body was discovered in bizarre circumstances in a client's apartment in Manly, New South Wales, Australia, in 1962, there were allegations of occult practices that were never

*substantiated and no culprit was ever charged.
But when her only daughter, Joyce, hung up her
own shingle, many practitioners in this branch of
horoscopic astrology—*

My eyes fly down the page and two passages leap out
at me as if outlined in flames:

*Joyce was known to have credited seeing Death
at several critical junctures in her life. Like her
mother, Joyce also died before she reached the age
of forty-five and it is well known that she foretold
the exact date and circumstances of her premature
and tragic death based on the Pleiades rising in
opposition to her ascendant in conjunction with
the sun in baleful opposition to Mars.*

*Joanne is said to have surpassed both her mother
and her grandmother in intuitive ability, but her
life has been marred by more than its fair share
of grief and tragedy due to a prolonged period
of that well-known condition 'Saturn hunting
the moon'. It is also well known in the horary
community that Joanne found, then swiftly lost,
her soul mate—a man whose natal Venus, it
may be added, was conjunct that most fated of
indicators, her natal vertex. After his death, she
is said to have been 'destroyed', but as Pluto is
her planetary ruler, together with the calming
influence of Neptune—marrying transformation
and arcane power with wisdom, sensitivity, vision,*

empathy and compassion—Joanne did recover
and continues to do great work in the field of—

There's one natal chart for Bev, one for Joyce.

One for Mum and one for…me.

Refusing to look at the charts—*our charts!*—I fire up my laptop and type in the URL for one of the pages I'm holding and it's really there, all out there, for people to see. We Crowes are a case history accessible to every wacko spiritualist nut-job on the planet with WiFi. There aren't any direct hyperlinks to our names, thank God, so we're unlikely to ever trend on Google, but some astrology tragic in Chicago, Illinois, has compiled a Ridley's on the best-known horary practitioners in recent history, and as I scroll through paragraph after paragraph of lunacy, I see that I get a mention, too:

> *It remains to be seen whether Joanne's daughter*
> *Avicenna (named auspiciously after the great*
> *Persian polymath) manifests any—*

Mum wouldn't even tell me her birthdate, but her chart, *her chart*, is right here. On the screen and in my hand. Wurbik would have seen this already, and Mal; anyone else who'd cared to look. Suddenly, all the weird little questions, the glances between the two men that day at the police complex, they all make sense.

I shut my laptop down and push everything aside

for later, only keeping the piece of paper with Hugh's handwriting on it in front of me. I tell myself that after today, I will never do this again. Because no one in Chicago, Illinois, or anywhere else in the world, has the right to know whether I manifest a common cold, let alone 'the knowledge'. After these two readings are done, I will never again frame a question for the heavens to answer.

Some things may have no answer, see. I accept that. But some questions should never be *asked*. Boon was right: this thing we Crowes can do is dangerous.

I hesitate for a while over whether to assign the quesited thing—the issue of another's murder—to the seventh house governing *other people* and *open enemies*, or to the fifth house governing *sex* and *pleasure*.

Something—the murder date, or maybe the weird *frisson* of discord between Hugh and Rosso, or just the way Hugh had looked: kind of wild and sick and desperate—makes me plump for the fifth house. The house and its ruler will largely determine the quesited thing, the answer, and I hope this *gut feeling* is right.

It takes me a few hours to progress the men's natal charts to the night in question. After I finish annotating the transits into the outer wheel for each man, it becomes clear that the two are implicated in some personal grief or misfortune for the same day and time period. The older one was physically injured—that much is obvious from the afflictions to Mars and Uranus and his progressed sun, with trouble coming through siblings, or family connections. But the younger man...

I lay my pen down and rock for a long time, my knees drawn up under my chin, hoping that none of what I'm looking at is true. At birth, the younger man's natal stars show multiple afflictions affecting his natal sun and moon. There are harsh aspects between Mars and the sun conjunct Venus, between Mars and the ascendant, between the moon and Jupiter, between both the luminaries and Mars. The 'potential' outlined in the man's radix is for abuse coming through the male parent, with deep hostility or neglect on the female side. Couple those stars with multiple afflictions to natal Mercury—governing the mind—and what you have is the 'potential' for a walking time bomb: an individual who is at once argumentative, secretive, destructive, deceitful and hypersensitive, but also exceptionally well spoken, intelligent, ambitious and decisive. Cunning, but resourceful. A survivor.

Okay.

Now progress the natal conditions forward to the evening of 9 July, 1984, throw several unusual conjunctions between Pluto and other fateful nodes into the mix—stimulated by transits of malefic Mars and Saturn—and this much is obvious: the younger man had some kind of meltdown that night, reaching a dangerous turning point. Violence and force were involved. While the man's own death is not indicated in his eighth house stars, death *is* indicated in that house via afflictions to Venus and the moon from a number of sources—Jupiter, for one, and the transiting lunar nodes. The man lost someone he considered a loved one (female); and the indications are that the loved one's destruction came by his own hand in a singular instance resembling madness.

I pick up my mobile and gradually the rocking slows, then ceases. It is 4.44am. In five, maybe six hours I will have to give my final oral English presentation of the year; no, scratch that—of my entire *life*. It will be a shambles, because nothing short of a blow to the head will let me get some rest now. It's like I have electricity running through my veins. I'll be lucky if I can string three words together. And I won't have any help, because Simon Thorn has earned the right not to speak; the right not to be pushed into doing anything, by anyone, ever again. If he wants to sleep with his boots on in my living room for the rest of his life, so be it.

There's a mobile number in Hugh de Crespigny's show-offy arsehole handwriting, on the last page of the printouts. Uncaring of the time, I type into my phone:

> *The progressed chart for the older man indicates he was badly hurt by a male sibling or family member (brother?) on the date in question.*

The one for the younger man indicates mental breakdown and force/violence used against loved one (female) resulting in loved one's death. I DO NOT want your money.

With a sharp pang, I add: *Please do not come here again.*

If I was older and more sophisticated, with a different face, and a whole different personality—arch, witty, fascinating—then maybe a guy like Hugh would come into my life and not ever want to leave it.

Yeah, I tell myself, *dreaming.*

After I send the message it's like this weight comes off me. But then I remember *the issue*, the one I shoved in the 'for later' compartment. If everything is connected, and people really do wander into your life for a reason, all those things I never believed in before but maybe almost kind of do now: then I need to breach the compartments, let the waters in. Let them mix and mingle. I owe it to Fleur to do it. And to Mum; because she would try and set things right, it was her way.

I pull up the mobile number for Don Sturt and just stare at it for a while. He might be on a stakeout and get my message in real-time—in which case he will most likely call me up and subject me to all kinds of awkward questions that I can't answer. But it's more likely he'll be asleep and this will be the last of it; for me, anyway.

Either way, once the message is delivered, it's no longer

my responsibility. If Boon is to be believed, it never was. It was already written, and all people like me amount to is Fate's dumb conduit.

I copy the two sets of birthdates, birthtimes and birthplaces provided by Hugh de Crespigny into the message for Don and tell him:

> *Progressed stars and transits indicate the older man was injured by male sibling or family member (brother?) and that younger man killed a female 'loved one' with force or violence on the night of 9 July, 1984. I was not given names. The source does not know I am sending this. Do not ask me how I got this. Please do not involve me any further. Avicenna Crowe.*

The message in no way breaches anyone's confidentiality, I reason feverishly. No names are involved. It could just be a stupid hunch, an awful coincidence, in which case Don can shrug his narrow, ropy shoulders, hit *delete* and get on with his life knowing he tried his hardest.

Filled with misgivings I hit *send*.

I look down at Mum's birth chart with unseeing eyes so that all the baby pinks and blues and greens go blurry and run together. Now that I have it I could make it *speak*. I could find out her state of mind on that Wednesday. I could find out from where the harm—if any—had come. Had a friend set off this chain of events? A co-worker? A...lover?

All her secrets—and now I know, she had them, she had them in spades—I could find them all out and fill in all the shadowy spaces in my mother I never knew existed.

Hell, I could ask the chart whether she's still *alive*.

And my own birth chart—it's right here. I could torture it, too. Set my life on some narrow pathway I might never get off. Find out how long I'll live, how I'll die; whether I'll ever be kissed, or have children, a breakdown, a lottery win, a house.

Or find someone to love me again, the way I have been loved my entire life.

For a second, before the tears stream down, a familiar cluster of stars in the first house seems to leap out at me. And I realise with a shock that *my* chart is the one from the front of all the journals, Mum's journals.

House Aries. My house.

What had Wurbik said? She wouldn't even start a case if the job wasn't compatible with *this* chart. Mine.

Find the pattern and you find the person.

Suddenly, I'm howling, ripping at all the papers, all the printouts, until there's a blizzard of torn paper, the pieces mixed up and scattered and impossible to put back together. The fate of all the Crowes, to be scattered and destroyed and made lesser, pulled to pieces: as a people, as a family. It's like we've always been the one person any-way—destined to die young; dying then being reborn, only to die again. Leaving our daughters motherless.

In the midst of the storm I hear the door open, and Simon's standing there, still in his clothes and boots, the left side of his face creased from sleep. He doesn't ask me what I'm doing. He just pulls me to my feet and wipes at my eyes with the pads of his bruised thumbs and rocks me in his arms until I stop bashing at him, bashing at the world, and he says, 'Cenna, *Cenna*, it's going to be all right.'

19

Suddenly, I am a pillar of stone in his arms. Nobody calls me *Cenna* but me. Mum and Vicki know it as my gamer tag, but they've always, always called me *Avi*. And *Changeling_29* never called me anything because it was his policy to never write back. Not even when I gloated and deliberately twisted the knife, for laughs.

'So is it true, then,' I mumble, 'what they said about you dropping Miranda Cornish because she couldn't *spell*?'

But what I'm really asking him is: *Is this okay, what we're doing here?*

Simon is standing very still; I can feel the tension and uncertainty in the way he holds himself so upright, he might snap from the strain. He doesn't often get caught out, or let things slip, but he knows it, and I know it, and I can't help the small, secret smile that curves up the corners of my mouth where it's hidden in the front of his scratchy jacket. 'You never even won a single *game*,' I say quietly into his shoulder.

'It was driving me crazy,' he replies, and he could be talking about Miranda and her loose grasp of the English language, or about all the games in which I handed him back his arse on a plate. I feel him slowly relaxing when he realises I'm not going to go berserk and scratch his eyes out.

'I saw you and Vicki playing once, in The Caf,' he says sheepishly into my part, his jaw all scratchy with dark stubble. 'You were sitting side-by-side, laughing your heads off. It was easy enough to invite you to a game after that. It was meant to be a test. But then I couldn't win, so I couldn't stop.'

He says it like it's my fault.

I raise my head then to his mauled face, my own all red and scaly, runny and unlovely, the two of us a pair. 'But if you win, will you?' I say uncertainly. 'Stop?'

And I mean *stop playing*, but I also mean: *stop wanting to know me or be with me, leave me behind once you achieve the shiny new life you've always longed for?*

It's palpable, how badly he wants that life. But I under-stand now why he deserves it and is the way he is. 'I'm never going to win,' Simon says simply, 'because you'll always be smarter than I am, and you're going to take out the Tichborne. I'm always just going to be standing in your shadow.'

It's not an answer, not really. But it was a stupid question. People who want guarantees are the kind of people who consult astrologers and I'm done with all of that.

I'd like him to kiss me, but I wouldn't know where to begin. So instead I say gruffly, 'What happens now?' Hoping he'll take it as an invitation.

He steps back and says firmly, 'We do the talk.'

Of course we do.

I'm so disappointed I actually sway on the spot, but I see the rightness of what he's saying. When you keep busy, you forget to remember, or to dwell. You take it one step at a time and then you find that you're…living.

We have the soup for breakfast because we are motherless now, and there are no longer rules to abide by. We can do what we like—but we'd give it all away in a moment to have them back, the way they were, at their best, when they loved us and were not overwhelmed by the things that caused them, in the end, to leave.

Simon drives us to school in his rusting, stinky bomb, pulling into his usual spot in the Year 12 car park, by the skips. It could be any other day. But plenty of people see us get out together, and the class is already talking about it when we take our seats, side-by-side, in the front row.

The mess his face is, this morning, makes looney June de Costi gasp out loud. Dalgeish practically smacks her ruby-red lips when she sees that we're both here, technicolour bruises, scars and all. 'When you're ready?' she trills from the side of the room, activating the *record* function on the tablet she's holding up with a purple fingernail. I can imagine all of them in the staff room later, having a gay old chortle, and my face goes so hot and red that Adam Carney, sitting in the second row right under my nose, actually laughs. 'Come on, Frankencrowe, balls of steel, man, balls of steel.'

Simon and I had agreed in the car that I'd go first because I had nothing prepared. I was going to wing it, pull something out of my arse, and it would be up to Simon to try and draw the whole thing together, get us back on point, whatever that was.

In summary, he'd say smoothly, *in conclusion*. And that would be the impression Dalgeish—all of them—would be left with: that we'd actually *worked well together, top marks for trying*. When of course, we hadn't; because we're both house *Aries*—I worked out that much from the way Simon had seemed to recognise himself in my chart—and we're both always going to want to dominate the proceedings.

'We're completely not compatible in *any* way,' I'd said fretfully, in the car, unable to look at him. 'It will be a disaster.'

Ostensibly, I'd been talking about the talk. And Simon, who'd been distracted by a taxi rear-ending someone in the lane beside us, had completely missed the point the way I'd wanted him to, and said, 'We're going to do great, if you just keep it brief and punchy. Leave the textual analysis to *me*.'

The lights are very bright in the classroom. I look down at the skin of my hands, which seems both yellow and red at once, stippled and blotchy. I close my eyes briefly and think to myself: *Words. Words are my currency.*

When I open them, and begin to speak, it's like the fear, the edges of the room, the eyes, all fade away. I speak of my mother and my grandmother and my great-grandmother before them. Of their secret marriages: with the stars and planets and luminaries, with the men who were not their husbands, with blue-eyed Death himself. I tell them of how my mother loved my dead father so much that I think she bought an old astrolabe and went out looking for him in a fit of madness. But something terrible and cruel and ultimately human intervened, so that she found Death again, anyway. On the summit of Mount Warning.

As I say it, I believe it to be the truth, the true story of what happened. Then the words rush forth, out of nowhere.

> *Let sea-discoverers to new worlds have gone,*
> *Let Maps to others, worlds on worlds have showne,*

Let us possesse one world, each hath one, and
is one.

Beside me, Simon rustles his papers, horrified that I have skied straight off the mountain into uncharted textual waters. (*Not* 'The good-morrow', I can hear him thinking, *we didn't agree to do that one!*)

But the rest of the room is absolutely silent as I add, 'This was them. Mum could read the stars, she could foresee all futures; it was her gift, both terrible and divine, wielded for such a mundane purpose: "*Will he marry me? Will he leave me?*" But all she wanted, I think, in the end, was him. "*One world*"; but not this one. Donne understood that. He understood death and love and God at some new and fundamental level, some eternal level. How two people can be so close, so *conjoined*, that they are like a compass, one arm anchoring the other, but still allowing it the freedom to move. The two moving always together. "*Thy firmness makes my circle just*",' I whisper. '"*And makes me end, where I begunne.*"'

There, Simon, I found my way back to the point, I think. *I am the point. There is no other.*

I bow my head when the grief cannot be held at bay. 'In our own small way,' I murmur, staring at the stained and rucked-up carpet beneath my runners, 'Mum and I were like the two arms of a compass, always moving

271

towns, moving schools, always together. But I wasn't enough to keep her here. And now the compass is broken and I don't know the way forward...'

I falter to an awkward stop, watching, horrified, as two fat tears fall out of my eyes onto my shoes. The front row kids see, and a murmur of restless noise spreads back down through the rows like wind rustling through fields of grass.

Simon smoothly steps into the gaping chasm I have created, talking confidently about a love so elevated above the profane that it is a love which transcends the physical, 'Moving into the realm of inter-communion of two minds,' he says breezily, like he didn't just turn off the life-support for his own mother.

He's so good at *pretending*.

Panic—that he's talking about *us*, that maybe this is all I have to look forward to in this life, two minds meeting on an electronic gameboard in cyberspace—makes me feel like throwing up, makes me run out of the room with my hand over my mouth in a flurry of *oooo-oohs* that sets everyone talking.

It's all been caught in high definition on Dalgeish's Samsung.

Unable to face anyone, I grab my pack and walk out

through the school gates. No one tries to stop me as my forcefield sizzles and sizzles away. Even the guys with lanyards and clipboards hustling for wildlife donations on the corner of La Trobe and Swanston leave me alone, actually peeling off to the sides when they see me coming.

As I draw closer to home, I delete my messages, one after another.

Wurbik's worried: *Call me.*

Delete.

Vicki's worried: *Call me.*

Delete.

Don Sturt next, saying Eleanor desperately wants to talk.

Delete.

Hugh de Crespigny, voice like molten honey, urgent: *I need to show you something. You need to* see *it.*

'Unless it's your huge, hard body, not interested,' I say out loud with a harsh, teary laugh, hitting *delete*.

Then there's a couple of consecutives from a heavy breather who hangs up after the requisite amount of hostile panting.

Delete, I go; my finger savage. *Delete.*

Though I do wonder, for a moment, how it is that the mouth-breathers have gotten hold of my mobile number, too, spreading like mould across my life.

I wave at Boon through the front window as I go by, but

I don't think he sees me through the reflected glare. And I realise, then, that maybe all you ever see is surfaces, and that even then, sometimes you don't even get that. One day soon I will have to sit down with Boon and ask: *What was she like? When she was truly happy?* But not now, not today.

Today, the question would be: *How could she leave me, when I still need her?*

But that's not a question it would be fair to ask him.

Mounting the stairs, fatigue is heavy in every line of my body. I am slumped inside my jeans and flannel shirt, like a creature made of dough, incapable of speech or thought. It's only because the stairwell lights are still blown on both the upper landings that I don't see it. I don't see the thing until my foot connects with it.

There's a hard metallic *thok* as I kick something on my front doormat into the base of the door. I bend down low, squinting to make it out in the faint light from downstairs, and my backpack swings around and hits me, hard, in the side of the head. In a fit of all-consuming rage, I twist and dropkick the bag, punting it all the way down the steps to the landing below.

On the mat is a flat metal box. Some sixth sense tells me not to touch it as I run back down to my pack, throat working with bile, to retrieve my Maglite. I don't even make it back to my landing before I've got the torch on, sweeping the bright arc of light in the direction of my door. The parts of the box that aren't rusty or a matte-grey from age and hard use pick up the light, throwing it back in my eyes.

As I draw closer, slowly, as if I've cornered a viper, I see a picture of a castle, no, no, a house—a big, grand, Englishy house—on the flat face of the case. And there's that dark-blue label, across the front of it, with white writing, in capital letters that say: THE OXFORD SET OF MATHEMATICAL INSTRUMENTS.

'Boon!' I scream, already running down the stairs. '*Booooooooon!*'

∾

I leave Malcolm Cheung and his team at my place with their dusting powder and illuminating devices, recovery kits and recording equipment. My *gut feeling*? They won't find anything inside my place. But I invite them to knock themselves out. 'If you see Simon Thorn,' I tell Mal, grabbing my pack as I leave, 'tell him to call me when the circus has left town.'

'Will do,' Mal says, getting a technician to bag up Mum's box of compasses. 'Don't go too far away.'

But I can't get far enough away. Mum's box didn't just find its way back to me on its own.

I insert myself into the edge of the small crowd that

has gathered to watch the police come and go from my building with their two-ways and hard cases. Down the block, a news crew is miking up, and I lose myself in the arcade over the road, not dialling until I get to the hot-bread shop on the other side. By tonight everyone will know where I live. They'll see the pictures and go: 'Isn't that the place right next to the dumpling house, two doors down from the sheepskin slipper emporium? God, I walk past there all the time.'

Before I can change my mind, I call Hugh de Crespigny's number and bark: 'What do you want me to see?'

What *I* need to see is something beautiful. I'm not usually so impulsive, and I already regret what I've done. But he makes me feel anxious and angry and alive, and so full of *want* that I'm able to forget, just for a while. He doesn't think we're done, and I'll go with it, do my own pretending, breathe that rarefied air until I'm no longer necessary.

I can't face the people I *do* know. I can afford to make a fool of myself with Hugh, whose laser-like gaze, for now, is on me.

'Avicenna? Hugh replies, startled. 'You called back. I didn't think you would.'

More calmly than I'm feeling, I advise him that I appear to have had a brief window open up, and he says he'll cut Econometrics and be right there, give him fifteen minutes.

Heart racing, I tell him which street corner to find me on, replying in a detached voice I'm proud of: 'Whatever, I'll be waiting.' And then I hang up.

20

He drives the kind of car I always imagined Simon would drive. A black, low-slung European coupé with tan leather seats and a 10-CD stacker with surround sound. Conscious I haven't dressed for the occasion, I lever myself down, wincing as I misjudge how far down I have to go, the hardware on the back pockets of my jeans squeaking across the leather.

Hugh's in retro aviators and a sleek open-necked shirt and jeans, hair styled as if by wind machine. *How*, I think, *do people in his vicinity actually* concentrate?

'I just get this feeling,' he says in a rush, 'that you can help me with what happened,' and the words seem to come at me from somewhere remote so that it takes a moment to assemble them into the right order. I think I'm watching his mouth in a predatory way, and I have to remind myself to look out my window and breathe. It's like I'm bathing in fire.

Something is very familiar about the route we take. There is that toffy boys' school, seen from another angle, the Shrine and the mad, multi-lane intersection near the hospital, the same strip of shops that normal people in their right minds would never shop at, everything sent over by plane or boat from France, Spain and Italy, hand-crafted by small and merry bands of artisans.

Of course, I think, as we turn into Eleanor's wide street of walled estates. *Of course we would be coming here.*

As we go past her property, the gates actually open and Don Sturt, in the delivery van, slides out. He stops to give way, his eyes widening as he sees me seeing him. There is an electric shock of recognition in the way he's frozen at the wheel his head turning just like mine is, as I drive by.

Then we're climbing uphill. Hugh stops the car at a huge set of stone gateposts topped by Victorian carriage lamps bigger and heavier than my head, and steps out. Through the sound of the running engine I hear him shout into an intercom, 'Stainer, it's Hugh de Crespigny, just a quick visit to the grounds.' Then the heavy steel gates swing inward and we're following a bluestone drive—through stands of English trees, leaves and conkers beginning to fall—that goes past the façade of a double-storey Italianate mansion with graceful arches all along the upper floor.

'The man who laid out the Royal Botanic Gardens had a hand in this place,' Hugh says, assuming I know what he's talking about. Where the driveway turns back around a large, three-tiered, cast-iron fountain, Hugh parks his car and leaves his sunglasses on the dash, hopping out and opening my door for me. I edge around him, clutching on to my mangy backpack as if it also functions as a shield.

'It's just over here,' Hugh says, body language anxious, a world away from the guy who faced down Wurbik in my apartment.

We walk across the emerald lawn, past beds of winter blooms, weaving between massive boles that reach up and up into the steel-grey sky, until we come to a pretty summerhouse, made of iron and glass, painted a blind-ing white. The structure is old, but well maintained, with wooden bench seats that go all around the inside walls like that scene out of the musical where the girl and her Nazi lover are having a lovely *pas des deux* in a rainstorm.

Where have you gone? my brain asks itself, because Hugh's just said something, and I saw his mouth moving, but I didn't actually understand what came out of it.

Being here with him is a huge mistake, because he says again, weirdly eager, 'So what do you *feel?*'

'W-what do you mean?' I stammer, trying to work out what he's really asking.

You don't want to overcommit here, some small, still-functioning part of my mind says dryly. *It's a bit early to be talking about feelings, isn't it?* But I'm blushing like a stop sign. I am an all-out unflattering red. I look up into the struts and panes of the summerhouse roof, wondering if there is a camera capturing every torturous moment, as if I'm being punk'd by the hottest guy on earth. Overhead, the clouds—massed and brutish-looking—move rapidly, like surging waves.

'Walk around,' Hugh urges me, actually propelling me by my back with the flat of his hand. 'What do you *feel?*' Again, there's that weird emphasis.

I walk around because he's making me do it, but all I see are lovely old wooden floorboards, adrift with dead leaves at the edges near the two entryways that face onto each other. 'Uh,' I reply uncertainly, 'cold?'

The wind chooses that moment to pick up, and it gives a whistling howl, sweeping through the summer-house doors, the concentrated gust moving straight through me. I actually shiver as Hugh stares down at me with this look on his face that is—disappointment, fury, grief—all rolled into one.

Not the look of love. Not that I've seen it enough to recognise it.

Then I get it. Why I'm here. I stop dead, shocked.

'I'm not, uh, actually *psychic*, Hugh. If that's what you mean. I don't *feel* anything.'

Except maybe underdressed and soul-wounded, in this lovely place made for undying declarations. What a *putz* I am. I could slap myself. *Feel*. Every word *can* have more than one meaning; everything is open to interpretation. I've known that since I was five and could read to myself.

'But you can see *death*,' Hugh says, his eyes so dark and fixed and tragic he could be drunk. 'It said so on the internet. It's what you Crowes are famous for. You must feel *something*. Especially here.'

I hug my pack tighter, actually lifting first one foot, then the other, as if I've blundered into a pool of blood, every part of me cold. 'You've got the wrong girl,' I say savagely when he stands there just gracing me with that look. 'For "psychic girl" you'd need to look under "P", mate, in the phone book. *Feeling* stuff is not part of my skill set, but my maths? My maths is really good.'

I'm already withdrawing from the moment, from his hand, from the summerhouse. I am actually walking back across the pretty green lawn and he is practically chasing after me. *What a dumb, dumb error*, I'm thinking as I swing my backpack onto my shoulder.

'He was fifteen years older, you know,' he calls out in this feverish, broken, confessional way. 'Already a lawyer, but he told anyone who would listen that one day he was going to *marry* her. People remember that; I've had it from more than one person. And he was supposed to be at our place in Portsea—I've worked that much out—but he drove back and she had a friend drop her here so that they could meet up when she was supposed to be at a party, and then something happened—something really bad—that changed everything. I would have had a different *life*. My father spends six months of the year in London, off his face on painkillers. And when he's here, he's not here. I hardly know him.' Hugh grabs me by the back of my right elbow, swinging me around so that I'm forced to look up at him. *'I hardly know him!'* he yells.

Well, boo hoo, I almost retort, looking around at the shockingly lush and expansive grounds, the white mansion set in their midst, as big as a cruise ship, *you rapist-murderer-harbouring, rich crazies*. But I don't have any proof, not really, so I bite my tongue when the words threaten to slip out: hard enough to sting.

Hugh's breathing harder than a short walk across a pretty lawn would credence. 'No one will talk to me about it,' he hisses. 'The official line is that he never left the beach house at all. The family protected him, every single one.'

'All I can tell you,' I say as gently as my fear and outrage will allow, 'is what I've already told you. Tell your father to see a priest. I can't help you anymore; I'm sorry.'

I'm shrugging Hugh's hands off—those big hands I had wanted on me—when a shout rings out across the grounds. There are two men hurrying our way, twisting and running between the stands of trees, trying to cut me off before I get to the car.

As they get closer I recognise the short, stocky one as Rosso and a wave of dislike breaks through me. The taller man with the hard body and head like a close-shaved bullet—in suit pants, shirtsleeves, leather shoes and corporate-looking tie—is a stranger. A stranger who could easily put you in a chokehold, facedown on the turf, and accidentally kill you on purpose.

Hugh doesn't let me go, but his hand on me relaxes a fraction as he says, 'Stainer. Ross.'

Rosso barrels right up to us and I see, with dull satisfaction, that I've got maybe an inch on him, the twerp. 'What's *she* doing here?' he says furiously.

'The cat's mother,' I say more lazily than I'm feeling, 'was just showing herself *out*.'

I wrench my elbow right out of Hugh's hand and start for the gates, which are closed. Something I'll worry about when I reach them, because I'll climb them if I have to. I have no dignity when I'm cornered.

'Miss,' the man called *Stainer* says, business-like, 'I'm afraid I can't let you out until we clear this up.'

I swing back around to face the three of them, standing there in a tight semicircle of belonging and easy familiarity, realising with fury that this must be Rosso's house. Maybe his credulous, social butterfly of a mother, Jacqueline, is prostrate inside that pile right now at the news of my own mother's disappearance.

I am enervated by misery at my own stupidity. Like some rich, hunky dude would seriously ferry me across town to his pretty summerhouse so that he could, what? Kiss me, then totally fall to his knees and declare undying love? Please.

I am my own worst enemy. I am, I am, I am.

'That man,' I spit, doing an air-jab in Hugh's direction, 'brought me here so that I could "lay my hands" on that summerhouse to see whether his father raped and murdered a young girl in there.'

Rosso actually reels backwards at my words, as if he's lost his footing. Then I remember that the only person who has so far connected Fleur Lucille Bawden to this place, in so many words, is *me*. Shit. But I'm looking more and more right, and I don't like it.

Thankfully, none of them have seen the look on my face, because Rosso has already turned on Hugh, grinding his finger into Hugh's chest and shouting, '*What* did you fucking do? It's gone beyond a joke now. She wasn't supposed to *come* here; it was just meant to be a "reading", a stupid piece of paper. It's fucking hearsay, you fuckwit. You don't bring people in off the street and give them fucking family rumours as truth and then release them back into the wild again. *Are you out of your mind?*'

Stainer is looking at both men with a touch of uncertainty that sits very uneasily on his face-of-granite hardness.

'Don't you wanna *know*?' Hugh bellows, getting right into Rosso's space. 'It's been hanging over all of us for *years*. It's fucked up all our lives, not knowing.'

Rosso drives his fist into Hugh's stomach, shocking us all. Staggering backwards, Hugh coughs and coughs as Rosso screams, 'Why would you want to jeopardise everything, you stupid *fuck*?' Panting, his fists still clenched, Rosso snarls, 'If he catches you here, doing *this*? Digging up past shit? Past *unsubstantiated* shit? He will fucking *kill* you. He'll rip your head off and feed it to you, or get someone to do it. Blood or no blood.'

Hugh suddenly rears up and grabs Rosso by the shirt collar and throws him to the ground, then they're laying into each other, wrestling and clawing and yanking and punching like they mean every blow, years and years of bad blood leaking out. I start backing away again, pleading with Stainer, 'If you'd just let me out now, I'd really appreciate it. Nothing to do with me, mate. Please.'

Shaking his head, Stainer points a small remote control in the direction of the gates, before moving to separate Ross and Hugh, and I hurry through the widening gap without looking back.

21

Hugh passes me at the tram stop on Toorak Road and doubles back. There are no trams to escape into, so all I can do is stand and watch the chrome grille of his coupé drawing closer. It reminds me of cartoon shark teeth.

He slides in at the kerb, right next to me, and lets the engine idle while the drivers in the cars behind him all pile up, beeping their horns and leaning out their windows, the *effings* flying. Still, Hugh just stares fixedly at me through the half-down passenger window, refusing to move along until I get in beside him.

I have a high embarrassment threshold and have every intention of looking the other way for as long as it takes, before getting on a tram. But the wind is really rising now, keening like a funeral mourner. Rain imminent.

I hate the cold. In all the moving around we've done, it's been the one constant—how much I hate it. The whole time since Dad died, I suddenly realise, Mum has been working her way down the eastern seaboard, working her way back from when we were warm and safe in the north, the three of us together, to *this*. Closing some kind of circle that's ending in wind and rain.

To a chorus of shouted oaths, kicking myself at my weakness, I get in, still hugging my backpack. Sitting with knees drawn primly together—as if that will somehow minimise my general surface area and volume—I catch sight of my reflection in the glass and grimace. My hair is hanging in tangled dreads all down my back and shoulders and my cheeks seem thinner, the bones and scars more prominent. I look like one of the witches out of *Macbeth*.

There are grass stains on Hugh's torn shirt and red marks on his face, but all he says in a normal-sounding voice is, 'The least I could do is drive you home,' and then he guns it, the coupé's engine roaring like a caged animal at the bottlenecks.

I study his profile, his downturned mouth, the line of his neck and jaw when he isn't looking. He's the kind of guy I would sleep with in a shot, I decide. I would give it up for a guy like this, no questions asked, because I'm as shallow as the next person. But Wurbik was right. Even if he could see past the scars, Hugh's not for me; he's not one of my kind. Being with him keys me up to a pitch that only dolphins can hear. Nothing would ever be easy. Around a guy like Hugh, I would always be falling over my feet and saying the wrong thing and kicking myself and kicking myself and kicking myself. I'd be flavour of the minute, not the month; I'd never even make it into the guy's fucking fifth-house stars, that's how fast he'd be through with me, and I might never recover. That's nothing to aspire to.

Still, it will hurt me every day, knowing he's out there, because I'm not going to forget him. I mean, who forgets meeting *the dream guy*? It's a once-in-a-lifetime thing. Some people don't even get that. But it's okay to let him go because he was never mine anyway, and I've at least seen him. I know he exists.

'So I'll live,' I say out loud without meaning to, like they do in the soaps.

I cover my mouth with one hand, appalled, and Hugh darts me a curious, sidelong glance. 'There's living and there's *living*,' he says distantly, gazing back out onto the congested road ahead.

But he's wrong. It's all the one state. It's just getting through, and not letting the absences overwhelm you.

'Well, goodbye, then,' I say as we drive under the painted arches of Chinatown, cringing at how banal and emotionless my words sound when all this, *all this*, is going on inside my head. This is the end of the road for him and me. There should at least be music. 'And thanks, you know. For the lift.'

Ugh. Somebody sew my mouth closed, please.

My hand is on the door; I'm all ready to leap out and run from how much I suck at small talk. Hugh slides the car into a loading zone opposite my building and turns to me. 'I'm sorry you had to see that,' he mutters. 'I'd like to see you again.'

I blink. Two complete non sequiturs. The only thing connecting the two statements? The word *see*. Bloody nervous word-game disorder.

Hugh hasn't turned the engine off, which makes it all sound even more matter-of-fact: that if he says he'd like to see me again it will, in fact, come to pass. He's a go-getter, a hunter. He never gives up. I know that. It's in his chart.

'I've never met anyone like you,' he says. Which sounds like a line, but it's *my* line and I will hug it to me and milk it later, when I'm alone, for meaning. Turning it over and over incessantly, like a polished jewel. I blink again, everything spun on its head, and Hugh's dark eyes are intent on me. 'You said you couldn't feel anything. But you knew about Fleur. No one will talk to me about her and you knew her *name*.'

I'm unable to summon up something sharp or sassy

in reply. I just can't. I'm suspended. He reaches out and actually touches the skin of my face: the scarred part, which warms instantly. And I don't draw away. 'Does that hurt you?' he murmurs, leaning forward so that our foreheads are almost touching. The pad of his thumb is resting against my skin and I want to close my eyes and succumb because this guy, *this guy*, is better than Bio-Oil, better than psychotherapy. If he doesn't see or mind the scars? Then there *are* no scars.

We're leaning in, about to fall, about to do all those theoretical things that theoretical people in books do with their mouths and hands, when a familiar pattern, a worn-out blue plaid, moves into the corner of my eye and just stays there.

I glance up, startled, so that Hugh turns his head to look, too. It's Simon in his knitted grey beanie. Standing very still across the road, right in my line of sight. Arms crossed, waiting for me. His eyes don't leave me for a second and the moment between Hugh and I is fleeing; it flies.

Maybe we can get it back. *Or maybe*, says the voice of reason in my head, reasserting itself huffishly, *you should just let it go, okay? You were saying* goodbye. *Quick ones are easier all round.*

My own body fighting me, I sit back from Hugh. 'I can't,' I say simply, 'not right now.'

Hugh's posture changes; going rigid. He knows it has something to do with the tall, beat-up-looking guy trying to melt the car from the outside with his grey-green eyes. He turns back quickly, moving so that Simon is entirely blocked from my view. 'This isn't the end of it,' he warns, stroking the skin of my scar again with the pad of his thumb, bringing the heat. 'I know where to find you.'

I move away from him, putting my pack back up between us like the fence that will always stand between the *haves* and the *have-nots*.

'Everyone does,' I reply quietly. 'Best of luck with your life.' Still holding his gaze, I open my car door and scramble out backwards, adding, like a gibbering numbskull, 'Really, I mean it. It'll be a great life. You'll do great.'

I almost add, thinking better of it: *Don't let having a murderous sicko for a father hold you back.* I shut the door—flushed and hot from shooting my mouth off like a fool. Over the roof of the car, all I see is Simon's taut, bleak face, bones and bruises prominent.

❧

The coupé moves off in a squeal of tyres—I register that, but I don't really see it go—as I dodge across the street towards Simon. What are we, really? I've got nothing to feel guilty about, but I feel it. I'm hangdog, hesitant, like

I've done something wrong, as I come up onto the kerb in front of him. Simon's voice is biting, his arms still crossed. 'Is that the rich guy Wurbik told me about? Why don't you ever answer your damned *phone*? You aced it by the way. Dalgeish wasn't even looking at me after you left. You held the floor then you wiped me with it. Prize is in the bag.'

His tone is as bitter as his body language and fury rises in me, sudden and sharp.

'How is it my fault if I did *better*?' I say incredulously. 'You had all the answers. You were *prepared*. You stayed on point. I cried all over my shoes, for fuck's sake. Give the fat, ugly chick a little credit for being able to—'

Simon cuts me off. 'Hook a stud? He only wants one thing, Cen; it's so obvious, it's nauseating.'

I mean, look at you is what Simon's really saying.

'And, like, I'd just give it to him? Right there in his car in the middle of Chinatown?' I screech, fumbling my house keys out of my bag and punching them into Simon's chest so hard that he rocks backwards. 'Like that's all a rich, good-looking guy would want from me. *Sex*, not conversation? Not answers? He wants to know whether his dad is responsible for a cold-case rape-murder. And if he happens to like me as well? Well, isn't that just my *luck*.'

Simon's mouth is opening and shutting as I snarl, 'Get out of my sight, you hypocrite. It's okay for you to want all of those things—the beautiful life, all the trappings—but not okay for *me*. When I want it, when I want to reach out and take it because, maybe, just maybe, something's being handed my way for a change, it's not permissible. My motives are suspect, or his are. *Don't judge me.*'

Simon tries to catch me by the sleeve but I step around him, almost dancing on my toes like a prize fighter. 'I hope I *do* win the Tichborne, because if I do I'm going to buy you a car you can actually sleep in which will take you right out of my *life*. Do what you like,' I add, pointing up at the darkened windows of my place. 'Make yourself a sandwich. Plot my downfall. Shit, play me a word in a game you're never going to win. I'm going for a walk.'

And a moment later I'm lost in the late-afternoon crowd moving uphill through Little Bourke Street, everyone hurrying to get somewhere, be somewhere. I duck through one alleyway, then another, finding that I know the streets like the back of my hand, like the local I never thought I was.

~

He calls and calls and I ignore him, not sure where I'm really going. People see the shine of tears on my face and stare; most just avert their eyes. When the rain comes down, in sheets, in torrents, I keep walking in circles and squares and zigzaggy lines while people rush and huddle and battle their pop-up umbrellas going inside out from the wind. The noise is immense, water rushing down the bluestone gutters, pooling in the dips and warps in the road. Soon my feet and shoes, the legs of my jeans are sodden. I pause outside the 7-Eleven on Exhibition Street feeling stupid about grand gestures, when this prickling starts up, in my gut.

Maybe I *do* feel things because I'm suddenly aware—an intense awareness—that I'm being observed.

I look across the road, my eyes searching the darkness under the deserted front marquee of the Comedy Theatre. But there is nobody there. Around me, people are hurrying to catch things—the pedestrian crossing, a blue bus, taxis. I am the only still point in a streetscape alive with motion. But the feeling won't go away; it crawls across me, like something trapped under my skin trying to burrow its way out, and I step into the brightly lit convenience store, spooked.

I check my phone and it chooses that moment to emit the sparkly *bling* sound that happens when someone plays you a word. Fingers fat and wet and clumsy from the cold, I open the app, thinking it must be Mum, even though it can't be. But I see that it is *Changeling_29*. Simon. Not with a word worth anything, but a message. My first message from him, ever.

Chilled to the core, I read: *Where are you?? Get home. I'm worried.*

Home.

And I realise it is. It's a fetid dump, but in so many ways I'm connected to it now and I want to be there more than anything. But it's at least three blocks away, more. Stupid, stupid, stupid.

Tears welling in my eyes, I brush them away viciously as the Indian guy at the cash register looks on with suspicion because I'm not buying and I'm not talking. I'm just dripping water onto the floor by the newspaper stand, shaking like a drug addict over the screen of my phone.

Fumbling at the keypad, I type with bloodless fingers: *I WANT to be home. Scared. Feel I'm being watched / followed.* My words crop up in a golden bubble at the side of the game.

Simon's answer comes back right away, slotting straight underneath in a bubble of white: *Where are you? Come to you.*

I think frantically, my eyes raking the windows facing out onto the Lonsdale and Exhibition Street intersection.

'Can I help you?' the Indian guy queries over my shoulder, but I just wave a hand in his direction, so that he takes himself back around the safety screen, pissed.

I know there is a narrow, dog-legged shortcut just around the corner that takes you back past the front of the Chinese Museum into Chinatown. I can wait there. In the museum, no one will want me to buy anything or move on, and it's public enough that nothing can happen to me if I stand, dripping wet, by the pretty girl at the front counter.

I type: *Chinese Museum, hurry.* Hitting *send*, then sending one more word: *Please.*

Simon's bubble comes back: *Cohen Place, got it. Coming.*

Then he does the same thing as me, sending another message hot on the heels of his last one: *And you're not, you know. Ugly. You're kind of unforgettable, actually.*

There's no time to savour the amazingness of that perfectly punctuated message right now. Later, we can thrash out the exact context and parameters of his words, but for now I shove my phone deep into my jacket pocket and head back out the sliding doors.

Going left up Lonsdale, I see the half-hidden opening to the laneway just past a deserted souvenir shop, its windows full of sheepskin scuffs and Aussie flags, clip-on koalas. A man emerging from a pokies venue that opens onto the laneway actually pauses in his stride to let me pass, alerted by something in my face, in the way I'm holding myself.

I burst through the doors of the Chinese Museum and the girl behind the counter nods in bewilderment as I gasp, 'Is it okay if I just wait here?'

That feeling, the crawling feeling, hasn't for a moment gone away. A chill moves through my guts when I see through the museum's long front windows: a dark shape emerging from the laneway I've just come from, wet grey hair plastered to his gaunt, familiar features.

As his head quests from side to side, turning towards the museum's doors, I back further into the building, hoping I haven't been seen. The woman calls out, 'Miss? *Miss!*' as I start running up the stairs.

22

Every room I pass is lit up like a Christmas tree, the light stark against the unnatural early afternoon darkness outside the windows. I hear heavy feet on the stairs below and make for the female toilets signposted for the third floor, intending to lock myself in until Kingdom Come, or at least until Simon does.

As I'm about to crest the landing outside the chamber of photographs, the lift between me and the restrooms opens and Don Sturt steps out, his hands already extended, like he's reaching for me. I let out a scream, so high and terrified you can barely hear it.

'Don't be afraid!' he pleads, taking a tentative step forward. 'Don't run!'

On the turning below me, the Chinese woman from the front counter has come to a stop, her eyes wide and frightened. A look passes between us: that I'm not dangerous, that I'm not the problem; the tall white man, the man who stinks of booze, is the one to watch. Don hasn't seen her, but I catch her beginning to back up quietly and head back down, her steps undetectable above the shudder and roar of the rain outside.

Help is coming, it is. I have to tell myself that.

I force myself to keep still, guts quivering as Don draws closer. I'm neither up nor down. I'm at a disadvantage, frozen here on the flight, looking up into his pockmarked face, the muscles of his seamed mouth, working.

'She saw the darkness in me,' Don pleads, his yellow-flecked eyes very wide, 'and she wasn't afraid.'

'I'm sorry,' I say, voice shaking. 'I don't understand.'

'I need you to know that when I left her,' he tells me, hands still out in a gesture like supplication, 'she was *alive*. We drove all day, and all of the next. I talked and talked and she listened and she was alive when I left her. She was fine.'

I shake my head, uncomprehending. But horror dawns when he says, 'She said you were the smartest person she'd ever known. She said you'd figure she wasn't dead, just gone, and she couldn't tell you, because then the magic wouldn't work. That's what she called it: *magic.*'

I sink to the stair I was just standing on, unable to hold myself up.

They tell you the darndest things.

Even if I could speak, there are too many questions. So I fumble for my phone, right there under his nose, and start recording him, every word. I mean, I'm just holding my phone in my hand, but he doesn't stop talking.

Swaying slightly, he says, 'Not like them others. We gave it to them; every man took his turn. And when they wouldn't, when they played up, tried to run away into the bush, we laid into them with sticks and bottles—after a while I had to drink myself stupid to block out the screaming. But not your mother. Didn't touch her. She was good when I left her. She was fine.'

Fine, that stupid word that's supposed to convey, what, *fineness*?

'Who are you talking about?' I whisper, this sick taste of iron in my mouth. 'What "others"?'

'Them girls from Armidale. Hitchhikers. Coming on for forty years. We showed 'em a good time then carried on the party. At Mount Warning.'

Something monumental has shifted in the man. It's like he's spewed forth some irritant that's been buried deep, like a bullet, or a fishhook, for years. He's actually hunched over, clutching at his stomach, purging his guts out. 'We left 'em tied up,' he whimpers, 'facedown choking, like, on their own blood. When they was found, they was bones. And all this time, I've kept it quiet, carried it in me, tried my best to make amends, do some good, make my peace, but your mum...'

Something, even in his speech, has broken down. The country boy he used to be is coming up through his pores, rising like a ghost.

'So she wanted to go somewhere she could feel the presence of death, that's what she said and did I know anywhere? Just asked me one day, out of the blue, on the way back from El's place and, and...' His eyes fill with tears as I watch. 'And I said I knew; I knew a place all right.'

My mouth fills with an onrush of saliva, like I'm about to throw up. Don took Mum to *that place*, where some atrocity was committed. She must have been so scared. To think she got into a van with this well-dressed, unassuming man, this trusted acquaintance of an acquaintance. And that underneath his expensive clothes and well-kept shoes is this monster inside.

'Never told, swore a pact, blood oath; no one ever caught, ever charged, everyone dead but me. Night sweats for years. Eleanor doesn't know—if she did, she never would've took me on, leant on me the way she does. But I told *her*.' His head swings back up, red-rimmed eyes focused on me. 'And now I've told you.'

What is it about us, I think, shrinking back, sliding down a stair, *that makes people hand us their darkness?*

Don takes a step forward, his hands still out, grasping, and I fall down the stairs in earnest then, phone still clutched in my hand.

I break out into the front foyer and the Chinese woman is on the phone, still giving frantic instructions, calling out, 'Wait! Wait, *Miss!*' when she sees me. But I don't wait, because Mum told me you don't wait, you never wait when things go bad, you get. I burst out, into the obliterating rain.

∽

In the tiny square outside the museum, I send the audio file to Wurbik's phone. Rain runs down my screen, into my mouth, the hollow in my neck. No time to explain. How to explain? That bad things bring other bad things out into the light.

I spin, unsure and directionless upon the slick cobblestones, the rain raining down; knowing absolutely where I am, but feeling lost.

Simon hasn't come. I wonder why I even expected him to—don't I always save myself, in the end? I shove my phone into the front of my pack, cutting across the small ornamental square, hurrying under the celestial arch and past the stone lion on the right, towards home: when I see him.

It's like he's stepped out of the future.

A tall, strikingly handsome man in a long camel overcoat and dark pinstripe suit, narrow-toed business shoes, a Melbourne Football Club scarf draped elegantly around his neck. He's coming up the hill towards me, unhurried in the rain beneath a black umbrella.

I see the same longish, dark-blond hair and one-in-a-million physique. He looks good, and he knows it, and he'll always look good. He's talking on the phone. I don't think he's even seen me yet.

But then he looks up, with his unreadably dark eyes under wicked brows, and I'm looking at the man of my dreams—Hugh de Crespigny—*in thirty years' time*.

As he gets closer, I see there are streaks of grey in his hair, the beginnings of crepey chicken neck happening, but it could be the same man. I actually back up in horror, thinking: *This can't be happening. I just left you, and you were young.*

It's like magic.

Heart thumping like a driving bassline, I turn quickly on my heel, walking back uphill, up Little Bourke. I give pretty good poker face. But I'm certain the man recognised that I recognised him, because the hard heels of his fine shoes are ringing out behind me, steady and unhurried

305

on the slick flagstones. And when I pick up my pace, he does too.

What had that snake Rosso said? *If he finds out you've been airing very private dirty laundry with a cheap palm reader, he will kill you himself.*

When I get to the theatre restaurant the front door is locked tight. I pull on the handle, sobbing low in my throat, but it doesn't give. Future Hugh is standing on the corner now, a block away, still talking on the phone. He's looking into the window of the noodle shop by the pedestrian crossing, checking out his own reflection in the electric streetlights, the beams of passing cars. Just his presence, menacing.

When the man's back is half turned, I duck down the driveway of the commercial car park a couple of shopfronts away, praying that he hasn't seen me and it's all a terrible coincidence.

I'm standing in the stinking alley, the rain falling from the early evening sky through a narrow gap between all the buildings. The back door's ajar, which means Newlands must be in.

Almost crying with relief, I pull the wire security door open and run through the deserted kitchen into the darkness of the backstage area, looking for a place to hide. Somewhere in here are stairs that take you to the upper floor. And there was that glow, coming from down below;

some kind of basement or cellar, I remember. Across the stage, on the far side from the kitchen passageway.

My eyes adjust slowly today. There is no light left in the day and no gap in the curtains facing onto the dining area. Backstage is absolute blackness, except for that below-stairs glow that begins, tremulously, to coalesce in the corner of my eye.

I almost call out to Newlands, who must be around. But I'm glad I don't when the unlocked screen door slams, then slams again seconds later. *Two* of them: their heels striking the distressed concrete of the kitchen floor as they poke around between the island benches, searching for me. And two options: straight out through the curtains at the front of the stage, screaming for *Newlands! Help! Police!* And hope that the front door will open from the inside. Or make for that faint glow.

I feel about with my hands out, like a blind person. A line of painted balsa wood cut-out trees runs either side of me. I abandon my pack and begin creeping towards the faint source of light, the glow abruptly vanishing as a new bit of backdrop crops up, set on a different plane from the first. I'm suddenly panicked, lost in the dark. But as I inch forward, the light returns. I must be midway across the stage by now.

My sneakered footfalls are absolutely soundless and I'm maybe ten feet from the opening, crouching low against a 3D polystyrene prop, when the sound of male voices emerges from the passageway. Then their footsteps are echoing on the same floorboards I'm standing on, and I know I've missed my chance to make it downstairs without being spotted. I'll be silhouetted against the light if I move now.

'You shouldn't be seen here,' says a hard voice I recognise as Stainer's.

I wonder if they can smell my fear, or maybe feel it, rolling off me in hot waves.

'You know how much I enjoy the thrill of the chase,' replies a deep, cultured voice, laughter in it. It's a beautiful voice; less a voice than an instrument. Authoritative, resonant. 'It's part of the *fun*,' the man continues. 'And I'm going to have fun with this one.'

'I have to insist,' Stainer says, his own words blunt with concern. 'Whatever you intend to do later, right now? You should wait in the car, *sir*.'

I'm craning my neck, trying to work out where they are, but their voices are floating, disembodied, echoing in the high-ceilinged space. There's a long pause, as if Future Hugh is weighing his risks. And then he says, briskly, not best pleased, 'Perhaps you're right, Stainer. My son, Ross, won't breathe a word, of course, but my nephew is in… an unpredictable frame of mind. Take the front-of-house area. I'll wait by the back door. Just in case.'

There's another long pause and then Stainer says, voice colourless and unemotional, 'Yes, sir. Just stay out of sight of the cars coming up and down the entryway, okay? She won't be far. The geriatric's probably out. And even if he isn't…'

I hear one set of hard soles moving away, striking concrete. Then the other man steps lightly across floor-boards until there is the sound of curtains being batted aside, an instance of weak, grey light, then the sound of heavy fabric falling back into place. I hadn't realised I was holding my breath until it comes out of me in a quiet *whoosh*. I need to move. I've got one foot on the top of the basement stairs when my phone, my bloody phone, utters that loud, sparkly *bling* sound—to tell me someone has just played me a word.

I don't wait to see what happens, throwing myself down the hard concrete steps, tripping badly off the last one and twisting my ankle. I land on my side, on the cold, dusty floor, with a dull *thud*.

As I breathe out hard in pain, overhead it sounds like wild animals stampeding in all directions. The basement is lit by a single dim pendant bulb and littered with junk: a bright-blue papier-mâché elephant with a hole punched in its side, giant fans, broken chairs, boxes and barrels and crates, a glittery game-show spinning wheel.

Right in the centre of the room, though, is a

weird-looking rectangular wooden structure fixed into the concrete of the floor, yellow-and-black warning tape stuck all around its perimeter. It has three weighted pulleys set into the top, but like everything else it affords me no place to hide. It reaches from the floor to the underside of the stage above, like a rudimentary archway made out of four heavy wooden beams, each one wider and more solid than a person. Like a rectangular box, only standing upright, all the sides open, facing onto mounds of old theatre rubbish.

I register all of this—that there's no cover, anywhere—as I'm pulling myself awkwardly up into a sitting position.

Rising with a cry of pain I can't quite muffle, I'm just standing there at the bottom of the stairs, favouring my right foot, when a man appears at the top of them.

It feels like a dream as he slowly walks down, his dark eyes never leaving mine. I back up, limping and sucking in shallow, painful breaths. One heel hits the edge of the peeling yellow-and-black tape and I'm backing straight through the centre of the boxy wooden structure, because it's the only clear path in the entire space, my sneakers snagging on the warped edge of a metal plate as I fall out the far side.

He keeps coming on: withered-beautiful, up close, and deadly; wearing every single one of his years and cruelties on his face and in his eyes.

Behind me is the vast, damaged bulk of the bright-blue elephant; on either side, broken chairs and heaped-up boxes. The room is a giant box—no, a box inside a box—with no way out except those stairs behind him.

The man who wears Hugh's face keeps crossing the room, passing through the standing wooden beams himself, before coming to a stop in front of me. He places his hands on my shoulders, running long, leather-gloved fingers through the ends of my hair while I look up into his face like cornered prey.

If I closed my eyes, right now, and placed my head against this man's rain-drenched lapel, it would feel like Hugh and smell like Hugh: expensive, well maintained, reeking of sex and power.

The resemblance is uncanny as he purrs, 'How could anyone prefer him to *me*?'

Disorientated, I realise belatedly that the man must be speaking of Fleur Bawden and the mistake she made: of loving his brother better.

Above us, I hear Newlands roar: *'What the devil is going on?'* and through the floorboards overhead there's a metal *clang*, then light streams down through the cracks, refracted into strange lines and patterns.

The man before me puts a hand over my mouth and pulls me, hard, into the iron line of his body, breathing, '*Hush now,*' into my hair.

I can hear someone above, walking in circles. Footsteps close, then dying away, roaming all over the stage.

Then the footsteps grow distant and the man with his hand over my mouth relaxes his grip only slightly and says, 'You're coming with me now, quietly, like a good girl. I'm glad I waited.' He clutches at me with his free hand and I actually gasp into his palm as he twists hard at my soft, female flesh and says lazily, 'You were worth waiting for.'

The lines overhead are dizzying, resolving and dissolving. I start fighting him then, really kicking out and biting, stamping and bucking, going wild because I know, *I know* there are some things you can't come back from, as he's pulling me around, smashing me in the side of the head, getting huge handfuls of my hair and wrenching until I'm seeing purple and stars and explosions.

'Come with me, you little bitch, or I will kill you here,' he hisses in this voice that's all the more terrible for being so controlled, so quiet.

He has me facing down and he's forcing me, really trying to push me to my knees, but I'm forcing my way back up, the two of us almost centrifugal, when I glimpse feet on the stairs: battered workboots, the brown leather so worn it's got this sheen of grey all over the surface of it.

Then his fist connects with my face and I can't see the boots anymore, I can't see anything. When I sag to my knees the judge turns me like a baby, hugging me to his broad chest and dragging me backwards between the first pair of heavy wooden beams, my heels again snagging against the edge of a warped metal plate, set into the floor.

Then we're under the archway and he's got an arm under my jaw, right across my windpipe, pressing down on it so that I've got no air left, there's nothing, I'm going to pass out. But as the edges of my sight start going black, I see the weight above us. It's enormous: as wide across as the gap between the beams themselves; three pulleys it takes to lift it, heavy enough to crush a man.

And I understand, at last: about the lines overhead, how they all go one way, in parallel, except for this one star shape, right in the centre.

'Simon,' I gag, rasping, kicking out, my heels beating against metal as the man struggles to contain me. 'The lever, push it!' I'm barely audible. '*Push it!*'

It is a Death's head rattle. As my eyes roll back, I actually look for him, the silver-haired giant with the eyes like sunlight on the sea. I can feel him in the room, walking amongst the boxes, watching over me.

Then I pull down on the man's little finger, the way Mum taught me, until I feel it snap in my hands. Wrenching myself sideways, I dive and scramble to get clear of the box with no sides, uncaring that I've left my hair and my blood everywhere.

It takes forever and it takes no time at all.

There is a sound like a heavy bolt shooting home, an iron arrow leaving a crossbow, and then there's a star-shaped hole in the sky, white light, the metal plate returning, sinking back down into the floor, empty. And screaming.

Nothing can block out the screaming. It goes on and on, the star shape remaining, jammed open by a man's arcing, writhing body. As I turn over onto my back, whooping and heaving to get air into my lungs, I see the rain coming down, together with the light. The light and the rain are the colour of blood. A rain of blood, falling all over me. I close my eyes.

AFTER

So you want to know how it turns out, right? Well, so do I. But I'm resisting the urge to look.

I still believe in happy endings. They just happen to other people, that's all. For people like me it is a little more complicated.

It could have gone either way, I remind Simon gravely, when I want to see him squirm. I do it a lot because it's fun.

If he hadn't run back and found Boon after making it to Cohen Place too late to catch me? Well, I'd be all kinds of dead. To needle him, I say that it was really Boon who saved me—for introducing me to Newlands in the first place, and restoring to me pieces of myself I hadn't even known were missing.

The judge—who'll never be pretty again—and Don Sturt are both Wurbik's problems now. Things eat at you long enough? They'll either kill you, or you'll kill to keep them secret. I've seen it for myself, firsthand. I know.

Elias Kircher knew it, too. He saw death coming and made sure the people who most wanted it made it to the party. The explosives were his own special touch, rigged by a special effects guy on the Gold Coast who thought he was doing it for a telemovie. The only way to get the job done properly, Kircher always believed, was to do it yourself; see it to the bitter finish. He must have recognised that quality in my mother.

And the word? The word that came through at the worst possible time and almost got me killed?

Was: *Luv.*

I like to think that, wherever she is, Mum was trying to reach me with the only letters she had left.

It's slang, sure. But it's clear enough. Well, as clear as her last message was before she left on her great journey, astrolabe in hand, kindled by some kind of weird blood magic: *always*. That's the way I imagine it, anyway: her setting off on a journey like some misguided, modern-day Orpheus going after her lost love. Because to imagine anything else is unbearable.

Words can have more than one meaning, I know that. But *always* on its own has a terrible certitude, an irrefutable finality. However, when you couple it with the idea of *love*, it goes beyond even borders, even death: it's transcendent, this idea that there will always be love, enough love, more than you could ever want; something constant. And, in those two words, she's somehow managed to reference the entire back catalogue of Whitney Houston, too—I can see her now, belting out the very tune at the top of her lungs, me hitting her with a pillow to make her shut it—so I'll take it all as a sign that she's okay.

I don't think she ever worked out that Fleur and Hugh were connected, even though they were a generation away from ever meeting each other. But she just had a way with people, with bringing things out into the light. So maybe it really is true what Boon said—that we're all just links in a gigantic chain; or a web, because life is circular, things come around again and again. Bad things beget bad things; but good things, too. Those dead girls from the 1970s? They're saying now the families will at least get some answers, and if it took Mum leaving to get that, well, she would have said it was a fair trade.

She never looked it, but Mum was strong and wise. And now I have to be all that, too, because I am the last Crowe left behind in this world.

Simon's taught me how to turn that sound off, that sparkly *bling* thing. He's taught me lots of things, in the days and hours since I looked for Death in the basement of the oldest theatre restaurant in Melbourne. When you're as damaged and spiky and *House Aries* as the two of us are, it is never exactly boring. More like a game of combat where we make up the rules as we go along and the play never, ever stops.

But he's refusing to cut a deal regarding the prize money. We're going to hear any day now, which one of us is officially more *alpha* than the other. But I'm holding to my side of my one-sided bargain. If I win it, he gets a car. On condition that he'll take me driving up the coast so that I can see it for myself, see Mount Warning.

They haven't found a body, and I'm holding on to that.

If there's magic up there, Crowe magic, I like to think that I'll feel it and figure out what really happened.

So. I could confine it all to paper, run my divinations, pierce the veil between *now* and *what comes after*. But this way, my way; there's no messenger, no message.

The future's just wide open, the way I like it.

ACKNOWLEDGMENTS

With loving thanks to my husband, Michael, and to our beautiful children, Oscar, Leni and Yve; who every day put up with me and love me exactly the way I am.

With thanks also to my parents, Yean Kai and Susan, and my sisters, Ruth and Eugenia, and new brother-in-law Quino Holland, for distracting the little people with games of Candyland and Connect Four and Uno. Thanks also to Barry and Judy Liu, Ben and Michelle Lee, and Sally and Marcus Price for their unflagging support.

To Michael Heyward, International Man of Mystery and Publisher Extraordinaire, and my editor, the fabulous and enormously dedicated Rebecca Starford, manifold thanks for letting me retreat to my cave and just write without expectations of suitability or marketability—how intensely liberating.

A huge thanks also to rights ninja Anne Beilby, marketing genius Kirsty Wilson, super publicist Stephanie Speight, design sorceress Imogen Stubbs, and to all at Text Publishing who have championed my work and given it wings.

Grateful thanks also to Mark Battye, Suzy Roberts, Sharne Bryan and Caitlin Bryan for reading my manuscript and gently pointing out the many glaring errors, inaccuracies and pacing issues. It would not be the book it is without your help.

Thanks also go to Alicia McLeay, Cassie Pittman, Kara Bobbera, Ainsley Hallman, Ben Doughty, Kirby Spicer, Regan O'Cleary, Daniel Mills, Sarah Beassley and Katie Kletzmayer for feeding and watering me during the writing year and keeping that corner table free.

Also, in memory of Ray Factor, master astrologer. I'm only sorry that this didn't make it into your hands before you left on your great journey.

And last, but not least, to Alison Arnold—who took a punt on a complete stranger—with thanks and best wishes always.

expressed by the characters, whose preferences and attitudes are also entirely their own. Any errors are entirely mine.

The extract from John Donne's sonnet 'A Fever' that appears in the epigraph, is taken from the 1635 compilation (made after his death) of some of his songs and sonnets. The extract from 'A Valediction forbidding mourning' that appears on page 92 and the extract from 'The good-morrow' that appears on page 270 are both taken from *Seven Centuries of Poetry in English*, edited by John Leonard, Oxford University Press, 1988.

Certain authorial liberties may have been taken with those buildings and places that do actually exist in the real world and, for those, the author apologises and begs your leave.